THE CHRONICLE

AWAKENING

BOOK ONE

PAUL SVENDSEN

About The Author

Paul lives in the west of Ireland with his wife Stephanie and an assortment of mostly rescued animals.

He enjoys trying to be self-sufficient, looking after the animals, writing novels, poetry, and writing and playing music.

Copyright © 2013 by Paul Andrew Svendsen
All rights reserved. This book or any portion thereof may not be reproduced or used in any manner whatsoever without the express written permission of the author except for the use of brief quotations in a book review.

Printed in the United Kingdom

First Printing, 2013. Second Edition

ISBN-13: 978-1493579488
ISBN-10: 1493579487

Email paul.svendsen@wtfaw.org

Book cover design by BespokeBookCovers.com

This is a work of fiction. Names, characters, businesses, places, events and incidents are either the products of the author's imagination or used in a fictitious manner. Any resemblance to actual persons, living or dead, or actual events is purely coincidental.

My thanks to Dad, Dawn, Lea and Tarnz, for providing feedback on the many drafts!

To Simon, my son, for not falling asleep whilst I read Awakening to him!

A special thanks to Stef, my wife and motivator. You kept me going when I felt like giving up.

And to Mum. She passed away in 2011 but will always inspire me to make the most out of life.

Chapter One

Krys glided high over old Spain. From her lofty viewpoint, she could see the great polar ice cap that covered nearly half the world and which had, along with violent storms and tsunamis, wiped out most of its original inhabitants. A descendant of the great golden eagle, Krys's species had evolved in the five thousand years since the great freeze, as had many of the other creatures who inhabited the planet.

With a wingspan of over three metres and weighing over twelve kilograms, the eagle soared impressively through her environment, a powerful and beautiful creature of the sky. She still possessed some white feathers in her tail, but at the age of five and a half, they would soon make way for the dark brown, almost golden plumage, that adorned the rest of her body. At the end of each of her wings, which she held slightly upwards to provide lift in her glide, her almost finger-like feathers gave her complete control over her environment, allowing her to make minute adjustments for lateral stability. Her tail feathers, held at the same angle, controlled her pitch. With six strong wingbeats, Krys changed direction towards a small clearing and hovered silently above, looking down as she had done many times over the last several weeks.

She did not understand what drew her so far from her normal hunting grounds to the place of humans – they were a threat to her kind – but something powerful called to her. Before the great freeze, her species had already possessed a limited ability to speak mind to mind. Five thousand years later, she and her kind could communicate clearly with each other via their thoughts. They could also communicate with several other species, although much of what they said remained unintelligible to her.

The voice in her head now though, was unlike anything she had ever heard before. It spoke softly in her mind, and had been drawing her closer every day. This morning she had told her life mate Krask of the voice, and he had immediately banned her from going near the humans again. She had promised that she would not, but then she could not resist the call when it came.

Looking down with her amazing vision, Krys could clearly see the humans. They were a powerful species and not to be approached. They could control fire and kill at great range with flying sticks. All great golden eagle chicks were told the tales of the deadly sticks adorned with the feathers of their prey. All eagles grew up wary of humans.

Today, Krys located a baby lying under the shade of a tree, about ten metres away from a pair of humans. As she flew over, it turned its head to look directly up at her. In that moment, Krys knew the source of the voice in her head.

Chapter Two

Bodolf and his pack of white wolves came off the ice and travelled south. Being away from the domain that they knew and understood made progress difficult. However, a force kept Bodolf driving further into this alien territory; a voice that kept drawing him to its source, taking him and his pack hundreds of miles away from home.

It had been days since they had last killed, and the pack's general hunger was causing fights and unrest. Bodolf knew that if he did not either find whatever it was that drove him soon, or admit defeat and turn back, he would lose control of the pack. Honi, his mate, would stick by him whatever he chose to do, but the rest were more of a problem.

"I am fed up with this, Bodolf. Why do you insist on taking us from our hunting grounds?"

The question, in Bodolf's mind a challenge, came from Ulf, the oldest of his offspring and the one who had been complaining the most over the last few days. Wolves like most animals, had developed the ability to communicate mind to mind over the centuries, using little audible dialog. They only used their voices for expressions of threat, fear, or passion. It was in fact the mastery of and subsequent reliance on the spoken word, which had denied most humans the ability to communicate mind to mind.

Ulf moved in the typical gait adopted by the pack when they were travelling long distances, head at the same level as his back, maintaining a loping run of around eight miles an hour, which they could sustain all day. Travelling ten metres behind Bodolf, Ulf did not expect what happened next.

In a blink of an eye the big white turned, his head raised, and his eyes fixed a primal stare at Ulf. With his mouth open wide and razor-sharp canines bared, Bodolf charged.

For Ulf, the one hundred and twenty kilograms of pure white evil triggered every defensive and passive response he had at his disposal. He knew that he could not match Bodolf and that these next few seconds could well be his last.

Bodolf recognised the instant submission signals from Ulf, who was already crouched on the floor with his mouth closed, not making visual contact, but something inside Bodolf had snapped. Used to being in control, he felt a lack of respect from the pack and anger at this tormenting voice in his head. He was so hungry and angry; Ulf became the target of all of Bodolf's frustrations.

Normally the leader would control the pack with demonstrations of his size and speed and the occasional growl and nip; however, this time he hit Ulf at nearly twenty miles an hour. As Ulf collapsed, Bodolf plunged his head down, jaws opening around his offspring's neck, and bit hard. Standing up to his full height, the pack leader dragged the wolf up by the neck and started to shake him.

"Bodolf…Bodolf, stop! You are killing him!" From somewhere outside of his rage, Bodolf recognised the call of his mate, Honi. But he wanted to keep shaking Ulf, to kill the challenger to his leadership, to take control again. He wanted to ignore Honi and teach this cur a lesson.

Then Tasha's warning of danger cut through his anger like a knife. Dropping Ulf in a limp, cowering heap on the floor, Bodolf immediately focused his senses on the new situation.

"Tasha, what have you sensed?" he asked his second-generation daughter.

"I have no smell of it yet, Bodolf, but I just heard a noise ahead of us that is from no animal I have encountered before," Tasha replied.

Bodolf informed the rest of the pack, still reeling from the attack on Ulf, that there could be danger ahead. All thirteen wolves melted into the undergrowth and stealthily followed Bodolf as he crept towards the point indicated by Tasha.

"Do you hear it Bodolf?" she whispered.

"Yes, yes, let me concentrate," he snapped back.

He could hear a low, guttural rumble accompanied by the noise of travel, but what a noise! A thousand wolves at full speed would not make such a clatter. Then he picked up a new scent. In all his time on the ice pack and during his brief foray into this strange land, he had not smelt anything like it.

Whatever made the noise suddenly went relatively quiet. He could still hear ragged breathing and other recognisable life sounds, but there was also a range of other noises that he could not identify. He could not distinguish the smell either.

Creeping forward, he came to a vantage point where he could see the source of these conflicting sensory inputs, but what he saw did not help his comprehension of the situation at all.

Five humans stood at the edge of the woods with their backs to Bodolf and his pack, looking out towards a clearing. As Bodolf watched, one of the humans used one of his forelegs to raise a long stick and hold it in front of him. Then he used another foreleg to pull out a smaller stick from an appendage and connect it to the first.

Chapter Three

Banain lay sheltered and contented under the shade of a large tree. His parents were several metres away; his father, Judoc, was cutting the undergrowth with a large scythe and his mother, Nimean, was arranging the cuttings into large piles for burning. The child was swaddled in a blanket; a mop of golden hair protected his exposed head. His dark blue eyes possessed a magnetic quality, and right now, those eyes were staring at a black speck that circled high above.

Although not old enough to control the rare gift he possessed, Banain could already send and receive messages with his mind. He had heard the shrill voice of Krys and the deep growling voice of Bodolf from many miles away. The voice of Bodolf had become much louder over recent days. At this young age, Banain had no idea of the power of his thoughts, or the consequences.

From the edge of the clearing, the militia sergeant fired his standard issue bow. The arrow climbed high before starting its descent. The leader of the five-man scouting party had wanted to kill the farmer quickly, just in case he had a weapon close by, but his aim was low and it hit the top of Judoc's thigh, bursting through skin and sinew.

Judoc collapsed to the ground, rolling in agony and trying to understand what had hit him. At first, he thought it must have been a snake or a trap, but then he saw the arrow. He knew he and his family were in grave danger.

Denied a further target for his bow, the sergeant indicated for his soldiers to attack with a downward chopping motion of his arm. Then he drew his sword and charged towards where his target had dropped.

Unknowingly, Judoc had sent out a mental cry of anguish when the arrow hit, a cry that only a creature with special abilities would be able to hear. The cry crashed into Banain's world like an unexpected and angry wave from a peaceful ocean. He had received messages from his parents before, but not like this. Even when they shouted at each other, it never affected the calmness of their inner thoughts. His father's waves of distress and fear assaulted Banain's brain, and for the first time he felt fear, and started to scream.

A hundredth of a second after hearing her son's scream, Nimean started running towards her child. In his short life, she had never heard him cry out. In fact, she and Judoc had been worried that he may have a problem.

As she ran toward Banain, she looked for Judoc. She had seen him a few seconds ago, but could not see him now. Then, on her right, she saw a band of men burst from the woods, heading straight towards where Judoc had been just a moment ago. Should she go to her husband or continue to her son? Her maternal instinct won the argument, and she kept racing towards Banain.

On the ground, Judoc grabbed the scythe that he had been clearing the brush with and used it as a crutch to haul himself upright. As soon as his head had cleared the scrub, he saw five men charging towards him. The closest had a feral grin on his face and held a sword high above his head, ready to bring it down. Adrenalin surged through Judoc's body, masking the pain and giving him the strength he needed to take his weight on his good leg and swing the scythe in a wicked arc towards the sergeant.

Charging at a full run and not expecting such a quick response, the sergeant could not stop his forward motion in time to miss the honed blade, which entered his body just below his leather jerkin and travelled inwards and upwards, ripping through his intestines and puncturing his lungs. His forward motion carried him further onto the blade, which snapped under the pressure. Almost dead by the time he hit the floor, the sergeant now lay on the broken scythe and his sword, Judoc's only weapon.

"Run Nimean, run! I have the measure of these men!" Judoc lied. He turned back towards the four soldiers. Without their sergeant, they were leaderless and unsure.

"Come on lads, he is one simple farmer." The speaker, a tall thin man with a large scar across his right cheek, moved towards Judoc as he spoke, swinging his sword from side to side.

The other soldiers did not look sure; the smallest in the group scratched his chin. "Why don't we just shoot him Scar, why risk a close fight? He already killed the Sarge," he said.

"Look, you idiot, the sergeant had the only bow, so stop bleating and let's kill this miserable farmer." Scar moved in, swinging his sword at Judoc.

Chapter Four

Still crouched watching the humans, Bodolf had also heard Banain's physical and mental scream. Then he had understood what he had been hearing for the last few weeks. The strange intrusions into his mind had come from the baby in the clearing.

When the humans were standing still, Bodolf's pack had been in stalk mode, but as soon as the humans started running towards the clearing, centuries of hunting instincts took over and the wolves, as a single unit, gave pursuit. Arctic wolves did not use speed as their main hunting tool, preferring to wear their targets down with a steady and relentless pursuit, but it surprised Bodolf that the humans were so slow.

Before the lead wolf was halfway there, his target collapsed. The smell of fresh blood heightened his killing instincts. Bodolf scanned the remaining, now stationary, targets, about to signal the pack to stop as well, when the soldiers started running again towards another human figure. Bodolf changed course for the creature in the lead, communicating his intentions to the pack.

Judoc reached down to the dying body of the sergeant in an attempt to free the trapped sword. He knew in his heart that he did not have time to free and use it against this second attacker, but he had to try. His hand closed around something and he pulled, falling backwards as it came free from under the sergeant's body. He held the bow and arrows in his hand, not the sword he was after, and looked up to see the scar-faced man almost on top of him.

As Judoc braced for the deathblow, the expression on the man's face changed from pure evil to shock. From behind him, a white blur materialised, landing on his back and launching him forward. Judoc threw himself to the right as Scarface, with this white devil locked onto the back of his neck, ferocious teeth biting through flesh and bone, crashed to the ground. Judoc had never seen anything like it before, and although saved from immediate death, he realised that this second danger could be much worse than the first!

Running just behind Bodolf, Honi watched her mate take down the human. She always stayed close to him when they were hunting, completely attuned to his needs. She had not understood what had been causing Bodolf to act so strangely for the last few weeks, but now she did. Any creature with even a small amount of telepathic ability would have heard Banain's mental scream. Succumbing to her protective instincts, Honi focused her attention on the cause of her mate's distress.

Turning towards the large tree, she increased speed and her eyes locked onto the small, noisy bundle. For a second, her maternal instincts towards a child made her falter, but the duty to her mate took precedence and she closed the gap to silence the noise.

From her lofty perch, Krys had seen the whole event unfold. Every instinct had told her to leave quickly, especially after seeing the large white wolves. Wheeling around, undecided about what to do, she too heard Banain's scream.

Then she knew what she had to do. Krys partially folded her wings against her body, moved her legs back towards her tail, and dived. Making small adjustments with her feathers, Krys honed in on the child. She could see one of the white wolves charging towards him and knew that it would be a very close thing.

Running flat out, with her head slightly cocked to one side so she could hear both in front and behind, Honi sensed a human closing in on the baby. She calculated that they would reach it before she did, so she changed her direction to intercept. She caught the human just before it reached the child, hitting from behind and to the right. The force of the attack knocked the human to the ground. Because of the last minute change in direction, Honi only managed to get her teeth into its arm. Just as she was about to go for the neck, she heard renewed cries from the child, which reminded her of her original objective. Dropping Nimean's arm, Honi moved in for the kill.

A little distance away, Judoc had managed to crawl from where Bodolf and the other starving wolves were feasting on the soldiers. He propped himself upright just in time to see Honi's attack on Nimean. He still had the bow and arrows. A bow was not his best tool, but he knew how to use one. Selecting a shaft as fast as he could, he let fly at the wolf attacking his partner. Just as the arrow left the bow, the wolf leapt from Nimean and started towards Banain again. The arrow passed dangerously close to Nimean as she rose to protect her son.

Judoc fitted another arrow and fired. As he followed the flight of the arrow towards the target, a golden brown apparition appeared from above, wings beating furiously to slow its descent and talons outstretched. Almost in slow motion, Judoc watched in horror as a massive eagle grabbed hold of his baby and flew back into the air. He saw the arrow glance off the side of the wolf's head just as it lunged for Banain and deflect into the eagle's left wing, passing through and exiting the other side.

The excruciating pain in her wing caused Krys to tilt crazily to the left and start to drop towards the ground. Drawing on every fibre of her reserve, she forced the wing to extend and, with centimetres to spare, managed to work it again. Then she started to ascend.

Below her, Bodolf was feasting on the corpse of the soldier he had just killed. Sensing Honi's distress, however, he leapt to his feet and scanned for her, annoyed to be side-tracked by the thrill of the hunt and the prospect of food. He saw Honi shaking her head and a great eagle flying over holding the baby he had been hunting all this time. Immediately focused, Bodolf raced to check his mate.

"Are you hurt?" he enquired. He saw blood on her head.

"Something hit my head but I do not think I am hurt. I nearly killed the baby, Bodolf, the one that has been troubling you, but an eagle stole it from me."

"Yes, I saw. We need to follow, now!" he said, turning in the direction the eagle had taken.

"Just leave it, Bodolf. The eagle will kill it and eat it. What can we do? Do we have wings? We should stay and feast here."

Bodolf knew Honi was right, but something deep inside him would not let go, so he turned in search of his wolves. Most of them, including Ulf, were still at the edge of the clearing where they were devouring one of the soldiers.

"Ulf, attack the eagle," Bodolf ordered.

Ulf pulled his head from the corpse, the command from Bodolf interrupting his search for the human's heart. All his primal instincts were telling him to ignore Bodolf and to continue his feast, but his strongest instinct, fear, fresh in his mind from Bodolf's attack, persuaded him otherwise.

How am I supposed to hunt in the sky? Do I have wings? Can I fly? All those questions flashed through Ulf's mind as he set off after the eagle. As he ran, Ulf shouted to the other wolves, "Bodolf says we must catch the eagle. Move across its path. It is low enough for us to reach the human child."

He calculated that, with the current angle, he should just be able to reach the child in time. He was already anticipating how pleased Bodolf would be with him when he brought him this baby prey, thinking perhaps he would even be allowed the honour of the baby's heart to feast on.

With the safety of height only a few wingbeats away, Krys spotted the five white wolves running directly towards her from the right. Instead of carrying on in the same direction, she turned towards them and screamed a shrill cry, causing them to hesitate. In that second, she flew over them, gaining height. With the weight of the baby manageable and the pain in her wing bearable, the eagle made her escape, but she needed to decide what she was going to do next.

The move was so fast and unexpected; Ulf and the others did not have time to counter it. Turning as hard as he could, Ulf gave chase, but the eagle, reaching well over thirty miles an hour and climbing, would not be his today. In despair, the wolf watched as his prey disappeared over the canopy of trees defining the edge of the great forest.

Gaining height with every beat of her powerful wings, Krys thought she had control of the situation. Then she looked down to see that the baby's swaddling was slowly unwrapping. She could not change her hold on the material and would not have the time or the opportunity to land before it unravelled altogether. Every second a bit more material loosened, and it would be only be a few more seconds before the baby would slide out and fall to its certain death. To go through so much only to see this child fall and die would be too much to bear.

As the main pack of whites streamed past Ulf in continued pursuit of the eagle, Bodolf said, "Call yourself a hunter? Come on, we must not let them get away!"

Ulf had wanted to challenge Bodolf, to point out the stupidity of chasing a flying animal, what could it achieve? However, fear won the day again and he, along with the rest of the pack, charged back into the forest in pursuit of the eagle and child.

The wolves, crashed through the undergrowth of the forest. Luckily, as they were large, ferocious and in a strong number, none of the inhabitants challenged them. In fact, if they had been hunting this way, they would have been surprisingly successful – they flushed out many small animals with their noisy charge across the forest floor.

At this distance, Bodolf knew exactly where the child was, although his mental calls were getting weaker. He sensed anguish in the transmission that both encouraged him to continue the chase and saddened him.

Travelling, as always, just behind him, Honi had also heard the same thing. She found herself questioning her normally black and white instincts, puzzled as to why she had hesitated when running for the child before and why she now felt concern for this human baby.

With no end to the forest in sight and his energy reserves failing, Bodolf knew he and the pack could not carry on this pursuit much longer. Back on the ice, they had pursued large animals for days, loping along at a steady eight miles an hour, but this relentless charge through thick undergrowth, roots, streams and foliage moved the wolves far from their comfort zone, and they were all tiring fast.

Krys screamed a message for her mate Krask to help her. She knew it could not be in time, but she had to try. She looked down at the baby – those deep blue eyes firmly fixed on hers – and died inside as she saw the last of the swaddling slipping away.

Just before the last piece slipped letting Banain drop to his death, the baby reached up with one little hand and clutched at one of Krys's legs, and then the other. This stopped the swaddling from slipping, giving him a small chance of survival. Krys could not believe what had just happened, but she knew they were still in serious trouble. She had to get him to the safety of her nest, but how long could those tiny hands hold on?

Chapter Five

Krask spotted his prey and moved into an attack glide. As his speed increased, he closed his wings tighter to his body, achieving over two hundred miles an hour. The large hare, sensing danger, started to run, but it was too little far too late! His ultra-sensitive ears could hear the rush of air as the thirteen-kilo feather-clad missile transformed back into flight mode. Krask's wings opened, his tail fanned and his talons came forward to grasp the hapless creature. These actions caused a large boom, the last thing the hare heard before he died.

Flapping to gain altitude once again, supper dangling below, Krask mulled once more over his earlier conversation with Krys. They had hardly ever had a cross word in the two years they had been mates, but then neither of them had done anything so strange before. Like Krys, he had the ability to communicate without voice, yet he had received none of the messages Krys claimed to have heard. He regretted the strong stance he had taken with her, admitting grudgingly to himself that he had simply felt envy.

He knew she was his, but he still felt the need to impress her. He had always been the best hunter and flyer – was his reaction because she could do something he could not? Heading back towards their nest high in the range of mountains to the west of him, Krask pondered these feelings and promised he would apologise to Krys when she got back.

The first call from Krys was so weak that Krask could not be sure that he had heard correctly, but the second call galvanised him into action. Dropping the hare, he wheeled, his powerful vision searching for his troubled mate. The call gave no reference to direct him, but he knew which way she had gone hunting and immediately headed towards that area. Unfortunately, this was in the opposite direction to where Krys and Banain were struggling to hold on to each other.

"Bodolf, please stop. We cannot keep this pace up any longer!" Bodolf had expected the call from Honi earlier, and it pleased him that she and the pack had kept up the gruelling pace without complaint for so long.

He could not believe how close he had come to finally stopping this voice in his head! Was it all going to slip away from him again?

"Okay Honi, we will stop and…" About to finish the sentence that would have stopped the pursuit, Bodolf suddenly saw patches of sunlight in front of him. For the last ten minutes, they had been in perpetual gloom under the canopy of trees, but as quickly as the forest had started, it ended on the edge of a great plain.

Bodolf and the thirteen wolves burst out into the bright sunlight, and they could see the eagle and baby.

"There they are, just a small distance away," Bodolf encouraged.

With their energy partially replenished by the thrill of seeing the prey again, the wolves leapt forward once more, starting to eat up the distance between them and the eagle with its human cargo.

Krys had decided that as soon as she passed the edge of the old forest and reached the plains, she could land and put the baby down to get a better hold on him. However, as she cleared the edge of the forest and started her descent, fourteen white shapes emerged and began running purposefully after her. Krys knew she could not land and take off in time. She also knew that the baby could not hold on much longer.

Chapter Six

Krask had searched the area he thought Krys would be in, but to no avail. He had not heard another word from her since those first couple of calls. He wheeled again and headed towards the area she said she had been visiting for the last couple of weeks – the area he had banned her from. Although he had only faintly heard Krys, he had recognised the anguish in her message.

Far in the distance and quite close to the ground, Krask spotted her familiar shape, which confused him more than ever.

It looked like Krys had been hunting as she seemed to be carrying prey, but from this distance he could not make out its type. Krask then spotted the white shapes on the ground running after Krys, placing her in immediate danger.

"Krys…Krys, I am coming. Drop your prey and climb!" Krask sent with every fibre of his mental power.

However, Krys just kept struggling along, with the white wolves gaining every minute.

Krask did not understand. Why didn't Krys drop what she carried so she could gain height and safety? In addition, what were these strange creatures chasing her? These questions and more flashed through Krask's mind as he readied himself for a shallow dive to close the distance between him and his mate as quickly as possible.

"Krask, I know this is hard to understand, but we must save this baby. I am losing him, and he will fall in seconds. Please Krask, help me!"

Krys sounded exhausted and more frightened than Krask had ever heard before. Getting closer, he could see the human form dangling below Krys, and he was amazed to see that his little hands were holding onto her!

"Krys, what are you doing? What is this? Drop that thing! Those creatures will drag it and you from the sky and devour you in seconds. Drop the baby Krys!" he screamed.

Suddenly, Krask saw one of the little hands lose its grip and watched in disbelief as Krys immediately dived, losing precious height to try to regain her hold on the child. He knew that she would not give in. She was going to save this baby or die trying!

Out of ideas and with the baby dangling by one hand, Krys knew Banain only had seconds left before he fell. In her head, his silent cries of fear were tearing her soul apart. She looked down into the deep blue eyes of Banain at the exact moment when he lost the last of his grip. With his full weight back on the blanket, it finally unravelled completely, and he started to fall. Krys watched in utter dejection as Banain dropped away from her.

Krask was travelling at over two hundred and thirty miles an hour, his wings folded tight into his sides. Krys was between him and the falling baby, but Krask calculated that he could just get past her. Then he had three problems. One: could he get to the child in time? Two: could he stop before hitting the ground? Three: could he get a hold on the child that would not kill it?

He was totally committed to the dive as he passed Krys in a blur. At this stage in a normal hunt, he would be extending his wings and slowing, but he still had a distance to go if he was to reach the baby before it hit the ground. He had never in his life flown this fast whilst so close to the ground. In addition, he was not at all sure he could stop on his own, never mind with the extra weight he was about to be carrying!

Krys's heart, which had been beating almost out of her chest with fear, was in meltdown. Not only was the human baby in mortal danger, her mate was also involved. She knew Krask was a fantastic flyer and she had seen him perform amazing acrobatic feats, but she was not sure even his great skills could get him out of this situation. She hated that she had put him in danger. Krys wheeled and followed Krask in his descent, hoping she could help in some way. To her dismay, she saw that the wolves had covered nearly all the distance between them, and she could clearly see the killing lust in their eyes.

At the very earliest he calculated that he could stop the dive before hitting the ground and still reach the baby, Krask went into full brake mode. He thrust his powerful talons forward, knowing that he could kill the child if he got this wrong. He also knew that he might have to damage the baby if he was to save it. The baby was falling face down with his arms and legs spread out, and his head facing away from Krask. It was almost as if the baby was trying to fly himself!

Krask's talons went either side of the baby's torso, with the wicked pointed tips coming to rest on the baby's chest. With every ounce of his considerable strength, Krask shifted his talons backward and upwards, tucking Banain against his chest. The ground was a rock-strewn blur close under the baby, and getting closer every second. With a last immense effort, Krask strained to arrest the dive and gain life-giving height. He was only a couple of centimetres above the ground – one rock, one small shrub or bush, and it would be over. Then Krask realised that they were climbing. Looking forward again, he was just about to breathe a sigh of relief when he saw a massive white wolf a short distance in front of him.

Chapter Seven

A feral stare locked onto Krask and the baby, and he saw a row of wickedly sharp teeth, ready to rip the life from the pair of them. Before he could think about avoiding this fang filled apparition, a shape dived down from above him and collided full on with the wolf. One second there was nowhere to go; the next Krask was able to pass over the fur-and-feather ball of two bodies in mortal combat.

"Krys…Krys. What have you done?" Krask cried. A coldness spread through his body as the enormity of her actions hit him.

"Save the baby, Krask. Whatever happens, save the baby. If you love me you will do this, not just for me, but also for the future of our kind. Please Krask, I love you so much. I know you will not let me down. I love you…"

Suddenly her voice was gone, replaced by a terrible void, a hole where her presence had been only a second ago. Krask wanted to drop the baby and dive down to help Krys, but he could not. Her words had affected him deeply, and in his heart, he knew Krys was dead. Circling around, he looked down at the bloody spectacle playing out below him. At his beloved Krys now engulfed in a sea of white wolves. A little way from the carnage and staring up at Krask and the baby, sat the white wolf that had so nearly caught Krask, and who had killed Krys. He arched his neck and howled. In the howl, Krask recognised feral savagery and hate towards both him and the baby.

Turning towards his now solitary home, Krask could not think clearly. In a few seconds his world had been ripped apart – his life mate was gone, and he was carrying a human baby. What was he supposed to do with it? He could sense that it was in distress. Then he realised that his talons were tearing into the baby's chest. Adjusting his grip and accelerating, Krask headed towards the lonely safety of his nest.

Chapter Eight

Bodolf sat and howled his frustrations at the disappearing dot in the sky. He had been sure that he had the baby, then that other eagle had hurtled into him, knocking him out of the path of his quarry. He was still shaking with rage and frustration, he could not see from his left eye and his whole head ached.

"You are hurt, my love," Honi said as she padded up beside him, mouth still bloodied from her share of Krys's corpse. She started to lick the blood from Bodolf's face, exposing four large, wicked wounds running from above his left eye down the side of his head almost to his jaw.

"I was so close to silencing the noise and now…" Bodolf dropped his head not wanting to look in the direction his quarry had disappeared any longer. He starting to feel the pain of his wounds as the adrenalin stopped pumping around his system.

"I know, my love, but there is nothing more you can do. The child is already many miles away; you cannot chase him in the sky! We must return to our home, to our hunting grounds, to our way of life."

"Honi, I cannot. While that human child lives I will not go back! We will follow him, and I will silence him. Get the pack together and let's move. He already has a big head start on us."

Ulf moved in front of Bodolf, his hair erect and bristling, his tail held high. The wolf knew that Bodolf was injured, and he knew this was his only chance to take control of the pack. Apart from that, he knew the rest of them did not want to travel any further into this strange land, and so he hoped they would support him. "We are not going anywhere, Bodolf. We are going home, back where we belong!"

"You were always trouble, Ulf. You should have left to look after yourself many seasons ago, but the coward in you kept you here. The only reason you challenge me now is because I am wounded and you think you can beat me, you cowardly mongrel." Bodolf snarled, turning to face Ulf. The leader stood so that the damaged side of his head and his injured eye were away from his opponent. He had not told Honi, but he could see nothing through that eye, and he knew this would put him at a distinct disadvantage in a fight.

"I stayed because it suited me, yes, but you had no right to drag us all this way for nothing. We are ice hunters. We are not of this land and we will die here. I do not want to fight you, but I will, and the rest will back me."

Bodolf looked at each of the pack members in turn. He did not believe Ulf, but he knew they had been through a lot, and it was true that this was not their fight.

"And what about you, my love, will you leave me as well?" Bodolf said, turning to Honi.

"That is unfair, Bodolf! I want to go home, you know that, but my place is with you. I will live with you, and I will die with you. However, please consider Bodolf, what can you do? The human baby is gone, who knows where.

How can we track it? How will we survive in this strange land? Please reconsider Bodolf."

"I cannot." With those words, Bodolf turned in the direction the eagle and baby had taken and loped off without a backwards glance.

Honi was lost. She loved both Bodolf and her offspring and did not want to leave them. She was also worried about her future in this strange land.

"Are you coming with us, Honi?" Ulf questioned.

"I can't leave him, Ulf. He is wounded and he needs me." Honi was not at all happy with Ulf's attitude, but she wanted to avoid a conflict in the pack.

Then Ulf changed her mind. "He does not deserve you; he is a fool and weak. I should have killed him, but I let him live."

Before Ulf realised what was happening, Honi had turned and leapt on him, pinning him to the ground, her teeth at his neck. For the second time that day, Ulf was in fear for his life.

"You are very lucky that you did not attack him, Ulf," Honi snarled. "Even in his weakened state, he would have torn you to little pieces before you had time to even think of attacking him. You have always been stupid Ulf, and now I have to decide between leaving you in charge of my offspring and staying with my love!" Every word she spoke accompanied further pressure on Ulf's throat.

Honi considered finishing Ulf, but she could not do it. He and the rest of the pack would have to fend for themselves. She let go and turned to face the others; she could see they were uncertain about what to do. Everything they knew had changed so much in the last few weeks, and now this!

"You must all travel back to the ice, my children. Whether you want Ulf to lead you is your decision, but you need to decide quickly. My place is beside Bodolf, but I do not think this warm land is a good place for our kind, so you should go back," Honi said sadly, turning away from the pack to follow Bodolf.

Chapter Nine

The nest that Krys and Krask had built together was in a small mountain range, which fronted onto the vast plain. Only eight miles long and four miles wide, the whole mountain range had been the sole territory of Krys and Krask for the last year, and there were no other eagles nesting there.

Krask's home was situated on a large ledge with an overhang that protected it from most of the weather. There was a small pool of water to one side where a stream trickled down, fed by melted ice from above. The nest itself, built of branches, was over three metres long, around two wide, and lined with dried grass collected by the pair from the plain below. Long vines growing above the ledge from Virginia creeper plants, adapted over the years to deal with the change in climate, extended down from the overhang to one side. They followed the stream of water downwards for quite a few metres. Where they crossed over the shelf they intertwined, providing good shelter for at least half of the nest situated underneath.

Krask stood at the end of the ledge looking back at the nest and the small human body he had dropped there on his return the previous day. The temperature had dropped well below freezing overnight, and he was sure that the baby would die soon. Had he been a normal human baby he would have, but Banain was very special. He was a one in a million baby, who had inherited abilities from his ancestors, which activated parts of his brain not used in the majority of humans and which now were working to keep his tiny body alive. Invisible to the naked eye, a small shield of energy surrounded the Banain like a blanket, protecting him from the elements. With his heartbeat and circulation almost stopped, Banain lay in this protected state. But he could not keep out the life sapping cold for long.

Krask really wanted to tear this thing apart for what it had done to his Krys, but her last words kept reminding him of her dying wish… "Save the baby."

"Save the baby." That was what Krys had asked him to do, and he had saved it, but at what cost? His beloved Krys was dead.

"Why did you disobey me, Krys? Why did you save this thing? Why have you destroyed everything we had together? Why did you die, Krys?" Krask screamed at the empty sky.

In that moment, everything that had happened to Krask over the last few days hit him like a hammer. His natural instincts took over, and an overwhelming wave of anger swept through every bone, muscle and feather in his body. He leapt towards the nest and Banain with one purpose. To rid the world of the thing that had killed his life mate.

Chapter Ten

Bodolf was in pain. The whole of the left side of his face was on fire, and he could not see anything through that eye at all. The eagle had left his limited vision many hours ago, and although Bodolf could still hear the voice of the child in his head, it sounded different. Whereas before it was more of a contented burble, it was now distressed and weak. He knew that he should be happy about this, but oddly, a part of him longed for the return of the contented burble.

One thing he knew for sure was that he could not keep on going without rest. The last few weeks had been extremely hard, and he needed time to recuperate and mend his wounds.

The terrain he travelled was as close to his icy home as he had seen since he'd left. The large, flat expanse of short, tundra-type grass covered in a thin layer of snow was similar to areas of his homeland, although the temperature was much higher, at around four degrees during the day and minus three to five at night. It was spring now, but it would be getting much warmer as summer approached. Since the great freeze, many plants and tree species had died, not able to deal with the drop in temperature. Five thousand years ago, the whole plain would have been full of olive trees, and the temperature in the summer would have averaged over thirty-five degrees centigrade, very rarely dropping below freezing, even during the winter. Even protected from the worst of the cold by its well-established canopy, the great forest had still shrunk to half its original size, only just beginning to push back again.

At home, Bodolf would have looked for a hillock where snow had collected, burrowed in and created a warm, cosy den. However, here he was not sure where to find shelter. He could, of course, just lie down and sleep, as the temperature was no problem for him, but his instincts told him that he needed to be out of view, so that he could recover without fear of attack.

To his right, Bodolf noticed something that looked like it might be suitable, and he turned to investigate. Drawing closer, he saw a square structure half buried in the ground, covered in green tentacles of competing growth, with a small tree that had pushed its way destructively through its middle, providing a leafy ceiling. It had a large opening in the front, with smaller openings to either side. There was also a small spring in a hollow just below the structure. It was unlike anything he had seen so far in his travels. His natural instincts were telling him to leave, but he needed to rest.

Bodolf did not realise that his injuries had damaged his sense of smell as well as his vision, so when the attack came, it was from very close by.

The six grey wolves had watched Bodolf as he had loped into their territory, and had been stalking him for some time. They slunk low to the ground, their tails wagging, all eyes fixed on this strange white quarry. At an instinctive level, they knew he was one of their own, and the females in the pack were already displaying mating behaviour. But the creature was heading towards their den, ignoring every warning marker established by the pack.

The grey leader rushed at Bodolf from behind, his pack streaming in after him. As he got close he realised just how big this beast was, and how fast!

Bodolf sensed the attack at the last moment and spun to his right, bringing his good eye into play, any pain from his wounds forgotten as a massive burst of adrenaline flowed into his system. His fur bristled, making him look twice as large, and his massive jaws opened wide, searching for a target. The grey leader was in mid leap and could not avoid Bodolf's jaws. He was gripped by the neck and thrown metres away from the white monster. He was dead when he landed, his neck broken.

The next wolf managed to get hold of Bodolf's back right leg and bit down hard. Four more wolves jumped in, one on his neck, and the other three targeting legs and parts of his huge torso. Bodolf felt the pain on his back leg and twisted his whole body so that he could use his jaws. Grabbing a grey wolf's leg himself, he bit, breaking through flesh and bone. The wolf howled in agony and let go of Bodolf's leg, but all four remaining wolves were still in the fray and he was weakening fast.

With a last effort, Bodolf brought his teeth down on another wolf's neck, but before he could bite, another pair of jaws had found his own. He lost the ability to breathe, his vision blurring as jagged teeth began to tear into his air passage.

Chapter Eleven

Krask leapt over to Banain's tiny body, fully intending to end the child's life, but as he lowered his wicked beak to carry out the deed, his eyes came directly in contact with Banain's. The eagle's eyes were about the same size as the baby's, with a brown outer ring and an almost black interior. But Banain's eyes, apart from being an amazing deep shade of blue, held something else. They were a conduit to his soul, and the instant Krask looked into them, he knew he could not kill this child. He did not understand why, but he knew he could not do it.

Standing up to his full height, Krask opened his wings wide and beat the air in frustration until completely drained of energy and emotion. He then calmly closed his wings and set about helping the child.

Krask could see that Banain had no feathers yet and was cold, so he settled down over the child, making sure he could still breathe. He sat on Banain for several hours, slowly bringing the child's temperature back up. When he considered he was warm enough, he inspected the child's body, in particular his wounds, which were badly infected and puffy. Krask collected feathers and other materials from around the nest and covered the little body with them. Then he leapt from the nest and headed to the closest hunting grounds to find food.

In amongst the materials Krask had scattered on Banain was the body of a small dead animal, which was full of maggots. Sensing a new food source, the tiny creatures started to wriggle towards the enticing smell of rotting flesh.

After finding a small hare, Krask returned to the nest and ripped small strips of meat from the animal, dropping them into Banain's mouth. At the edge of the ledge, a small stream of melted ice from the snow-capped mountaintop high above ran into a small pool before continuing its journey downwards. Krask drank water from the pool, and then regurgitated it into Banain's mouth. The child coughed and spat out both the food and the water, but Krask kept repeating the feeding process until Banain swallowed some water and a little food.

Krask carried on with this procedure for five days, and then noticed that Banain's wound was full of large maggots, which had done their job and eaten all the infected areas of the wound. Krask picked up each of them, enjoying the tasty morsels of food, and fed some to Banain.

Although not out of the woods, Banain was surviving, his little body adapting to the harsh environment. The raw protein from the food caught by Krask on his daily hunting trips was helping his body fight the infection and cold.

Krask kept up this level of care for the next three months, until one day, when he returned from the hunt, he was shocked to see Banain standing erect out of the nest, tottering towards the sheer drop below!

Chapter Twelve

Honi had not realised how long her argument with Ulf and her talk to the rest of the pack had taken. However, she did realise that she was quite a distance from Bodolf. She was exhausted from the events of the last few hours, especially the flat out run in pursuit of the eagle and baby and the fight with Ulf. She could not see Bodolf, but his trail was not hard to follow – his fresh blood splattered on the frozen mostly white tundra at regular intervals was an obvious indicator, along with his distinctive musky scent.

After about an hour, Honi also started to pick up other scents, which she recognised as territorial markers from other wolves. She realised that Bodolf's trail headed right into the middle of their territory and broke into a run, fearing for the life of her mate.

After a few miles, she came to a point where Bodolf's path turned to the right, and she noticed a structure in the distance. She could also just about hear the sounds of a ferocious battle and knew Bodolf was in mortal danger.

Just as Honi broke into a full run, she heard movement right behind her. How could I have been so stupid? she berated herself. Wrapped up with finding Bodolf, she had failed to check around her and she was going to pay the price for that mistake! In front of her, she could see Bodolf under the bodies of several grey wolves, and instead of helping, she was bringing more enemies to the fight. She did not have time to look behind, she just charged straight in, targeting the wolf locked onto her mate's neck.

Grey wolves had become much more intelligent over the last five thousand years and had sophisticated mental communication abilities. However, this was of no use to the grey clamped onto Bodolf's neck. Even as he received the mental shout of danger, the nighty-five kilo bulk of Honi smashed into him. It did, however, save Bodolf's life! On hearing the mental warning, the grey wolf released its grip as it tried to see where this new danger was coming from; had this not happened, the impetus from the collision would have ripped the greys teeth through Bodolf's throat and windpipe.

Instead of going for the kill on her current target, Honi rolled and immediately turned to remove more of the wolves from her mate. If he was going to die, she would be by his side.

What she saw when she turned astounded her. Bodolf was lying on the floor unmolested; the grey wolf with the broken leg was lying dead beside him. The other four grey wolves were huddled together in full submission mode. Eight white wolves surrounded them, moving in for the kill.

In her mind, Honi received a strange message, certainly not from any of her pack. "No kill, no kill, submit white wolves, no kill."

"Wait!" Honi barked out the order to her pack.

Padding up to the four cowering animals, Honi stared at each of them in turn. She had never heard any other species communicate with their minds, except for the human baby and the eagle. Although what they had said was gibberish to her. However, she had understood something from these grey wolves and wanted to find out more.

Satisfied that the greys were going nowhere, Honi quickly went to Bodolf and checked for signs of life. She could hear his heart beating and a slow but steady breathing. She could do nothing until he woke except keep him safe.

"What are you doing here?" she said, turning to the eight white wolves standing in a semicircle around the huddling greys.

The answer came from Urska, a three-year-old female. "We could not leave you and Bodolf. Ulf ordered us to follow him, but we decided that we would rather be with you than follow him, no matter what the danger. Ulf took Jinska, his mate, although we do not believe she wanted to go, and the boys Horth and Sriank. He was not happy, Honi, but being a coward as you said, he would not fight to make us obey him. He slunk off to the North, and we came after you and Bodolf. Are you displeased, Honi?"

"No, my children." Honi called the pack her children, but in reality, it included wolves from several other packs that had mated over the years. However, Urska was her blood daughter. "I am so very pleased and surprised to see you! Bodolf and I would be dead had you not arrived when you did."

"Not so, Honi. You had already killed one grey, and would have dealt with the others had we given you time," Urska replied.

Honi was pleased with the answer; it showed the correct level of deference.

"Urska, keep a watch on Bodolf please, I want to examine these greys more closely and decide what to do with them."

Honi padded back to where the greys were huddled, wagging tails between their legs, lips grimaced into smiles and their eyes averted from the fearful, white she wolf.

"Who spoke in my mind?" she demanded.

The greys stayed in submissive mode and Honi heard nothing. She must have been mistaken before, although she was sure that she had heard something, and she was sure it was not from one of her pack. What was she to do with them then? If she let them go, they could alert more grey wolves in the area of their presence and be back with more. If only Bodolf was awake, he would know what to do.

In fact, she knew what Bodolf would not have done – he would not have told the pack to stop their attack. He would have eliminated every risk. It was this single mindedness that had attracted her to him in the first place, not that she had had any choice in the matter.

When she had first seen Bodolf, she was just thirteen months old. He had raided her parents' pack, having left his own in search of a mate. In his first couple of attempts, the pack had seen him off, but he never gave up trying. One night when she had been almost asleep, huddled with her pack for warmth, she had heard a strange voice in her head. It was the first time she had received a mind message, and she was not sure what it was. She could not understand all the words, but she understood the message behind them: he wanted her and would do anything to have her. It was the strongest sensation she had ever experienced.

Honi had realised that if she did not go to this wolf, there would be a fight between her family and this stranger. So she crept out of the den, guided by the reflection of the full moon in the eyes of her abductor. As she closed the distance between them, he turned and padded off, and a single, recognisable word entered her mind: "Follow."

Follow! Honi had never been an obedient wolf; she'd always had a rebellious streak. It had resulted in several painful nips from her elders. She had just left her pack for this wolf and "Follow!" was her thanks?

Honi could still remember the howl of shock as she had leapt at Bodolf and had bitten him at the base of his tail, right at the sensitive part. He had whirled around so quickly she could hardly believe his speed, and for one moment, she thought he was going to kill her there and then. Instead, he just stopped.

Towering over her, he had looked deep into her eyes, and she had realised that he was the most handsome wolf she had ever seen. He was snow-white, but with a small black mark over his left eye. His eyes were a rich gold colour. It had seemed to Honi that she was looking into his soul, and she liked what she saw. She remembered how calm he was when they heard the whole of her pack barking and bounding through the snow towards them.

"Follow," he'd said. And she had ever since.

"Honi, Bodolf is okay, I think, although he needs much time to recover. His wounds are many and deep. What shall we do with these greys?" Urska said.

Shaken out of her memories, Honi got back to the matter in hand. "Thank you, Urska. It is a shame, but we cannot let them go. We do not know enough about anything here, and they could come back with more of their kind. We must kill them!"

"No kill!" It was that voice again.

"Who was that? Speak or you will all die!" Honi demanded.

"I Brek, now clan leading, no kill," the voice replied.

Honi surveyed the greys again. One of them, the largest male, was looking straight at her, still in passive mode but showing some signs of bravery. In the circumstances, Honi respected that.

"You attacked my mate. He is badly injured," Honi snapped at him.

"He wounded already. He invades our territory, and we defend," the grey countered.

"Can all you greys mind talk?" Honi asked, still finding it strange to be talking to this grey.

"Yes, we group you," the grey answered.

"You what?" Honi asked. This wolf was very hard to understand, and she was getting frustrated with the conversation. She was also tired. She knew she should kill these greys, but she had always had a gentle side to her nature, on which Bodolf would often comment. She decided that she needed time to think about the best thing to do.

"Urska, I know you are tired, as we all are, but I am not sure we should kill these greys," she said, turning to her daughter.

"Bodolf would," Urska answered, not in a conceited way, simply stating a fact.

"Yes, I know, but these greys have the ability to mind talk. We are in their land; they could teach us much." As Honi said the words, she realised that it was important for the future of the pack to learn as much as possible about the greys and the other animals living there.

"Some of us need to stay awake whilst the others rest," Honi said.

"I'll stay awake," Urska replied.

Once more, Honi was pleased with Urska. Turning to the greys, she said,

"You will wait. Try to leave and you all die."

Then she lay down beside Bodolf and was quickly in a deep sleep.

Chapter Thirteen

For three months, Banain struggled to survive the mental and physical traumas he had endured. When he had heard his father's and mother's tormented screams, he had gone into shock, and when Krys had grabbed him, carrying him high into the air, his mind could not take in all that was happening.

The one thing that had helped him survive was the fact that for whatever reason he had been taken, it had been done out of love for him. He had heard Krys's voice in his mind for some time, and he had known she did not want to harm him.

He had sensed the anguish from Krys as they'd flown higher, and he had known that he had to hold onto her. Then he had experienced a dark void as her mind contact had suddenly ceased, just after he had not been able to hold onto her any longer. When another creature that looked like Krys had caught and held him, his mind could take no more and shut down, putting him into a semi-coma.

This had probably saved him during that first very cold night. With his breathing and heartbeat slowed, he was able to conserve his core heat. When he had woken up, he was under the warm feathers of Krask.

After almost choking on the horrible food and foul tasting water, he had also had to deal with the gnawing pain from his chest. He had wanted to scratch at the wounds, but some inner guiding sense had told him not to, and so he had put up with the pain and food and stayed in a semi-comatose state most of the time, trying to recover from his physical and mental ordeal.

Banain had also been subconsciously probing Krask's mind. He did not understand it yet, but he had been born with very advanced mental powers, which were already helping him communicate at a subliminal level with almost any creature within range. However, he had far more potential than just being able to use his mind to talk. Banain knew that Krask was in turmoil and that he was in anguish over the loss of Krys. He also knew that Krask would not hurt him and that the haughty eagle cared for him in his own way.

During his first months with his birth parents, Banain had started to learn human words and was building up quite a vocabulary. Since the rescue by Krask, he'd had to re-learn everything. Although Krask hardly said anything aloud, he never stopped talking in his mind!

When Krask was at the nest, Banain had to endure the less-than-gentle attention of the big eagle. Three to four times a day, Krask had pushed him around the nest as he cleaned up after Banain. From these cleaning sessions, Banain had learnt quite a few words from the mind of the eagle. He was also learning all about his food and hunting, as Krask would recite his latest hunting trips as he tore the new catch to small shreds and fed Banain before feeding himself. If Banain tried to move or climb out of the nest when Krask was there, the big eagle would nudge him back to the middle saying, "Do not go out the nest! It is very dangerous for babies out of the nest. I do not want you to fall and die; Krys would never forgive me!"

Banain had tried to mind talk back to Krask, but the eagle had just looked at him quizzically and made a sort of tusking noise. Banain found this very frustrating, but the more he tried to communicate with Krask, the more Krask went, "tusk, tusk, tusk" nudging him to the centre of the nest at the same time.

For the last week or so, when Krask was away from the nest, Banain had finally managed to get some control over his limbs. To start with, he had managed to sit himself upright, and then he had finally managed to move a small way on his hands and knees. It was not easy to move around the nest as it had high sides, but every day, when Krask was away hunting, Banain was building up his strength and coordination.

Then he had learnt how to stand and toddle around the nest, but the sides were still too high to climb, and Krask had been adding more sticks recently, making them even higher.

Banain's gift allowed him to learn things at a very fast rate, even at this early age. Now he was looking at the high sides of the nest again, and wondering how he could get out. About a month ago, he had managed to use his thumbs independently from his fingers and had spent a lot of time picking up sticks and lengths of dried grass, experimenting with them. To an onlooker, it may have seemed as if he was just playing with the bits in the nest, but Banain was working towards a solution to his confinement problem.

Every day he would bind together more sticks with the grass, and every time Krask returned, he would unknowingly destroy Banain's work during his clean-up process.

Although Banain would have eventually found a way out of the nest, how he first left the safety of his makeshift cell was nothing to do with his intelligence. As he was exploring a new fortification built by Krask just a few hours before, the weight of Banain's body found a weak spot in the structure and he fell, accompanied by a load of debris, onto the floor of the ledge.

Winded, Banain just lay there for a while. Then, gathering his wits, he sat up and used the side of the nest to haul himself upright. From the nest, all he had ever seen was the sky above him. Now his newfound freedom rewarded him with a visual feast and he could finally connect the strange noises he had heard from the confines of the nest, to their sources. Like the trickling sound of the water running down the mountain into a tiny pond, and the rustling of the vines against each other, as the wind blew through their leaves.

Banain let go of the side of the nest and started to walk towards the edge of the ledge. He felt drawn towards the amazing panorama in front of him. From this lofty viewpoint, he could see in the foreground the vast plane stretching into the distance and the green canopy of the great forest, and then in the very distance and dominating the skyline, the white expanse of the ice cap.

Banain was aware of the edge of the ledge, an inner sense already alerting him to its danger. He did not intend to go any closer, but then he heard the mental and audible scream of warning from Krask. This caused him to lose his footing, fall towards the edge, and roll over the side.

Chapter Fourteen

When Honi woke and opened her eyes, she looked towards Bodolf and met his unblinking gaze. "How are you feeling my love?" she asked.

"I hurt in many places. Where are we, what happened to the grey wolves?"

"It is a long story, but we are all safe. You need to rest and recover. You must sleep. I will bring food later."

Bodolf struggled to raise himself, but the fierce pain in his neck and leg told him it was not a good idea, so he collapsed back onto the floor.

"What do you mean we are all safe?" he asked, trying to twist his head around to see who was there with his good eye. He was sure he had seen some of his pack and some greys! He was frustrated that he could not smell anything.

"Most of the pack is here, they followed you my love, and we are all safe. That's all you need to know for now. You must sleep and regain your strength."

Bodolf was losing consciousness again anyway and was drifting back towards a deep, healing sleep. "I saw grey wolves here Honi, I must be dreaming," he whispered as he drifted off.

Honi knew she had a problem with the greys. She should have just killed them and been done with it, but the longer she delayed the decision, the harder it was to make. She wished she could think like Bodolf. Everything was black and white in his world; all other animals, apart from other white wolves, were either food or enemies.

Honi padded over to where the grey wolves should have been and was dismayed to find them gone! Lying on the floor was the inert body of Urska. Fearing the worst and berating herself for leaving Urska with such a responsibility, Honi rushed to the white wolf, looking for the injury that had killed her.

As she approached, Urska jumped to her feet and immediately went into submissive mode. "I am sorry, Honi," Urska whined. "The greys were all fast asleep; I only closed my eyes for a second!"

Honi wanted to bite Urska so hard! However, she knew that the pack was very tired and the heat of this place was very difficult for all of them.

"It's okay, Urska. They are gone and we can do nothing about it. Wake the rest of the pack, though, in case they come back with more of their kind."

At that moment, both Honi's and Urska's keen hearing picked up the sound of a group of animals moving towards them. It was a strange sound, similar to something heavy being dragged along the floor. Honi immediately recognised the profile of one of the greys coming towards her as Brek. Behind him, the other three grey wolves were dragging the carcass of a wild pig towards the den.

Honi watched, amazed, as the carcass was dragged to her feet and left. The greys retreated a short distance.

"Pig good, you eat," Brek said.

"Why did you come back, Brek?" Honi replied. She'd thought that the next time she saw the greys, it would be with a large group.

"We small pack now, easy to kill. You strong pack, we join. We know much, you need us, and we need you."

"The decision is not mine, Brek. Bodolf is our pack leader – it's his decision," Honi replied, still amazed by the greys ability to mind speak.

"We understand Honi, but we stay until he decide, yes?"

Honi considered the situation. She could not see that Brek or the other greys were a threat. If they had wanted to attack, they had had the opportunity already. Honi was okay with the plan, but she was not sure what Bodolf was going to say.

"Okay Brek, we wait until Bodolf decides," she said, wondering if she had just made a big mistake.

In fact, it seemed that she had not. Over the next few days, there was an agreement that no greys would go near Bodolf as he was recovering. The last thing Honi wanted was him thinking that they were under attack from a pack of grey wolves. The greys were a fountain of knowledge. They knew just where to go for the best hunting, and they introduced Honi and the rest of the whites to the delightful taste of the berries from the white ash bush, and other things such as snails, frogs and large insects, all of which the whites found a welcome change to their diet.

The greys also benefited during the hunt, as the whites' size and stamina allowed them to bring down much larger prey than the greys would normally be able to manage.

The newly integrated pack had constructed dens within a short distance of the water source, all facing towards the south. Bodolf was lying close to the wall of the square structure. Honi had managed to get him to drag himself inside through the large opening in the middle. He and Honi occupied the old pack leader's den, which was against the far wall inside the structure. He was getting much stronger, and Honi knew she would have to tell him of the greys soon. She hated keeping things from him, and she was very worried that he might think she had not trusted him.

"What is bothering you, Honi?" Bodolf asked, just as Honi was working out a way to tell him.

"Well, Bodolf, I need to tell you of a decision I made," Honi said, automatically going into passive mode.

"Really! I hope it was a good decision. I have been worried in the last day or so. As my sense of smell is coming back, I am sure I can smell greys. Anyway, no matter, what was your decision Honi?"

Not looking at Bodolf and flattened to the floor with her tail between her legs, Honi whispered, "I let the greys live, Bodolf. They have been helping us."

Bodolf stood up slowly; he had a look on his face that Honi had never seen before.

"You let the grey wolves live, those who attacked and nearly killed your mate. You have let Brek and his pack dictate how we should live. You have eaten all manner of strange foods without sharing with me. How could you do all this?"

It was the longest speech Honi had ever heard from the big, white wolf, and quite out of character.

"My love, I am so sorry. I could not kill the greys, and then they started to help us. If I had given you the new food, you would have asked questions. I just wanted to wait until you were well enough before worrying you with these small matters."

Then something clicked in Honi's mind. "My love," she said, standing up as she drew out the last word, her eyes now firmly fixed on Bodolf's and a deep suspicion forming in her mind. "How do you know Brek's name? And how do you know about the new food?"

Bodolf turned and sauntered to the door, all signs of his injuries gone. He looked back, and Honi swore she could see his conceited smile in her mind, as well as on his face.

"Oh, I have been talking to Brek for several days, Honi. He has been bringing me some very tasty morsels when you have been out. I particularly like the berries. We have also been talking about hunting and many other matters. I knew you did not want me to know about the greys, so thought it best not to tell you. Do you think you could get me some berries, dear? I am a little peckish." With that, Bodolf strolled outside and padded over to have a conversation with Brek and the other greys.

Honi was furious with Bodolf, but relieved at the same time. Perhaps she had been wrong to keep the information about the greys from him, but she had done it with the best intentions. She followed Bodolf out, padded up behind him and nipped him hard on the sensitive area below the tail.

Then she walked off, tail held high, satisfied with his howl of pain.

Chapter Fifteen

Bodolf and his white pack were lying low on a ridge on the snow-covered plain. He had spent the summer months recuperating from his wounds, allowing Honi and the pack to take care of him. He had found the greys to be an interesting lot, and although Bodolf found it frustrating communicating with them, as they said so much that he just did not understand, they did know a great deal about hunting in that area.

That day he had insisted on going hunting despite the protestations of Honi. His wounds had healed, but he only had about twenty per cent vision in his wounded eye. He needed to build up his strength, stamina and hunting skills again, as he wanted to get back on the trail of the baby, although he had said nothing of this to Honi. He had not heard the little voice in his head for a while, and although he did not think the child was alive, he needed to go and find out for sure.

It had started snowing a couple of days ago, much to the delight of the whites, although the greys were not so pleased. Bodolf had taken charge of this hunt, and after locating a large, lone bull, had given directions for the greys to go upwind, whilst the whites circled downwind to conceal themselves in the snow. The bull was a descendant of the Spanish bulls bred for fighting before the freeze, and was much larger and more dangerous than its predecessors were.

Brek had questioned attacking this animal; he was black and around one thousand kilos of muscle with a pair of wicked looking horns. Before every hunt, it was customary for the wolves to stand in a circle, almost nose to nose, their tails wagging, and it was during this wolf pre-hunt meeting that he and the other greys voiced their concerns.

"This is a big animal; he will feed us for many days. It is the time of mating and we need to keep our strength up," Bodolf said.

Honi gave him one of her looks, which he noticed but ignored.

"It is also a chance for the youngsters to show what they are made of." With that, he loped off to take position downwind of the bull that was unaware of them, busy trying to reach the tough tundra grass through the covering of snow.

The plan was that the greys would charge at the bull, which would panic him, and he would run towards the whites, who would jump up at the last moment and take him down. As Bodolf and his group watched, the greys came into the range of vision of the large bull. It immediately stopped eating and turned to face them.

"Attack!" Bodolf shouted to the greys, but it was the bull who attacked first. With a lightning burst of speed, it lowered its head and charged at Brek and his greys. Bodolf watched in horror as a pair of very sharp horns, powered by one thousand kilos of angry muscle, bore down on the startled wolves.

To his credit, Brek was also very quick. Regaining his wits, he leapt to the side just in time for the horns to pass harmlessly by. Then Brek set off at a full run towards Bodolf's position, the rest of the greys following behind him. The furious bull turned, charging after the fleeing wolves.

On reaching Bodolf, Brek did not stop or slow, he just said, "All yours Bodolf!" and kept running.

Bodolf could have sworn Brek was smiling as he passed, but he had a bigger problem to deal with. A one thousand kilo problem!

Bodolf had never seen prey initiate an attack before, but when the bull ran past still chasing the greys, the whites were back on home ground. As one, they leapt from concealment and split into two groups, one following to the left, and the other to the right. Normally, with a quarry that was afraid and running, they would have held back and waited until the animal was exhausted, but Bodolf took no chances this time. He charged straight at the back of the animal, targeting the soft perineum, and bit down hard. Three of the other whites also attacked the fleshy under parts of the bull, causing massive blood loss, whilst the others kept pace, not wanting at this stage to go near the dangerous front end of the animal.

Within a few moments, the bull had slowed and then stopped. He was losing blood so quickly that he could hardly keep his head lifted. Bodolf released his grip and leapt up onto the back of the collapsing animal, along with the rest of the pack.

By this time, Brek and the greys had realised that the bull had stopped chasing them; they turned and returned.

They found the bull dead, Bodolf sitting on top howling to the sky in thanks for the kill.

"Where have you been Brek? You missed all the fun. Although it was quite a sight to see your reverse hunting techniques!" Bodolf did the wolf equivalent of a laugh, and then, along with Honi, buried his head in the prey to feast on the heart, whilst the rest of the pack waited for them to finish.

After all had eaten their share of the kill, the rest of the carcass was ripped apart and carried in chunks back to the den, which was only a couple of miles away.

That evening Bodolf lay with Honi. He was just about to tell her of his plans to continue the hunt for the baby, when Honi dropped a very large bombshell on him.

"Bodolf, my love, we will be having some new additions in the spring."

Bodolf was torn; he knew that even with Honi in pup they could go to the west and search for the child, and if they had been on the ice that was what they would have done, but here! No, he could not risk taking Honi on such a dangerous journey, and he could not risk leaving her in this strange place.

"This is wonderful news!" he said, his emotions torn.

"I think we should go back home. They should be born somewhere they are more suited to, not in this warm place," Honi said.

"I cannot leave here, Honi. I will stay with you and we will make a home here with the greys, but I must stay!"

Honi knew that she would not convince Bodolf to leave, and so she accepted the compromise. "Okay, but no hunting the child until the pups are of hunting age." Honi looked deep into Bodolf's eyes and saw agreement there, but only on his terms.

Chapter Sixteen

Krask could not believe what he was seeing. Banain was walking! However, he was walking towards the edge of the ledge, and certain death. He let out a warning screech as he dived to reach the child before he fell. To his horror, he saw Banain stumble, tip over the edge and fall. He was too late!

As Banain rolled over the edge and started to drop, something unbelievable happened. During his last three months in the nest, devoid of activities, Banain's mind had been developing in another way. As well as the gift of mind-to-mind communication, Banain also possessed the ability to control objects. So far, he had only used this skill in the nest to move small twigs. Now, the fear of death triggered the survival instincts in his brain, and in a split second, his subconscious mind took control of his body and skills. His whole world slowed down, as his upside-down body went past the lip of the ledge and headed downwards.

As Banain turned his head, his eyes locked onto a vine hanging just beside him. The fibrous tendril sprang as if touched by electricity and wrapped around his legs. Banain's mind repeated this process to more and more of the vines, so that by the time he came to the limit of the tendrils' reach, they had arrested his fall. He swung gently, held securely under them. For a part of Banain, it was like seeing the events unfolding as if a spectator and being cut off from control of his mind, which was acting of its own volition. He watched as the vines started pulling him upwards, more of them snaking down and around him, until his small body was almost covered in a green lifesaving cocoon. The vines, still controlled by his subconscious mind, rolled him gently upwards until he was over the lip, and back to the centre of the ledge.

Once safe, Banain's subconscious mind disengaged, and the vines immediately relaxed, remaining loosely wrapped around the child. The power required to control the vines had been tremendous and had almost completely drained Banain's reserves. In fact, he was in great danger of not being able to recover from his mental ordeal. His mind shut down, and Banain went once more into a semi-comatose state.

Krask almost flew into the side of the cliff! His normally ice-cold mind could hardly compute what his eyes had seen. One moment Banain was falling to certain death, and the next it seemed like the mountain plants had come to life and rescued him! It had all happened so fast that even Krask's amazing vision and quick mind could not keep up with events.

Recovering his flying composure at least, Krask landed next to Banain and gently lowered himself over the very cold little body. He sat on the child for the rest of that day and all night, until the sun rose the next morning.

Oh Krys, I wish you were here. Although I was the hunter, you were always the practical one, and you knew there was something special about this child. Could even you have guessed this though? he thought to himself.

Krask remembered the times when he and Krys would fly side by side in their mating routines. They would have a stick or stone, fly high and drop the object, then dive to catch it, each trying to outdo each other with their rolls and twists.

As he gazed into the distance, he imagined he could see his beloved flying towards him, returning to him, but he knew he would never see Krys in this world again, and a single tear dropped from his eye. Gathering himself, he sang the song he used to sing with Krys. It was an ancient song of love passed down through generations. Every golden eagle learnt the song when they were very young. Krask had sung it to himself a lot recently, and he started to sing again.

"In red tinged night and golden dawn.
Our love, our life, our spirit born.

Above the clouds, above the clouds

We find our mates, souls to entwine.
Our love to last the test of time.

Above the clouds, above the clouds

When our time comes, we will go proud
And rise as one, above the clouds

Above the clouds, above the clouds."

As he finished the song, Krask wondered if he would ever see Krys again above the clouds. He could not see any situation where he could replace her; they were supposed to be together for life!

As Krask was musing, a very gentle voice filled his mind and sang almost perfectly, "Above the clouds, above the clouds."

Krask froze in place. The voice had been so small and perfect, but where had it come from? Gathering his wits, he sang, "In red tinged night and golden dawn"

After a few seconds, the voice came again. "Above the clouds, above the clouds."

Krask then realised where the voice was coming from. Standing up, he moved a short way from Banain and turned to look at him. He watched in amazement as the small child grabbed hold of the vines around him, pulled them away and then raised himself to a sitting position. Banain's deep blue eyes locked firmly onto Krask's, and in the eagle's mind he heard the song of love replayed word for word in Banain's soft, gentle voice.

Whilst Krask watched, Banain got on his hands and knees, and then raised himself up to a standing position again. Then he toddled over to the pool at the back of the ledge, dipped his hands in the water and sucked it from his palms and fingers.

"Water, nice water," Krask heard in his mind.

Krask realised that when he had been giving water to Banain, he had been saying "nice water" to the baby, who more often than not had spat it out.

Banain was on the move again, this time to the edge of the ledge. But to Krask's relief, he stopped well short. Then he turned and approached Krask.

"Food?" Banain said.

"Food," Krask repeated.

"Yes, food, hungry," Banain said again.

Krask realised they had not eaten since the previous day. He hopped over to the other side of the ledge and picked up the body of the large hare he had caught. It was lucky that he had not dropped it when he had witnessed Banain's incredible rescue the day before.

Picking it up and moving back to Banain, Krask started ripping shreds from the animal, but instead of letting Krask put the food in his mouth, Banain reached over, took them from Krask's beak and fed himself.

Chapter Seventeen

For the next two years, Krask tried to teach Banain everything he could about the world, as he knew it, but he realised that Banain was already outgrowing any lessons he could teach. After all, what use was all his experience in flying and hunting when this wingless child could not use any of it! Although Banain never complained, Krask knew the confinement of the small ledge frustrated the child. Banain could run and jump, and would scare Krask to death with his crazy antics, running around the ledge, dangerously close to the edge.

Banain's development would have amazed most humans; far more physically and mentally advanced than most children his age, at three Banain was already looking like a small boy rather than a baby. Although Krask had never seen Banain display his mental abilities again, the child did use the vines as a climbing aid and would leap on them, swinging below the ledge and scrabbling back up again. Banain also spent hours tying together vines and pieces of wood. Krask had no idea what the boy was doing, and whenever he asked, Banain would say, "Just playing." Krask was convinced there was more to these actions than just play.

Krask's whole life routine had changed. Looking after Banain had become his reason for living. In a way, Banain was a substitute for Krys and the babies they should have had together. Apart from bringing food, Krask spent a lot of time gathering the items requested by the demanding child. He had carried over lots of materials to make Banain's nest warm in the winter, which he had then helped Banain use to make an enclosed nest under the long lengths of vines that already crossed over the ledge.

Banain had also been eating strange things recently. One of the branches Krask had brought for building works had blackberries on it, and before Krask could say a word, Banain had grabbed a couple and popped them in his mouth. Then, with a big smile on his face, he ate a lot more. That evening the child had had violent stomach cramps and had made a terrible mess for Krask to clean, but over the next few days, he kept asking for more.

Krask pretended he could not find any although he knew where they grew; he was not convinced they were good for the child.

One morning, just after Krask had set off for his day's hunt, his keen eyes spotted a flash of white on the plain below, moving towards the base of the mountain. Adjusting his flight feathers, he started a fast glide in that direction. As he got closer, the forms of three wolves came into view – two of them snow-white and one grey. They were moving purposefully towards the mountain and his home.

Although Krask knew Banain was safe on the ledge, he felt almost sick with fear as he recognised the wolf that had taken his beloved Krys.

Krask turned back towards the nest, climbing hard. He had to find a couple of updrafts and felt exhausted when he finally gained enough height to land. Looking around the ledge, he could not see Banain, but that was nothing new. He was probably in the structure he had created under the vines and where he slept protected from the elements. He had still not grown any type of fur or feathers, but between them, with Krask providing most of the raw material, they had managed to fashion a sort of cover to keep the boy warm.

"Banain, come out quickly!" Krask shouted.

There was no reply, so Krask hopped over and pushed his head through the vines. There was no one inside! Panicking, Krask inspected every part of the ledge, but Banain had gone.

Chapter Eighteen

Since his subconscious mind had rescued him from falling over the ledge, Banain's conscious one had been working on developing his skills. Krask had thought that Banain was bored on the ledge, but the truth was far from it; he had spent hours every day building up his mental abilities, focusing on small objects and moving them with his will. As his grasp of how to use his power grew, so did the size of the objects that he could influence. He learnt that to move something, he needed to visualise where he wanted that object to be and how he wanted it to get there. In this way, he could move things, envisaging them moving fast or slow. The trade-off for using his skills was that they took an enormous amount of energy, and he could only maintain the skill for a matter of moments before needing several minutes to recover.

He had also managed to gain more control over his mental telepathy powers, finding that he could focus on a single mind, sending and receiving only from that entity. This meant that he was no longer sending unsolicited messages to any creature able to receive them, such as Bodolf.

He connected with many insects, and especially enjoyed the connections he made with ants. It was like sharing an amazing network controlled by a very simple language consisting of only two words: "food" and "danger". He had first gained an insight into their world by watching a long trail of them marching to and from a squashed berry. Concentrating on one of the ants, he had started to receive a harmony of chants: "food, food, food". Switching his attention between a few of the industrious creatures, he had sensed that each ant was also laying down a scent trail, which changed in type according to what each creature was doing. If he pushed a stick into the trail of the ants, the chants would immediately change to "danger, danger, danger", and within a short time bigger soldier ants would turn up to do battle with the stick. Banain found that he could also suggest the word "danger" in an ant's mind, which would trigger the same response.

As his skills developed, Banain focused his mind further from the nest, until he made contact with another creature far more advanced than the insects. He sensed that it was quite close, and moving towards the end of the ledge and looking around, Banain tried to see where this creature was.

Although Banain was incredibly agile and strong for his age, he had tested every nook, cranny and handhold to find a way off the ledge, but to date, he could not. He was intrigued to know where this creature was.

Without disclosing his presence, Banain entered the mind of the creature, trying to make sense of what it was and how it communicated. Unlike the insects, there was a lot going on in this mind, and he could not understand most of the thought processes. After a little while, Banain had to withdraw, as it was draining his mental energy. Lying down to rest, Banain promised himself he would communicate more with this creature.

Over the next few weeks, he learnt more. He managed to identify the words for fear and food, by associating them with the emotions that triggered the use of the words. In addition, he knew that the creature loved food, especially berries and succulent grass.

Banain decided it was time to make contact. Even at this young age, his experience with insects and other small mammals had shown him that if he just barged into another creature's mind, it caused panic. Some creatures had been so frightened that they had died from shock. Banain had learnt that being in a mind that dies is almost like experiencing the death yourself. He had decided that he did not want that experience again.

When he did speak in the creature's mind for the first time, it was very gently, and he just whispered the word, "Food." He sensed interest from the creature so repeated the word. "Food."

"Food?" the creature answered, sounding anxious but showing more signs of interest.

"Yes, food here," Banain sent. He hoped that, like him, the creature could sense direction from the messages.

"No food here!" the voice said in his mind, much closer.

"Yes, food here, call for food," Banain added and then listened.

"Bah!" The call was close, just below the ledge, it seemed. Banain moved quietly to the edge and looked down, but he could see nothing, just a sheer drop.

"Baaaah. Baaaaaaaah! Food?" The sound and thought came from directly beneath him, but he could see nothing down there.

Banain found a shrub with berries delivered yesterday by Krask and tied it to a length of vine, then gently lowered it over the edge. After lowering it around ten metres, the creature rewarded him with a mental message.

"Foooood!" This was the response Banain had heard many times before when the creature had found food, so he stopped lowering the vine and waited, hanging precariously by his toes over the edge. From an area that seemed to be inside the mountain, a black nose protruded towards the berries and the animal gently nibbled a few of them from the closest branches. Getting bolder, the top of a black head, adorned with a pair of curved horns, emerged, took a good hold of the branch and yanked it inwards.

Banain was nearly pulled from his precarious position on the side of the mountain and had to let go of the vine quickly, using all his strength and skills to scrabble back up to safety. But he did not mind – he had found a way off the ledge!

Chapter Nineteen

As soon as Krask set off from the nest, Banain followed the same routine he had been using to leave the ledge since that day; with the help of Lepe, the mountain sheep, he had discovered the hidden trail below. He climbed on top of his nest house and scrambled along, and then down the front as far as the interwoven vines allowed. Focusing his mind, Banain concentrated on the area where he knew the ledge to be and envisaged a vine rope ladder he had placed there attaching to the bottom of the overhanging vines. From below, the ladder uncoiled itself and snaked up the side of the mountain, twisting itself around the overhanging vines. After he had climbed down, he used his mental power to bring the ladder back to the floor again, where he covered it with sticks and leaves.

He sank to the floor, exhausted by the effort of using his mental powers, and closed his eyes, trying to recuperate. After a few moments, he experienced a warm, wet sensation on his face, followed by a painful dig in the ribs. He opened his eyes to see his best friend Lepe standing in front of him. He had given him the traditional sheep welcome – a lick and a poke!

"Lepe!" Banain rebuked.

"Ah, poor human lie on floor when Lepe need food. Come on, we go." With that, Lepe turned and bounded along the very narrow track carved into the side of the mountain.

Gathering his strength, Banain raised his small body upright and started after the hungry sheep.

"Today we go down the valley, lots of food! Banan slow, Lepe always waiting!" the impatient sheep complained, pronouncing the name "Banan".

"I can't jump like you Lepe, but I am getting faster and one day I will catch you!" Banain shouted.

Over the last few months, the pair had built up quite a friendship. Lepe had strangely stinted, but comprehensive speech ability.

"Ha-ha, you funny Banan, you never catch Lepe. You slow human." With that, Lepe bounded along a part of the trail that had all but collapsed, and in an amazing feat of dexterity, the four-legged rock jumper disappeared from view. As usual, Banain had to navigate this part of the trail with caution. Although his years of living on the side of the mountain had hardened and strengthened him, there were long jumps between the rocks, and a very long fall if he misjudged.

For any human, the sight of the three-year-old child dressed in an outfit made completely from eagle feathers and flax would have been very strange. A circlet made from strips of flattened flax surrounded Banain's head, holding his mop of long blond hair away from his eyes. On the top three quarters of his body, he wore a type of feather smock, synched in at the waist with another length of flax. His lower legs and feet were bare. Soft down stuffed inside the smock helped to keep Banain warm, but would slowly work its way out as he moved. The outfit was the latest collaboration between Banain and Krask. Krask often complained that if Banain took any more of his feathers, he would lose the ability to fly!

Within ten minutes of leaving the ledge, Banain and Lepe were halfway down the mountain and had travelled via a tunnel to the other side. From this point, Banain could see the green and white valley below and the sparkling water of the lake that was on the edge of the clearing. The winter snow had receded from most of valley and the floor was full of new shoots and flowers.

"Remember Banan, keep look for Claw Killer. She think we food. Me escape fast, you dinner," Lepe said.

Banain sent a quick okay back to Lepe in his mind, conserving his energy to keep running. He and Lepe had already experienced a couple of close shaves with the Claw Killer, as Lepe called her. However, he could sense if she was close by; he also knew that he was not her normal prey, and that she lost interest in him if he sent the right signals.

By the time Krask had returned to the ledge to find him missing, Banain and Lepe were nearly on the floor of the valley. Because Banain was not expecting Krask to be back for most of the day, he was not listening for him and he did not hear his anguished cry of despair.

Once in the valley, Banain headed for the lake. He had taken to going into the water recently, much to the distress of Lepe, who could not understand why any creature would want to enter that cold, wet and dangerous stuff!

Banain found that once he got over the initial cold chill, the sensation of being in the water was fun. He had learnt to move around in the water by kicking with his feet and pulling with his hands. He planned to play in the water for a while, and then go and collect some of his favourite plants, herbs and tubers to eat. Again, Lepe could not understand why Banain made such a fuss about looking so hard for food when the whole plain was full of it! All you had to do was lower your head and eat.

Banain entered the water, waited for the initial shock of cold to wear off and then started moving deeper. He enjoyed the effect it had on Lepe. "Hey Lepe, look where I'm going!" he shouted.

"You stupid human, Banan, that far enough. Come back now, yes!"

Banain like the fact that this was something he could do that Lepe could not.

"You're stupid Lepe. You can't go in water like clever human," he replied, laughing.

"You not clever when water eat you!" Lepe said, pacing nervously along the shore of the lake as close to Banain as possible. He wished he could overcome his fear of the water that his friend loved so much.

Whilst the two of them traded insults, neither of them saw the shapes of the three wolves entering the valley and moving towards the lake from the opposite side.

Chapter Twenty

Bodolf was frustrated. For eighteen months, he had been the dutiful leader and father. Honi had produced a fine litter of eight pups last spring, and a year later, she was due to pup again. The other wolves had been busy as well, and the den area had been constantly full of yipping pups careering around the adults, who every now and then would nip an overaggressive pup as they practised their hunting skills. There had also been a couple of pairings between the white and grey wolves. The resulting offspring were off-grey and, to Bodolf's mind, strange looking creatures.

During this time, several of the group had left to set up their own packs, so there were about the original number of mixed wolves remaining, including the new yearling pups, who were just becoming useful hunters.

Bodolf no longer had a clue who belonged to whom, nor did he really care, except for one of the male cubs called Arkta who was in fact his son and who had taken to following Bodolf everywhere. At first Bodolf found Arkta annoying, but over time the pup had become a very competent hunter, which Bodolf respected.

All Bodolf had wanted was to restart his quest for the child. He had not heard him for a long time when he had received a very short but clear call in his mind. It sounded like "Kepe" or "Lepe". Bodolf was not sure what it meant, but he knew whom it had come from and from where. A few nights ago, he had told Honi of the message and the need to find the child. Although he had not wanted to leave her, he was confident that the pack could look after themselves without him. After a lengthy discussion, Honi had grudgingly conceded, knowing that she could not stop him anyway.

Just over twenty-four hours later, Bodolf, Arkta and Brek the grey were entering a valley in the shadow of a small mountain. They had travelled the eighty-odd miles at a good pace and had only stopped for a few hours' sleep. They had been careful not to trespass into other greys' territories. Bodolf had intended to go on his own, but as he left the den early yesterday morning, Arkta and Brek had padded up alongside him.

"Nice morning for hunt, Bodolf," Brek had said.

"I am not hunting, Brek, I am going somewhere on my own," Bodolf had replied.

"Oh, where you go?" Brek had enquired, annoyingly.

"That is my business. And what are you doing here, Arkta?" Bodolf had snapped, his patience wearing thin.

"Oh, I am just going to Krask Mountain to search for a legendary child," Arkta had said casually.

Bodolf had stopped dead in his tracks. He had hoped no one knew about his quest for the child, but of course, these greys did nothing but gossip. He knew that he was not going to convince them to stay behind without a fight, and he just wanted to get on.

"Okay, you can come, but do not slow me down!" he had said.

Twenty-four hours later, Bodolf was pleased that he had the pair with him. Brek was an expert at avoiding other greys and skirting their territories, and Arkta had boundless energy. With Brek's directional help, the pup would run off every now and then and reappear a short while later with a hare or other small animal hanging from his jaws.

After several hours of searching around the foot of the mountain, they came to a small opening through the middle, with a steep climb up between two vertical pillars of rock. Climbing up to the top of the narrow trail, the gap opened up to reveal a small valley with a lake.

As Bodolf examined the terrain, movement in the lake caught his attention. Focusing his senses, he recognised the blond head of a human child. Although bigger than when he last saw him, he knew it was the child he had been looking for. In stalk mode, Bodolf, Arkta and Brek crept down the valley towards the child and the sheep that appeared to be with him. Bodolf's mouth was drooling in anticipation.

Chapter Twenty-One

Krask was beside himself with fear for Banain. What had happened to the child? The most likely answer was that Banain had fallen from the ledge. Krask launched himself into the air, spiralling down to the base of the cliff, and looked for Banain's little body. Finding nothing under the ledge, Krask widened his search area, thinking that, somehow, Banain had survived and was trying to find help, but there were no signs of Banain at all.

The other option was that another animal had taken him. After searching as far away from the nest as he calculated Banain could have travelled, Krask decided to climb higher to see if he could spot anything, including those three wolves.

It took some time to gain altitude above the mountains, but as soon as he did, the eagle's keen vision spotted something moving in the small valley in the middle of the mountain range. He wheeled around and headed in that direction, although he could not believe this could be Banain – it was too far from the nest.

As Krask got closer, he recognised the distinct shape of Banain. He was just entering the lake. There also seemed to be a mountain sheep standing at the water's edge, watching him. Puzzlement and enormous relief flooded through Krask as he folded his wings and dived down towards the strange pair. He was going to give Banain such a peck for doing this, he... Krask's thoughts were interrupted as he spotted something else moving at the edge of his field of vision.

Focusing on this new area, Krask made out the shapes of the three wolves slunk low to the ground and moving with stealth towards Banain and the sheep. Changing his direction towards the wolves, Krask dived even faster, eating up the distance between them, but in his mind, he knew Banain was in grave danger. What could he do against these three ferocious hunters? He sent a warning to Banain. "Banain, run, you are in danger!"

Well out into the lake, Banain heard the warning loud and clear. Looking up, he saw the distinctive shape of Krask diving like a rocket towards a point just on the far side of the water.

"Killers, Banain, hunting you, you must run," Krask sent urgently.

At first, Banain was not too worried; Krask had probably seen the Claw Killer. He concentrated on his communication abilities and cast out for contact. Over the last few months, he had honed his abilities so that he was able to make contact with other minds from quite a distance. What came back chilled him far more than freezing water could ever do. He instantly recognised the mind of Bodolf and sensed the aggression and need to kill in the creature. More than that, he realised Bodolf was close, and that he was coming for him!

Panicking, the child turned towards the shore and paddled as fast as he could, but panic was freezing him – he could not remember how to swim! Banain tried to gather himself, but as he kept breathing in water, he found he was going downwards rather than forward.

Bodolf was only metres from the shore of the lake. He could see the child splashing in the middle, but as he had hardly ever seen liquid water in this amount, never mind been in it, he elected to go around. Brek, however, was happy in the water, as he was used to crossing the wide rivers on the plains to the north of Bodolf's dens. Arkta bounded into the water for the first time in his life without hesitation, focused on the most direct route to the prey.

Krask headed for the lone wolf on land: Bodolf. Extending his razor talons, he aimed for the back of Bodolf's head, but a sixth sense alerted the big wolf to the eagle, and at the last minute, the wolf veered to the left, bringing his undamaged eye round so that he could see the overshooting Krask. He snapped at the wing as it brushed past him, but the eagle was going too fast and shot upwards again, circling for another pass.

Bodolf set his sights on his human quarry again, confused by what he was seeing. He had closed the distance to around twenty metres and could see Brek and Arkta in the middle of the lake swimming strongly, but he had no sight of the child.

Banain made one last effort to get to the surface. His lungs were bursting, and he was on the verge of passing out. With tremendous determination, he pushed upwards and started to rise, but not fast enough.

Then he felt movement in the water beside him and could see thrashing legs and a black body.

"Hold on me, Banan, hold on me!" It was Lepe.

Seeing the danger to Banain, the plucky little sheep had run into the water and now swam beside him, treading water. The two wolves in the lake were very close now.

Instinct took over, and Banain grasped hold of the nearest part of Lepe to him, his horn. Lepe twisted his strong neck, pulling Banain onto his back, and turned towards the shore. As soon as his hooves found the bottom, the sheep accelerated onto the shore and then towards the track leading back up the mountain.

Both Brek and Arkta had been very close to Banain when Lepe had rescued him, but had lost some ground when the sheep found the floor first and accelerated out of the lake. Finding their footing as well, they set off in pursuit of the sheep with its small human rider. Bodolf was closer and was about to leap at the pair as they emerged from the water, when Krask screamed right behind him. He felt a sharp pain in his right ear as the eagle raked him with his talons. This distracted Bodolf for a few precious seconds, allowing Lepe to gain some distance.

Regaining his wits, Banain held onto the racing sheep with all his strength. Twisting his head, he was just in time to see Krask's second attack on Bodolf, and he noted the two other wolves closing the distance. Concentrating his mind, Banain sent a message to someone he knew would be a dubious ally, but even his undeveloped child's mind realised that he and Lepe were in grave danger, and they needed help.

Lepe reached the bottom of the rocky trail which led up to the tunnel and the ledge below Krask's nest. Had he not been carrying the fifteen kilo child, he would have headed into the rocks and used his agility and rock-hopping abilities to lose his pursuers, but he knew he could not manage anything but a straight run whilst carrying Banain, and he was tiring fast.

A gap of about ten metres separated Bodolf from Lepe and Banain, who were just entering the tunnel, and it was a further ten metres to Brek and Arkta. Bodolf, closing the gap fast, heard a strange screeching noise behind him, but decided to ignore it and keep after his quarry.

Brek and Arkta were taken completely by surprise by the full on attack from the screeching, teeth-and-claw-bristling cougar. Spurred into attack by Banain's food call, the big cat was committed to a downhill journey, which should have put her in a position right behind the slow moving sheep with the strange cargo, when she saw the three wolves. The first one passed below but the second two were coming head on, so she had no choice but to accelerate down the rock face and attack.

Momentarily stunned by the ferocious attack, Brek and Arkta stood side-by-side, backing slowly down the mountain, with the cougar spitting and snarling, but not attacking further. It was a standoff, and they were out of the chase.

Lepe was exhausted. Exiting the tunnel into the bright morning sunshine, he tried to jump over the difficult section just before the nest overhang, but he lost his footing. He knew he was going down, so in one last effort, he threw Banain's body to the right as he fell to the left. Still connected to Lepe's mind, the instant that Lepe made his decision, Banain knew as well. He tried to hold on and sent a message to Lepe to stop, but it was too late. His small body, thrown against the side of the cliff, rolled safely onto the floor, but Lepe's body started to plummet towards the rocky floor below.

For the second time in his life, Banain was in contact with a mind as it died. This time it was a close friend. It was like a physical blow tearing at the inside his mind and soul, but his anguish would have to wait. Bodolf, who had not been far behind, was just a couple of metres away and preparing to make his final leap at Banain. Lepe had thrown the child over quite a large gap in the rock, and this now created a barrier between Banain and Bodolf. The wolf, crazed with the desire to kill, sprang over the gap, jaws wide open and ready.

Krask had lost sight of Banain and the sheep as they had entered the tunnel, and had to climb hard to get to the other side to see them again. As he cleared the top of the ridge, he was just in time to see the white wolf bunching to jump the gap that separated him from Banain. Diving again, and with a mighty scream of rage, Krask hit the wolf full on as he was in mid-leap. The blow was enough to disrupt the wolf's jump and he landed short of the other side, his front legs on the ledge, but most of his body and back legs hanging in mid-air.

Bodolf clawed the rocky mountain surface with his front paws, trying to get some purchase, but the ground was full of loose stone, and the more he scrabbled, the further backwards he went. Bodolf knew he was not going to make it. He lifted his head to look at his quarry only a few metres away, immediately drawn into the deepest blue eyes he had ever seen in his life.

As he watched, slowly losing the last of his grip, he saw the child turn his head away to look up the trail. He cursed this human child who had brought him to this, wishing with every fibre of his body that he could somehow make him pay for what he had done to him. He did not even deem to watch his last few moments of life! Then, from the direction the child was looking, from under loose leaves and debris, an object rose out of the ground, flashed past the child and flew down below Bodolf. The child's head had turned to follow the object, and Bodolf noted that his deep blue eyes were strangely altered, almost pulsing with energy. He then felt something wrapping around his chest, winding around his torso, gripping him in a vice like hold. He looked down to see a vine tendril wrapped around him, following its writhing length back to near the child, he realised it was not attached to anything. It was as if the vine was alive, acting on its own to pull him from certain death. His backward motion arrested, very slowly, he felt himself hauled towards the safety of the ledge. A few moments later, he was able to pull himself to safety, all life leaving the vine, which fell lifeless to the floor.

Trying to recover his wits, Bodolf looked at the child again. Banain looked back at him his eyes regaining their steady steely blue for a few seconds, then closed as the small human boy who had just saved the large wolves life, slumped into a deep sleep.

Chapter Twenty-Two

Krask was in trouble. After he hit Bodolf, he did not have room to stop before crashing into the wall. Just managing to scrabble onto the ledge on the other side, he found himself trapped between the sheer side of the cliff and two large wolves: one white and one grey. He spread both wings and screeched in defiance at them, but both wolves were preoccupied with the events unfolding on the other side of the ledge. Looking that way himself, Krask could not believe the scene developing in front of him. He watched in disbelief as Banain saved Bodolf from certain death and then passed out from the effort.

"Banain, wake up, you are in danger!" he screamed at the child.

"He is not in danger from me, eagle!" another voice in his head said.

Krask looked around for the source, but apart from the wolves and Banain, no other creature was nearby.

"What is this creature? Why has he saved me, when I would have happily killed him?" the voice said.

"Who are you?" Krask demanded.

"I am Bodolf."

Krask realised it was the large white wolf standing over the sleeping figure of Banain, and met his steady gaze.

"You killed my beloved Krys," Krask almost hissed, remembering that day with bitter clarity.

"I thought her brave but stupid to sacrifice her life for a human. Now I think I understand why she did it, although I do not understand at the same time. If it is any consolation to you, she took nearly all the sight of one eye from me," the wolf said, settling onto his haunches.

"What do you mean, wolf? You are not making sense." Krask looked around for a way to escape from his trapped situation. He did not trust the wolf.

"I have travelled from my homeland in the North all the way to this hot, strange land in pursuit of this child. I thought my mission was to kill him. Now, when I could do so with ease, I cannot! So what is his purpose? What is my purpose?"

"I felt the same way after my beloved Krys died to save him. Her dying message to me was 'look after the child'. To start with, I did it because it was her wish, but very soon I was also in the spell of this strange child."

"What a strange sight we must be, three wolves, an eagle and a human child!" Bodolf said.

"How is it that you know my language?" Krask asked.

"I do not, I thought you were speaking in wolf tongue, wait a moment.
Brek, Arkta, can you understand this eagle?" Bodolf asked the two wolves who were looking at him quizzically.

"How do you mean, understand the eagle, Bodolf? We thought you struck dumb! You're just sitting there looking at it. Should we kill it?" Brek stood and turned back towards Krask.

"No Brek, wait, something strange is going on here. Be patient," Bodolf instructed.

Brek looked back at Bodolf, and he and Arkta sat back on their haunches again.

"My wolves cannot hear our conversation Krask, apparently only you and I can communicate."

"Well I hear both, with all the yapping and squawking, but what about Banan? He need help!" Lepe said as he appeared on the track, ran towards the two wolves and the eagle, jumped straight over them and the gap, and landed beside Banain and Bodolf.

The sheep was so quick that neither the wolves nor the eagle had time to react. One minute the track was clear, and then this mad sheep jumped over everyone and stood over Banain, licking him in the face and poking his ribs with the point of one horn.

"Come on Banan, no more sleep. Nasty wolves here to eat you. I rescue again!" Lepe said, lowering his horns towards Bodolf, who was having a hard time taking all this in.

Before anyone could say a word, Banain's eyes opened. He looked at Lepe and a huge smile spread over his face. "Lepe, you are alive!" Banain shouted in the sheep's mind. "But I saw you fall over the edge!"

"Of course Lepe alive! You stupid as usual, Banan. You think Lepe not know other tracks?" The little sheep laughed.

"So you knew when you fell that you were not in danger!" Banain said.

"So you knew when you went in deep water, I not like. Anyway, Lepe save slow Banan again from very big wolves." Lepe looked nervously at Bodolf, who was towering over him and not looking happy.

"Thank you, Lepe. I know you saved my life, but I thought I felt you die. I just don't understand." Banain was confused. He knew he had felt death in his mind whilst connected to Lepe, but here the little sheep was, talking to him.

Looking over the gap, the child saw the two other wolves staring at Bodolf; one was a smaller grey wolf, but the other was a white, almost as large as Bodolf. The white looked straight at Banain and the child instantly connected with him, enabling within the wolf the ability to communicate with other creatures. This ability was one of Banain's gifts and currently he did not have the ability to control it. Completely drained, Banain slipped back into unconsciousness again.

"Wolf, are you going to kill the child?" Krask asked Bodolf.

"It is all I have dreamt of for years... However, I cannot. In reality, I do not know what to do. Everything is so strange, so confused. Now I can understand this sheep as well!"

"Okay, so stupid wolf not knows what to do. Lepe know. Wolf goes away and Lepe look after Banan."

"Maybe stupid wolf will have a meal of sheep," Bodolf growled.

"This is not helping, Lepe. Apologise to the wolf before he eats you!" Krask said, still not sure about his situation, trapped between the other two large wolves and the cliff edge.

"Sorry Mr Wolf but–"

Before Lepe could dig a deeper hole, Krask interrupted. "Look Bodolf, there are many things that need to be discussed, but now is not the best time. Why don't you go back to the valley and rest and I will meet with you there later?"

Bodolf turned and stared at the large eagle. At this moment, he had every advantage. He had the eagle trapped, the child at his mercy and the cheeky sheep as a bonus. He could kill them all and go back to a normal life. At any other time, this was exactly what he would have done, but everything had changed when he had looked into the child's eyes and Banain had saved him from falling to his death.

Being a hunter himself, Krask had a good idea what was going through the big wolf's mind. He had been in contact with Banain for several years. He did not understand the child, but what he did know was that he had a special gift, and, strangely, so did Bodolf.

"Bodolf," he said to the contemplating wolf, "have you ever considered why, out of the many thousands of animals, and living so far from Banain, you heard his voice? There must be a reason for it, you must have a purpose with this child, and I don't think that purpose is for you to kill him!"

Bodolf knew the eagle was right, but the wolf instincts in him did not want to give up this advantage. "How do I know you will come, eagle? I have you all here. Why should I trust you?" As Bodolf said the words he knew the answer, but it was his last stand.

"I will come, wolf. We connect to this child in some way, so there is nothing to gain by avoiding you. Our destinies are the same and we need to decide what we are going to do, but as I said, now is not the time," the eagle stated, looking at the collapsed figure of Banain.

"Okay, we will go and wait in the valley, eagle, but do not make me wait too long," Bodolf said, turning towards Brek and Arkta. "I know this is strange, but we must go back to the valley," Bodolf said.

"After killing these creatures?" Brek asked.

"No Brek, we leave them and return to the valley. You must do what I ask, and I will explain later." Bodolf searched both of his travel companions for signs of dissent, but sensed none.

"Okay," Brek said in a matter of fact tone. He turned and loped back down the trail.

Arkta was going to tell Bodolf that he could understand the eagle and the sheep, but something stopped him from saying anything and he too turned and followed Brek.

"Wait, you two. I saw a large creature just before the dark passage when I was chasing the sheep, so we should be careful," Bodolf warned.

"We killed it, Bodolf. Looks like the only kill we get today," Arkta said.

Bodolf took one last look at Banain, turned and backed up to give himself room to leap across the gap.

"Wolf want push?" Lepe offered.

"I am curious about the child so he lives. I respect the eagle so he lives. You on the other hand, I see only as food! But I will wait until you have more meat on your scrawny little body," Bodolf snarled.

With that, Bodolf exploded into motion, leapt the gap easily and disappeared in a second down the trail.

Chapter Twenty-Three

Three hours later, Krask was standing by Banain who was sitting on the floor looking very contrite. Having seen the child recover enough to use his powers to gain access back to the nest, Krask had quizzed him about what he could do. Although amazed by Banain's abilities, he was also very annoyed and upset that the child had not confided in him.

"I am sorry, Krask. I didn't want to worry you," Banain said sheepishly.

"Worry me!" Krask exclaimed. "How worrying do you think it was to come back to the nest and find you gone, Banain? How worried did you think I was when I saw you in the lake, being stalked by wolves?"

"Not Banain's idea goes to valley, my idea," Lepe said, who still stood on the ledge below.

"I don't care whose idea it was, you were both in great danger and I promised my beloved Krys I would save you. Instead, I nearly sent you into the mouth of the wolf she rescued you from!" Krask said, realising how close he had come to losing the child.

"Never mind, all okay now. We go valley, see wolf, eat nice food, no problem," Lepe said.

"You two are going nowhere!" Krask exploded. "You have got yourselves in enough trouble, and I am not letting you near that wolf again. I am going to Bodolf alone, and if you leave this ledge before I get back, I will eat you myself, Banain!"

With that, Krask launched himself into the air, adding his final comment before flying off. "I eat sheep as well!"

Bodolf, Brek and Arkta were lying under a tree by the edge of the lake, close to where Banain had been swimming. They had feasted on the cougar on the way down the mountain trail and were now in a semi-slumber. Bodolf had explained as well as he could what had happened on the ledge.

Arkta was the first to hear the keen of the golden eagle as it circled high above, and alerted his travelling companions to its presence. Rising and moving into the open, the three wolves stood in a semi-circle looking up the descending form of Krask.

Landing a few metres away from them, Krask folded his wings and silently questioned his own sanity. "Banain is at the nest recovering. I thought it best to come and speak to you alone," he said to Bodolf.

"That is not the truth. You do not trust me, eagle, but I understand that. I would do the same in your place. Let us talk of this child and what hold he has on our lives," Bodolf replied.

"I will talk, but I feel exposed here on the ground, wolf," Krask said, nervously looking around.

"Don't worry, eagle, I will ask my companions to make sure we are not interrupted. Keep watch and make sure we are not disturbed," he said to Arkta and Brek, who padded a little way off from the pair.

"Oh I feel so much better now, wolf!" Krask replied sarcastically, accepting that he had little choice in the matter.

The two of them talked for several hours. Although in reality, Krask did most of the talking, recounting Banain's upbringing and the skills that the boy had shown. They had in fact stopped talking about Banain, unable to decide what to do next, and were discussing prey and hunting in the area, when something that would change both of their lives forever occurred.

Bodolf, with his highly developed hearing, heard the noise first, but could not distinguish what it was. Stopping his conversation with Krask, he turned his head, triangulating the sound with his ears, and identified a point just beyond the shore of the lake. Krask also looked where Bodolf was staring.

The noise, similar to a rhythmic high-pitched chanting, made Bodolf feel a cold deep inside, a chill unlike anything he had felt before, even in his homeland. Then it appeared to Bodolf that everything froze in place, but not quite. Things were moving, but very slowly. He realised that he was also immobilised, the sensation similar he imagined to being encased in a block of ice, he could look out but had no control over his limbs.

"Bodolf, you are the chosen, this has always been so." The voice, or rather the harmonisation of voices, almost sang in the Bodolf's mind.

"What are you? And why can't I move?" Bodolf growled.

"What we are, is unimportant, Bodolf. You cannot move because it is only in this nearly timeless state that we can communicate with you. It takes a great deal of power to communicate with you here, so please listen carefully. The child, Banain, is vital to the survival of the new world, and it is your destiny to use your skills to help him. You have been chosen to see that he survives to fulfil his destiny," the voices sang in Bodolf's mind.

"What, you want me to protect the child I have been hunting all this time because I have a gift that nearly caused me to kill him?" Bodolf was struggling to understand what was happening.

"It is unfortunate that we could not communicate with you earlier, Bodolf, but since the great freeze we have been forced further south and we cannot communicate in freezing water. This lake is the closest we can go north. You are very special, Bodolf, and are destined to play a major part in his future. Banain needs you, Bodolf."

"I have my own life, my own pack, my own world. I can teach this human child nothing. I do not know what you are but I have had enough of this. Get out of my head!" Bodolf shouted, trying to wrestle his mind away from the voices.

"Please reconsider, Bodolf. You do not have to teach the child, others will do that; you just need to protect him and help in other ways. He must make a journey far to the south and he needs your help. We have placed the location of the place Banain needs to go in the mind of the eagle." The voices were getting weaker as they spoke. "The child needs you, Bodolf." And then they were gone.

"What just happened Bodolf, you disappeared for a second and then reappeared?" Krask said, his feathers standing out in reaction to the event he had just witnessed.

"You heard nothing of the conversation?" Bodolf enquired.

"What conversation?" Krask said, looking at Bodolf quizzically.

Bodolf explained everything that had happened. When he finished, Krask spread his wings and ruffled his feathers trying to regain his composure again.

Settling back, he said more to himself than Bodolf, "So I have the location in my head. You need to protect the child, and it is Banain's destiny to rescue the world from something… Okay then wolf, if what you are saying is true, what are we waiting for?"

Bodolf stood up and turned to face Krask. "Are you mad, bird? I am not going anywhere other than back to my mate! I have rescued this human child already by not eating him. I will not be part of this…this madness!"

Bodolf turned and stalked away from Krask, the other two wolves falling in behind him.

"Bodolf, you can't go! What of your destiny, what of Banain?" Krask called after the wolf.

"You save the world, bird, and good luck to you!"

Chapter Twenty-Four

"Where are we going?" Banain asked again as he walked across the valley a few days later. He had never been further than the lake but was excited about the prospect of traveling through the landscape he had only seen from Krask's lofty nest

"We are going on an adventure, Banain, as I've told you lots of times already. But you must do everything I tell you, okay?"

Krask was circling a hundred metres above the figure of Banain, who was dressed in his eagle feather smock and leaving a trail of soft down behind him with every step.

"Where is the wolf? Is he not coming with us, Krask?" Banain asked for around the third time in the last ten minutes.

"No, Banain, I told you, this is just an adventure for you and me," the eagle said, trying to control his growing frustration. He knew this was a big event for the child and did not want to upset him.

"And me! You forget to invite Lepe, yes?" Jumping out from under the cover of a tree, Banain's friend ran up to the boy, licked him in the face and poked him in the rib with his horn, his customary greeting.

"You are not invited, sheep!" Krask screeched, diving down and landing in front of the pair of them who were chasing each other round and round in circles.

"You will only get us in more trouble. I have enough problems looking out for Banain on this journey without you to look after as well!"

"Journey... I like journeys. Where are we going? Is there nice food? What–?" Before the excited sheep could finish the sentence, Krask gave him a sharp peck on the rump.

"Look, Lepe, this is not some adventure," Krask started.

"You said it was an adventure," Banain interrupted.

"Okay, yes, it is an adventure, but it is only for me and for Banain. That is because I need to protect him from harm. You will ruin the adventure and put Banain in danger if you come as well, Lepe."

"So you not want Lepe because you need protect Banan from wolves?" Lepe asked.

"Yes, wolves and other dangerous things," Krask said, starting to believe he was getting somewhere.

"But you can't protect him from sheep!" Lepe countered.

"What do you mean I can't protect him from sheep? That is a stupid thing to say."

"Did you see Lepe before jumped from tree? If Lepe wolf, Banan dead. How you rescue Banan anyway? Can you carry him? Can you fight everything on your own? No, you need Lepe," the sly sheep said.

Krask hated to admit it but the annoying sheep was right. He could not stay high enough to look for enemies and be close enough to help the child if he missed something, which Lepe had just proved was possible.

"Okay, Lepe, you can come, but you do everything I say, okay?"

"Okay, eagle. Come on, Banan, Lepe see great food when he wait for you, come on."

With that, he ran off, Banain following behind him, a big grin on his face.

Krask watched them go, exasperated. Taking off, he climbed to a height where he could see Banain and the sheep running from one place to the next, the sheep stopping to nibble at tender shoots of grass and Banain picking berries and tubers.

"At least they are going roughly in the right direction," Krask thought to himself as he circled, picking out familiar land features and enjoying the feeling that the freedom of flight still gave him.

In reality, he was not sure where they were going other than to the South. Although Bodolf had told him he had the location in his head, he could find no clue or memory of it. He just hoped that he would soon.

After just a couple of hours travelling, Banain was tiring. Whilst Krask glided above on the thermals and Lepe jumped about full of energy, the child was finding the going tough. They had only just started, but his little legs were already aching and his feet were sore. Apart from going down to the valley with Lepe, which only took around ten minutes, he had never walked any kind of distance before.

Soaring above, Krask was beginning to realise the enormity of the challenge facing them. As he looked down at the tiny figure and the vast expanse of terrain in front of them, he realised this was the easy part. After a few miles, the terrain to the south changed to more rugged mountain foothills, and then there was a large mountain range and then the ocean! He did not know how far south they were going, but any distance at all was going to be a challenge. He also knew that although the tiny figure of Banain looked almost comical in this vast wilderness, the child was more advanced than his small frame suggested. The eagle knew that the toddling child possessed great strength, determination, and an intelligence that equipped him with very advanced survival skills.

"Hey Banan, I bet you not ride without falling off Lepe!" the sheep said, laughing at Banain as he ran round and round him.

"I bet I can. I did it when we were being chased, didn't I?" Banain replied.

"Okay, we see," said Lepe, stopping and allowing him to climb on his back.

Krask listened and watched the exchange between them. He had to admit that he was surprised by the little sheep, and more than a little impressed.

With Banain riding on Lepe, their pace picked up, and after a few more hours they had covered a good distance, but with the weight of the small child on his back, even the plucky sheep started to tire, and the pace slowed again.

"Listen Lepe, there is a rocky outcrop a little further ahead. I think we should stop there for the night. You will see it in front of you soon," Krask called out from above.

"Okay, eagle, if you are tired we stop," Lepe replied, attempting a joke, but Krask could hear the tiredness in his voice.

"Yes, I am tired, Lepe. You have done well today, and I am grateful you are with us," Krask said and flew on ahead to scout out the proposed night's nest site.

A few hours later, as the light faded, the three travellers stood, sat and lay near the top of the rocky outcrop. Krask was standing up finishing off a large hare, which he had caught and shared with Banain. Lepe had been off browsing and was lying down chewing the cud, and Banain was sitting near Krask, picking up feathers dropped by the eagle when he had preened earlier. Occasionally he would pluck a fresh one.

"Stop that, Banain, I still need those," the eagle said good-naturedly.

"I need more to stuff in my cloths to keep warm. They fall out when I move," Banain complained.

"Well try to leave me some please!" Krask said, hopping a couple of feet away.

"Where we go Krask? How far?" Lepe said. He stopped chewing for a moment and burped.

"I don't know, Lepe. Bodolf said that I have been given the location but I am not sure how to understand it. He also said we have to travel south. I am hoping that I will recognise the place when we find it."

"Ah, okay. Well Lepe carry Banan, no problem," Lepe said, but Krask was worried that this little sheep's heart was bigger than his ability. He had already seen how much

Lepe struggled towards the end of the day, and the journey had only just started.

"We all need to get some sleep," Krask said after a while. "I know this area well and do not think any predators live near here, but I cannot be sure. I do not have good night vision but I will do my best to keep watch whilst you two sleep."

When he did not receive a response, Krask looked over to see the sheep lying on his side, curled protectively around the sleeping child. Krask hopped to the top of the rocky outcrop and started his night vigil.

Chapter Twenty-Five

For the next couple of days the trio established a travel routine – Banain walked for a while and then rode on Lepe when he got tired or when the terrain got too difficult. They would stop for a few hours in the middle of the day to rest and forage for food. They were managing to travel around fifteen miles a day. In the evenings, Krask would find a place for them to nest, but the farther he moved from his home ground, the more difficult it became to be sure they would be safe.

On the third day, they came to a river. Krask had scouted out a place where the water was wide but looked shallow. A little downstream, there were the remains of a massive construction, which had collapsed many years ago. The water retained by the bottom section of the structure, gathered until it was high enough to pass over the top, creating a mini but powerful waterfall on the other side.

"I think you can cross where you are Lepe," Krask said, circling above the pair.

Lepe, with Banain on his back, took his first tentative steps into the water.

"Lepe no like water, Banan. We find other way." With that, the sheep backed onto dry ground again.

"You have to cross, Lepe, it's the only way. I have scouted for many miles and there is no other crossing. The water will not go above your knees, Lepe, it is shallow,"

Krask encouraged, knowing the small white lie was necessary.

"I can swim and cross this easily," Banain said to both, sliding down from Lepe's back and wading into the river.

"No Banain, let Lepe take you. You are too small, and you will not make it!" Krask shouted, diving down to try to head the child off, but it was too late, Banain was already well into the middle of the river.

"Come on Lepe, it's not deep!" Banain shouted to the sheep who was running up and down the riverbank.

Seeing that Banain was nearly three parts of the way across, Lepe decided that it probably was safe and entered the water himself with a giant leap. The sheep began to leap towards the opposite bank, staying in the water as little as possible.

Looking down, Krask watched the pair crossing the river. Lepe had nearly caught up with Banain when the child suddenly disappeared under the water completely. A second later, Lepe vanished as well.

Chapter Twenty-Six

Bodolf was in anguish. He had hardly said a word to Brek and Arkta on the way back to the den. He questioned his own decision not to help the child.

A day after returning he was standing a little way from the camp, mulling over what Honi had said to him the night before. After he had told her of the events that had taken place regarding Banain, he had thought she would have been pleased with his decision. But although she said nothing, he could tell that she was disappointed.

"You do not agree with my decision do you?" he had said.

"It was your decision to make, Bodolf, and I am so pleased you came back to me, but I just have a feeling that your destiny is tied up with that of the child Banain," Honi had replied. "I do not think that you will be able to rest until you have fulfilled that destiny."

They had said no more about the subject that night, but deep down Bodolf knew that she was right. He knew he had a decision to make, and it was not an easy one.

Bodolf's keen ears picked up the sound of a creature travelling fast towards him, and a moment later his nose confirmed that it was Nardic, a very pregnant grey bitch whose mate's leg he had broken during his first encounter with the greys, and who was then killed by the rest of his pack. Nardic and Arkta had recently mated and Bodolf was surprised to see her parted from his son only a day after returning from the trip.

"What is your hurry, Nardic? And why are you not with Arkta?" Bodolf questioned.

"Bodolf, you must come quickly. Arkta is tracking many humans who are coming this way. He told me to come and get you," Nardic panted, exhausted.

"Okay Nardic, go back to camp and tell Honi to get the pack together. Tell her to put sentries out and be ready to run if the humans approach the camp." Bodolf did not wait for a response, with his nose to the floor he set off at a fast run, backtracking Nardic's trail.

After around twenty minutes, he picked up Arkta's trail and followed but more slowly, every sense aware.

Arkta's trail told Bodolf that the wolf had been in stalk mode. The terrain was very flat, and had it been the winter, they would have had no chance to hide on the exposed tundra. Now there was around a metre-high growth of broadleaf grasses covering the plain, which gave good cover even for the large, white wolves. Even before he spotted the crouched form of Arkta, he could hear and feel a rhythmic thumping noise, accompanied by a squealing, grating noise. As he crept up alongside the crouched form of Arkta, he did not have to ask what the wolf had seen, his senses were being assaulted by the cause.

On the plain in front of him were hundreds of humans. They were similar to the ones he had seen attacking Banain's parents all those years ago, and they had what he recognised to be weapons bristling on their bodies. Some of the humans were walking to a rhythm in large groups, making a thump, thump, thump sound as they drew closer. There were also large moving structures carrying men and things that Bodolf had never seen before.

"What is this Bodolf? They look like Banain but much bigger!" Arkta said.

"They are the same species but they are very dangerous. I have seen them use those appendages before to send sticks of death great distances. We must be very careful," Bodolf replied.

"I think they head towards the great forest," Arkta said, creeping further forwards to get a better view.

Both wolves then heard another sound to the right and downwind of them. It sounded like many stampeding plains beasts, but accompanied by sounds of squeaking and human voices shouting. Bodolf and Arkta quickly changed position so that they could see the source of the new noise. Eight humans mounted on large four-legged creatures, similar to the ones Bodolf had seen on the great plain, were travelling very fast and were heading straight towards the den.

"Arkta, you go back to the den and warn the others. Tell them to leave and not attack the humans. I will try and lead these away from the den," Bodolf shouted, turning to head off the threat.

But Arkta had already leapt up and was charging towards the human riders, who had noticed the white wolf and were turning towards him. "Sorry Bodolf, but I am faster than you and you are needed at the den, and also I think for something greater!"

Bodolf froze for a few seconds, not sure what to do. He knew that Arkta was better equipped to lead the threat away from the den, but he hated putting the young wolf in such danger.

After taking a circular route back to the den, Bodolf gathered all the pack together and led them a distance to the west until they were well clear of the human invaders.

They waited several days for Arkta to return, but there was no sight of him. In addition, scouts sent out by Bodolf to search for him reported that the humans had stopped moving at the edge of the great forest and were building a massive den. They were also trapping many animals from the plain and imprisoning them in enclosures. Lastly and worst of all, the humans had trapped and enslaved many greys, although for what purpose, no one knew.

Bodolf decided that it was not safe to go back to the den and organised a wolf gathering to discuss what they should do. After much debate, they reached an agreement to move to the relative safety of Krask's mountains.

At the end of the meeting, Nardic requested to speak to the pack. "I know that Arkta is not dead, I would have felt something if he was," she said simply.

"I am sorry Nardic, but we must do what is best for the pack. You and many others will pup soon and we must get somewhere safe. We have already waited long enough for Arkta to return. Every day we remain on the plain increases the chance of more of us facing the same fate," Bodolf said, torn between his duty to the pack and his duty to his son.

"But we do not know what that fate is. Arkta may be in the hands of the humans, as are many greys. We cannot abandon him or them, Bodolf! If you cannot help, then I must stay and find him." With that, Nardic stood and started to walk away from the circle.

Bodolf rose, hackles rising. "Come back to the circle, Nardic! This meeting is only over when I say so."

He knew that he could not let a comment like that go and keep the respect of the pack. Nardic turned and crouched back, tail between her legs. Bodolf, clearly torn by the events, also sat back down.

Honi realised that since his experience with Banain, Bodolf had not been the same. She knew the enormity of the situation was weighing heavily on his mind and that he was in a constant battle with himself, trying to decide the best course of action. These most recent events with the humans only served to deepen the doubts he already had about his actions regarding the child.

"I understand your feelings, Nardic. But as leader of the pack, Bodolf has a duty to protect everyone. I have a suggestion, Bodolf," Honi added.

"Please go ahead, Honi," Bodolf said, thankful for the lifeline.

"We all agree the main priority is the safety of the pack. However, we also need to find out what is happening to the greys and what happened to Arkta. Brek has already been to the mountain range, so why not let him lead most of us there, whilst you and a few hunters stay and see if you can find Arkta?" Honi hoped she had not overstepped the mark.

Bodolf looked at his mate and around at the other wolves. "It is a good plan, Honi. I should have thought of it myself. Who will stay with me to find Arkta and find out what is happening to our kin at the hands of these humans?"

A positive response came from nearly every one of them. Bodolf said he would wait until morning to select the wolves who would stay.

The meeting broke off and Bodolf went to lie with Honi under a small scrub bush, which had been home for the last couple of nights.

"I am losing the ability to lead, Honi. I should have thought of that idea," Bodolf said, morosely.

"Bodolf, my love, you have things weighing on your mind that no wolf should have to deal with. Do not be so hard on yourself. I know you will always make the right decision, you just need time to be sure what that is, and only you have the gift to know," Honi said, grooming Bodolf gently with her tongue.

"You are right, my love. I have a great decision to make. My first reaction regarding Banain was based on years of only wanting to kill him. If he grows up to be like the humans on the plain, perhaps I should have done so when I had the chance," Bodolf mused aloud.

"I suspect, like wolves, that there are good and bad humans, Bodolf. I believe, and I think you do as well, that Banain is not only good, but very special too."

Bodolf answered Honi with a rhythmic breathing that told her he was asleep.

The next day Bodolf selected three male whites to go with him. Nordic wanted to go with Bodolf but realised it was not possible in her condition. There was no drama in the parting of the pack. Brek led the main pack west towards the relative safety of Krask Mountain. Bodolf and his small group set off towards the east and the very dangerous den of the humans.

Chapter Twenty-Seven

Banain felt the water go over the top of his head and a strong current pull him farther downwards. His time spent in the lake back at the valley meant that he knew to kick out for the surface. Looking up, he could see that he was rising. With a few more strokes, he made the surface and swam towards the shore, grateful when he at last felt gravel under his feet.

Turning around, Banain scanned the lake for Lepe, but he could not see his friend.

"Krask, where is Lepe?" he shouted.

"I don't know, Banain. He went under the water just behind you and I have not seen him since!" Krask replied, sounding worried.

"Lepe…Lepe, can you hear me?"

There was no answer.

Banain broke into a run towards the structure holding the water back. When he reached it, he ran out along its length until he arrived at the middle where the water was forced into the small gap to cascade down the other side. Looking out across the lake, he still could not see his friend. Concentrating his mind, Banain focused on the water of the lake, wishing he could see Lepe. He felt the usual warm sensation in his head when he used his powers. Then when he looked down it was as though there was no water in the lake and he could see everything. It appeared that there were fish just swimming in mid-air, with logs and debris gliding in the sky above. Momentarily distracted by what he was seeing, Banain then started looking for his friend, eventually spotting him trapped by the force of water against the side of the structure, just under the exit. As he watched, the little sheep gave a kick and freed himself, but was now moving towards the turbulent exit and the jagged rocks below.

Banain again concentrated his mind, envisaging the body of the small sheep safe and on dry land. Next to the near-drowned form of Lepe, the water started swirling faster until it was like a small, twisting water tornado. It moved towards and enveloped Lepe, propelling him up to the surface and then above, carrying him to the shore twirling like a top. As the waterspout reached land, it dissolved back onto the ground, dropping Lepe on the bank, the impact forcing his lungs to spasm and cough up the water he had inhaled.

Banain watched the whole event as if in a dream. He knew that he was responsible for what was happening, but at the same time, he felt detached from the whole event. As Lepe landed safely on the floor, Banain sank to the ground a blinding pain in his head building to a crescendo, before he was plunged into the darkness of unconsciousness.

Krask had witnessed the whole event and was diving towards Banain even before he collapsed. Landing by the unconscious child, Lepe checked for any injuries and was worried to see blood coming from his nose.

"Banan okay?" the weak voice of Lepe enquired.

"I am not sure, Lepe. He has blood coming from his nose and he is unconscious."

It took over an hour for Banain to wake up, and when he did, he had a thumping headache. As he opened his eyes, he saw the concerned faces of Lepe and Krask looking down at him.

"You okay, Banan?" Lepe said, giving him a lick but deciding not to give the usual poke with his horn.

"Yes, thank you, Lepe, although I have a terrible headache," Banain said as he struggled to a sitting position.

"I hope you both learnt a lesson here. You nearly died because of a foolish risk. We have a long way to go so you have to do as I tell you. We will say no more of it, now let's find somewhere safe for the night," Krask said sternly.

"And food!" Lepe added.

"You are obviously feeling better, Lepe. Yes and food," the eagle said, springing into the air in search of an evening's nest site and something to eat.

They did not mention the event again, but both Lepe and Krask were worried about the effect Banain's powers were having on him.

The next day at dawn, Krask took to the air and flew high, scanning the horizon. To the north, he could still just about see his home range of mountains, and to the south, he could see the blue of the great lake. The lake formed a border that was uninterrupted as far east and west as Krask had ever travelled. However, he had sometimes seen land further to the south, when the visibility was good.

As he looked to the south, a very small mountain right on the edge of the lake caught his attention. It stood at the lake's narrowest point and had beside it a large natural harbour.

Something inside Krask told him that this small mountain was where he must take Banain, and he calculated that they could make it by nightfall.

Encouraged by the news, Banain and Lepe made good time all day. By early afternoon, the small mountain looked bigger and not too far away. As they drew close, the rugged lowland mountain terrain gave way to scrubland and then to the strange landscape that Krask had seen in several places, although not as large as this.

Rising out of the ground were rows of large symmetrical constructions, overgrown with creeping plants twisting in and out of them and with trees heaving and buckling their symmetry as they strove to reach the sky above. Banain looked around in amazement as he passed between them. They had square openings all over and seemed menacing somehow. The flat tracks between the constructions rose up on large stilts to pass over other tracks. Large sections of track were missing or hanging at crazy angles from the supports, and in places, more shrubs and trees had pushed through the tracks making progress difficult.

"What is this place Krask?" Banain asked.

"It is told that these are the remains of great nests where many thousands of humans lived. It is also told that the humans were destroyed by terrible storms and floods," The eagle answered solemnly.

Banain felt a wave of grief engulf him, as he imagined thousands of his kin losing their existence here. He felt an attachment to them and for the first time that he could remember, wished for company of his own kind.

Oblivious to the child's thoughts, Krask gave directions from his lofty viewpoint, moving them closer and closer to the small mountain. Then a strange noise started coming from the constructions on either side of the pair. It sounded like the chattering of many teeth. Banain and Lepe stopped, looking around them for the source of the noise. Krask had not heard the sound and wondered why the pair had stopped.

"What is the matter?" he enquired.

"There is a strange noise, Krask," Banain replied.

Then, from both sides, troops of apes leapt out of the derelict buildings and rushed towards the pair.

Chapter Twenty-Eight

In the darkness, Bodolf crouched at the top of a ridge at the border of the great forest, looking down on the activities of the humans, as he had for the last two days. The fires all around the human den sent frightening warning signs not to approach. However, he could hear by the rhythmic chants from the humans that he and his three companions would have to do just that very soon.

After leaving the pack, he and the other three whites had headed towards where the humans had set up camp on the edge of the great forest. They'd had to avoid several groups of humans with their large moving constructions, although this was not hard with the amount of noise they made when they travelled. They had skirted far to the north, entering the great woods, and then travelled back as close as they could get to the human den using the cover of the forest.

What Bodolf saw was hard to comprehend. The humans seemed to be carrying out two activities. The first was the destruction of the great forest. They were cutting down the trees, clearing swathes of the forest every day and using the large plains beasts to drag the trees back to the den they had created. Then they would lift the trees onto the moving constructions, which left the den and headed west on a regular basis.

The second activity was more worrying and repugnant. They had set up several areas where they kept captured animals from the plains. Every day they killed some and then burned them over the great fires – the meat from the bodies was their food.

It wasn't that Bodolf was against the killing of animals to eat; he and his kind hunted and killed all the time. It was the lack of respect towards their prey and the prolonged ordeal they had to endure before the mercy of death that bothered him. The fear emanating from the trapped animals in the enclosures bombarded his senses.

The burning was another strange and unsettling sight for the wolf. In the frozen wastes of his home, he had never seen fire. Since being further south, he had seen the wild, unpredictable fires that swept through the tundra now and then and knew of their power and pain if you went too close. The humans, it seemed, had learnt to master fire and make it their tool. This was the most worrying and frightening aspect for Bodolf.

He smelt the fear from all the animals trapped by the humans and heard mind messages from some of the prisoners, including Arkta.

For some reason Bodolf could not get Arkta to hear his reply; the wolf was frozen in fear and anger. Every few hours one of the humans would approach the wolves with a large pole and beat them with it until they were in a frenzy. Last night, the humans had taken Arkta, along with two other greys, to a large pit surrounded by screaming humans. They had fought each other in a ferocious battle. Arkta, being bigger and stronger, had won, killing one of the wolves and seriously injuring the other. The humans had then re-chained him and thrown him part of the wolf he had killed to eat.

Bodolf knew he had to rescue Arkta and the other animals, but the plan he had devised was very dangerous.

"Are you sure we can get through the entrance, Sark?" Bodolf asked the slightly smaller white wolf crouched on his left hand side.

"Yes, Bodolf. It was tight for me but I managed to dig some more, and I am sure we will all be able to get through the gap," Sark replied. Bodolf could hear the fear in Sark's message and felt it from the other wolves. Although they were all brave hunters, they were all frightened by man's control of fire. Nevertheless, they had to face it if they were to save Arkta, and they had all agreed to Bodolf's plan.

"Okay, remember, after we have freed Arkta, head back to the forest. They cannot catch us with their plains animals there. Sark, you lead," Bodolf said, rising and moving down the slope after the crouched shape of Sark.

A wall constructed with trees from the great forest laid on top of each other, surrounded the humans' den. There were two entrances, one facing the forest and one facing the great plain, which the humans could open and close by pulling the large barriers in front of them. On either side of the entrances, large fires were kept burning all the time. Bodolf had ruled out these entrances.

Sark led the group to the gap in the wall that he had discovered a few hours earlier when he was scouting. Stakes driven deep into the ground prevented digging around most of the den, however Sark had discovered that there were a couple of stakes missing in this spot, and he had managed to dig down, enlarging the gap enough that they could crawl under the trunks and inside.

Bodolf had realised that they had to act that night, convinced that the gap would be discovered in the light of day.

"It's just here, Bodolf," Sark whispered and disappeared down the hole. Bodolf followed Sark's scent and pushed himself into the tunnel made by the smaller wolf. For a moment, he could not make progress, but with a final push of his back legs, his head popped up on the inside of the wall. He moved quickly to the side to let the other two wolves scrabble out.

"Follow me," Bodolf whispered and crept forward towards the noise of the cheering humans. The smell inside the human den was almost overwhelming for the wolves. The stench of the humans themselves was bad, but the smell of fear from so many animals denied their natural instinct to run from danger was overwhelming.

Bodolf led the group past a large enclosure full of plains bulls; the massive animals were crowded in the corner. A large fire roaring in a container suspended high in the air just by their enclosure was frightening them. The fire also illuminated a circle of humans looking into a large pit in which a grey wolf was fighting to the death with a large bull. A second wolf was already lying dead on the floor, gored through its stomach. The wolf was trying to find a way to get past the lethal horns of the bull. On the plain, wolves would never choose to fight like this, preferring to follow the prey and attack in numbers. Trapped in the pit, the bull had the upper hand, and as Bodolf watched, it managed to pierce the grey with a horn and toss it across the floor. This caused the crowd of humans to cheer and roar even louder.

The pit gate opened and two humans went in, each carrying lit firebrands. They used the brands to frighten the bull into the far corner, and then Bodolf saw Arkta on his way towards the pit.

As the humans released Arkta to face the bull, Bodolf and his small pack attacked.

Bodolf ran straight at the human who was trying to close one of the gates and leapt straight for his throat. The wolf bit hard and ripped in one savage motion; the human fell to the floor, his lifeblood pumping away. Bodolf then moved on to the human who had just undone Arkta's chain. Beside him, the other whites killed the human at the other gate and continued towards the ones carrying the fire torches. Within seconds, the whole place was in turmoil. Rooted in shock by the events unfolding in front of them, at first the humans did not know what to do. Then they started rising and running towards the gates to assist their human companions.

With no fire to keep the massive black bull away, his rage targeted the nearest enemy, which was Bodolf. Snorting, he lowered his head and charged towards the white wolf, who was trying to get Arkta to respond to him. "Arkta, you must follow me!" Bodolf shouted at the traumatised wolf.

Bodolf looked over and saw the bull lowering its head to charge. He knew he only had seconds to save his son. He nipped the white firmly on the rump, as he had done on many occasions to get attention from his pups. Arkta turned and made a savage attack on Bodolf, going for his neck. Only his amazing strength and agility allowed Bodolf to twist away from the attack in time. Then he counter attacked, barrelling the younger, lighter wolf across the floor of the pit, saving both of them in the process, as the bull roared past, missing them by millimetres.

Straddling his son and looking into his eyes, Bodolf said, "Arkta, it is me, Bodolf. I am here to save you, to take you from this hell. Please Arkta, hear me!"

Bodolf saw recognition in the young wolf's eyes. "Bodolf…it's you?"

"Yes…Yes, it's me, Arkta, but it's a dead me and you if we do not get out of here!"

With that, Bodolf jumped up from Arkta and surveyed the scene, which was not good. The three whites were battling a growing number of humans at close quarters by the gate, and the bull was preparing for another charge. After weighing up the situation, Bodolf ran straight across the path of the bull, who charged after him in pursuit. Instructing Arkta to head for the gate, he then led the bull at full speed there as well.

"Run for the gap whites…Run for the gap!" Bodolf shouted. He joined the other whites, ran between them and the legs of the humans, and headed towards the small gap where they had entered.

Behind them, the bull had reached the gate and was charging into the crowd of humans who were too late closing it. Still fixated on the wolf, the bull charged on, tossing humans aside like toys.

"Bodolf, we will never all get out of the hole before the bull or the humans catch us!" Sark shouted.

Bodolf realised at once that the small, white wolf was correct. Thinking frantically, he changed course and headed for the large pole that held the fire high in the sky, then ran under it and into the compound with the other bulls.

"Are you mad, Bodolf? There are more of them here!" Sark shouted, but it was too late, Bodolf was committed to a very dangerous plan.

The bull, having seen Bodolf change course, followed him and ran straight into the pole, flattening it in front of him. This sent burning logs and embers flying towards the rest of the frightened bulls in the enclosure.

The panic was instant. As one, the bulls ran away from the flames, crashing through the wooden poles as if they were matchwood, tearing through the human den, trying to find a way of escape and flattening any structures or humans in their way.

"Follow the bulls!" yelled Bodolf, positioning himself so that he was almost between the back legs of the rearmost animal. The bull that had been chasing him got caught up in the stampede mentality of the rest of the herd. On seeing the gates guarding the exit towards the plain, that were lower than the surrounding walls, the lead bull changed direction and charged at the structures which were never designed to stop anything coming from the inside. The gates collapsed under the weight of the bulls; they stampeded out to the freedom of the plain, closely followed by the five white wolves, and a further eight grey wolves still roped together.

"Follow me," Bodolf sent to all, hoping that the other greys would not be in the state Arkta was, and would be able to hear him. Turning, he raced towards the cover of the forest, running for a good ten minutes before stopping in a small clearing.

Turning and looking behind, Bodolf watched as the four whites burst into the clearing followed by the greys, only two of them still tied together. He was so happy that they had managed to free not only Arkta and the wolves, but also the other animals. He was also sickened by what he had witnessed, and resolved that he would do something about it. For now, getting as far away from this place as possible was the main objective.

Chapter Twenty-Nine

From high above, Krask watched as a sea of apes emerged from every derelict building around Banain and Lepe. They ran towards the pair, but then stopped, forming a large circle around them.

"I am coming, Banain!" Krask shouted, folding his wings and diving.

"Do not worry, Krask. The apes do not intend to harm us," Banain answered, sounding strangely calm.

Krask landed between the pair and the ring of silent apes. From the middle of the circle, a large yellowish-brown male moved forward from the main group.

"My name is Grindor. I welcome you to the Rock of the Immortals. I know you will have many questions, but first let us get you to the sanctity of the caves where you may rest. Krask, I take it you will not feel comfortable underground, so please feel free to find a spot that suits you. Lepe, I think you will want to stay with Banain. Although you're not allowed to pass inside the mountain, you can stay close by." With that, a passage opened in the group of apes. Grindor turned and led the way through.

"One moment, monkey, I am not leaving this child with you!" Krask shouted after the disappearing figure of Grindor.

"Don't worry, Krask. I know none of these apes means me any harm. I have never had so many friendly voices in my head. It is wonderful! Anyway, I have Lepe with me. I will be okay, I promise," Banain said.

Krask was just about to say something rude about the sheep, when he realised that this was what was supposed to happen. He had done his job and delivered Banain safely. A great sadness swept over him as he realised that from this point on, he would no longer be a father to the human boy.

"You will always be my father, Krask, and I will always love and need you," Banain said, as if from inside his mind.

"You can read my thoughts, Banain?" Krask exclaimed, shocked.

"Sometimes Krask, when your emotions are strong."

"So you will be okay without me?" the eagle said, unsure.

"I will never be without you, Krask, or you me. We are linked for life," Banain said, looking at his protector friend and, as far as he was concerned, his father.

"For now though, I know I must go with Grindor, and it does not sound like a place where you would be comfortable."

"I shall stay close by in case you need me," Krask said.

"Thank you, Krask." Banain turned to look at Lepe. "And what about you, are you coming with me?"

"Ha, of course Lepe come with you! How you survive without me? Lepe do not trust monkeys, but like idea of live on big rock."

Krask took off and headed for a large structure on top of the rock to rest. Banain and Lepe followed Grindor for about a mile through the structures until they came to a large, open area. In front were more ruined buildings, but these were completely overgrown with snow creeper vines, their white flowers creating a surreal landscape. The vines continued from the buildings, creating a white carpet on the floor up to the foot of an almost volcano shaped small mountain. On its north and east side, the base of the mountain reached and disappeared into the waters of the great lake.

"That is the Rock of the Immortals, Banain. Our species have lived there for thousands of years. Deep within is where we communicate with the immortals and where you will spend much time. Come, let us enter," Grindor said, moving towards the rock.

Banain was about to follow the ape, but he realised he could not enter the cave now. The conversation with Krask had affected him deeply. Although not worried about being with the apes, he needed more time with his friends. "Grindor, I am not happy to leave Krask like this, and I do not feel ready to enter the cave. I need some time."

Grindor stopped, turning to look at Banain. All the other apes started chattering their teeth. "Do not be frightened. My companions only react like this because the immortals predicted this, Banain. Follow the trail up to the top of the rock. There you will find a suitable spot to rest and be with your companions. When you are ready, call me and your training will begin."

Grindor and the other apes did not go into the tunnel. They just dispersed in different directions. Within a few moments, not one was in sight.

"This strange place, Banan," Lepe said, looking around at everything with suspicion.

"Yes it is, Lepe," Banain said simply, and started up the winding trail leading to the top of the rock.

Reaching the top, the pair found Krask, who was surprised by Banain's actions, but secretly quite pleased.

"I don't know why I didn't want to go in the tunnel, Krask. It just felt wrong somehow."

"Banain, you are very young, but you already face the world like a man. Once you enter the mountain and start your training, your limited childhood may be over. Perhaps that is what you fear losing?"

"Perhaps, Krask," Banain answered, still not sure.

"Or Banan not like smelly apes or smelly tunnel, prefer look for nice food with Lepe, although I not see much on this rock! What are we going to eat? The apes forgot that didn't they," the hungry sheep complained.

As he finished his sentence, a group of apes came up the track towards them. They were all carrying different types of fruit and grasses. They laid the food on the floor in front of the trio, chattered their teeth and then ran back down the track again.

Lepe was first to select a pile of herbs and grasses and was soon munching away contentedly.

For the next few days, the trio enjoyed resting, eating and spending time with each other. On the third evening, as the sun set on the great lake in front of them, they sat together full of the latest food brought by the apes. Krask had not been hunting, and Banain could tell he was itching to be back in the air again. Even Lepe seemed strangely subdued.

"I think tomorrow I have to go into the mountain. Banain said.

"Lepe will stay," the sheep said, but Banain could sense doubt in the small sheep.

"I am not sure what is going to happen, Lepe, or how long I will be inside. You will be lonely and bored out here. I think you should go back home with Krask,"

"I think you are right, Banain, there is nothing more we can do for you here. I will make sure Lepe gets back safely," the big eagle said, stretching his wings.

"Baa, Lepe get back safely on own! Not need stupid eagle. Not need stupid Banan!" he said and bounded off down the track.

"He is upset and worried, Banain. Give him some time to come to terms with things," the eagle said.

Lepe ran down the track, startling a group of apes who were walking up as he charged down the narrow path. Why the stupid human was sending him away after everything he had done, he just did not understand. At the bottom of the mini mountain, Lepe ran until the great lake blocked further progress. He stood looking out, shaking with anger. Then he heard a noise like a high-pitched chanting in his head, and he found himself unable to move.

"Lepe, you are a noble animal, and we thank you for all you have done for Banain," many voices chanted in his mind.

"Who are you and why I not move?" Lepe fired back, trying to force his muscles into action, wanting to get away from this strange sensation that was trapping him against his will.

"We are the immortals, Lepe, and again we thank you for bringing Banain to us. His survival is very important for the future of this world. Without you, he would be dead," the voices continued.

Lepe could not help but react to the praise. A warm glow spread through him, but they would not sway him that easily. "If I so good, why he send me away?"

"Lepe, you cannot enter the mountain with Banain. Only people with very special skills can stand contact with us for long periods. Inside the mountain, our strength is one hundred fold the power we have out here. There are other effects as well, Lepe, that we cannot explain to you. Please trust us; we will not harm your friend. We must go, Lepe. Outside of the mountain, we can only communicate like this for a short while. Please understand and thank you, Lepe." With that, the voices were gone and the world started moving again.

Banain watched Lepe come back up to the campsite. He was worried about how he was going to repair the relationship with his friend. Perhaps there was some way he could stay.

Lepe walked over to the child, gave him a lick and a poke with his horn and sat down to chew on some tasty morsels left by the apes. "Lepe think eagle need my help getting home, so I go with him in morning," the sheep said nonchalantly between mouthfuls.

Both Banain and Krask looked at him in obvious surprise.

"Yes, I decide Banain need time here on own. You call if need me, yes?" Lepe said, looking at Banain.

"Of course, Lepe. You are not angry with me?" he asked, completely taken by surprise at the sheep's change of attitude.

"Of course not, Lepe need proper food and mountain." He then started chatting about his day and other normal things, stopping any further discussion about them leaving.

The next day, the three of them stood at the base of the rock and Banain called for Grindor. For a while nothing happened, then an opening in the side of the rock appeared. One moment there was solid rock, the next Grindor was standing in an ornate opening leading into the interior of the mountain.

"Are you ready, Banain?" Grindor asked, looking intently at the child.

"I think so," Banain said and turned to Krask and Lepe. "Travel safely. Do not let Lepe get in trouble, Krask."

"Baa, it is the eagle that needs Lepe," the sheep said half-heartedly.

"We will be fine, Banain; you just concentrate on whatever it is you are going to do. Come on sheep, it will take ages to escort you all the way back, so let us get going."

Lepe was going to make a retort back to the eagle, but instead he walked up to Banain, licked him and gave him a poke in the ribs, and then he turned and charged off in the direction of home. Krask looked once more at Banain, and then he leapt into the air to follow Lepe.

Grindor turned and walked back into the tunnel. Banain watched his friends leaving, he felt an almost palpable ache as they moved away, he could not remember ever being without Krask, and since making friends with Lepe they had become inseparable. A wave of loneliness spread over his body and he nearly turned to follow the pair. Once again, the side of his brain that had driven a small child to do so much already took over, and Banain turned and walked into the mountain, tears rolling down his cheeks.

Chapter Thirty

Bodolf and his enlarged pack, including those rescued from the human den, were around halfway between the great forest and Krask Mountain. The journey had been very slow due to the number of human hunting parties out looking for the den invaders who came two nights ago. The eight greys said they had come from all over the plains, and the method of their capture was the same. The humans would charge into a den on what they called "horses". Then they would club unconscious as many wolves as they could, throwing those who did not die into a large moving cage. Bodolf had seen first-hand what happened to those who survived.

Arkta had been very quiet since the rescue. Although Bodolf expected him to be affected by his experience, there was something about the young wolf's attitude that was worrying. So far, Arkta had said nothing about his ordeal.

As they moved cautiously along after yet another close encounter with humans, Bodolf tried talking with him again. "I am worried about you, Arkta. You have been through a lot but you are free now," he said as gently as he could.

"I am free, but what of the others? These humans are enslaving everything. They are vile and we should have killed them all before we left! Instead, we ran away like curs with our tails between our legs!" Arkta shouted at Bodolf.

Both wolves stopped and faced each other, Arkta in a fully aggressive stance.

"What are you saying, Arkta? We rescued you and the other greys and we need to get back to the rest of the pack," Bodolf said, still shocked by Arkta's outburst.

"You'd already made your decision, Bodolf. You moved the pack away to safety, and that is what you will continue to do. The humans will not drive me. I will kill them all," Arkta growled and then howled to the sky, the eight greys joining in with him.

"Whilst you are in my pack you will do as I say, Arkta. You may be young and strong but you are still no match for me. Do you challenge me?" Bodolf demanded. Despite his fondness for Arkta, he had to maintain control and could not allow his authority to be undermined.

"No I do not, Bodolf, but I will not stay with you either. I am going with the greys to hunt these humans. Do not try to stop me or you will not just be fighting me," Arkta said, and the eight grey wolves formed a line either side of him.

In response, the three other whites stood beside Bodolf. An ugly and volatile mood was brewing.

"Arkta, this is not our way. We hunt for meat and we respect our quarry," Bodolf said, trying to reason.

"Pah. How can you say that, Bodolf? You brought the whole pack here hunting for a human baby, didn't you?"

Bodolf could think of no answer. Arkta was correct; he had brought them there, and now a desire for revenge against the humans who had tortured and nearly killed him, drove his son.

"How long will you hide away, letting our kind be tortured and killed by these humans? I looked into their minds, Bodolf. They see us as tools to serve their purpose, to amuse them. Not even food, just toys. If you will not act, I and others will!"

Arkta waited for a response from the great white wolf, but Bodolf just stood looking at him, a great sadness in his eyes.

Turning away, Arkta loped off, back towards the human den. The eight greys followed close behind.

Chapter Thirty-One

The inside of the immortal rock was like nothing Banain had ever seen before. As the wall magically closed behind him, his eyes became accustomed to the subdued light within the tunnel. The walls themselves glowed with a gentle light that changed in tinge from green to blue, creating a very calming effect. Rubbing the last of the tears from his eyes, Banain concentrated more on this strange place. Although the floor was firm, there were no sounds of his feet walking on it; everything was subdued, except, he could just hear a distant chanting that grew in volume, the deeper he spiralled town the tunnel after Grindor. As they descended Banain also noted a slight cooling in temperature, not uncomfortably cool, but noticeable.

After a while, the quality of the light changed, becoming strong and a pure white. The chanting was clear now, like the singing of a thousand children, high-pitched and strangely hypnotic. The tunnel opened up to reveal a large cave with a round pool in the middle.

From the pool, a column of water rose almost to the ceiling two metres above Banain's head. The water, suspended in a perfect cylindrical shape, was crystal-clear. As Banain moved closer, he saw a creature unlike any he had ever seen before in the middle of the column. It was about one metre high and the same wide. Its outer body was a translucent blue, revealing its inner organs, which were a darker blue, except for a centre organ, which was a vibrant red. It had between ninety and a hundred blue tentacles reaching from under its body; they undulated hypnotically.

"Please sit here." Grindor's deep gravelly voice pulled Banain out of his trance. He sat on the seat sculpted out of the floor of the cave as indicated by the ape.

"Banain, this is Turritopsis. It is your point of contact to the immortals. You are seeing a much-enlarged view of it provided by the magnification qualities of the water in the column. I will leave you," Grindor said, turning to leave the cave.

"Why do you call Turritopsis 'it', Grindor, and how do I talk to it?" Bodolf enquired, mesmerised by the floating entity.

"The immortals have no gender, Banain; they are neither male nor female. Turritopsis will explain everything to you," Grindor said, not pausing or looking back.

Banain sat waiting for some time before the mesmerising chanting swelled, becoming louder, and then a strange sensation came over him. Unlike outside, in the cavern the immortals were able to create a time bubble which encompassed the whole area, allowing communication and movement to whomever was within. It required a tremendous amount of power, supplied by millions of immortals, linked together in an underwater chamber below the cavern.

"Welcome Banain," a new, more focused, single voice sang in his head. "I am Turritopsis. Think of me as your connection to the immortals. You are very special, Banain, and we need you very much."

"I don't feel special, and I miss Krask and Lepe…Turrupsis," Banain said, struggling with the name. All of a sudden, the child felt lost and alone in this strange place. "Why couldn't Lepe come here with me? I miss him," Banain said, tears welling again.

"Banain, if you stay, you will never be alone again. We will show you how to use your skills properly, and with the correct training, you will be able to keep in contact with your friends wherever they are. However, you must learn how to use your skills properly and that will take time. Also, please call me Turr."

"How long do I have to stay here?" Banain asked.

"You will age ten years to learn what you need to unlock the potential inside you, Banain."

Banain could not even envisage how long ten years was at his young age. He had already had to face so much, and now it seemed like he was going to be trapped deep underground with only Turr for company for the rest of his life. And what of his friends? Lepe and Krask would not remember him after all that time, and they would be old! He did not know how long Krask would live, but maybe he would die before he finished his training. Banain's young mind was having trouble working all this out; he stared at the floor trying not to let tears well again as he struggled with all Turr was telling him.

"Banain, we understand your concerns, but please listen to what I will tell you now before you make a decision,"

Turr said, as if it had read every thought in Banain's head, which in fact it had.

"The immortals are the most ancient species on the planet. We cannot die of natural causes. When we reach maturity, we have the ability to regenerate, retaining the memories and experiences of our previous existence. We also live in a shifted time to other creatures on the planet. I will not try to explain the reason for that now. The main thing that concerns you is that it is only possible to interact with other creatures by speeding up time for them, so that they are in harmony with our own.

"This is important, Banain. For every hour you spend in this cavern, your body will age by twenty-four hours. We calculate that by the time you have finished your training, around one year will have passed outside. Therefore, everyone outside will be one year older, but your body will be ten years older. If you agree to the training, you will spend around six hours a day in this place with us.

"Under this floor is a vast sea cave. In the cave, over ten million of us share our power, enabling this link with you. During the other hours, you will be training with Grindor, learning the skills and building the physical strength you will need to manage the powers you have been gifted with.

"Do not make a decision now, Banain. Go with Grindor who will explain what the physical training will involve. Then you can make a decision. But before you go, let us give you a small demonstration of what you will be able to do after training. Whilst linked, Banain, we are able to give you the gift of vision. You just need to imagine where you want to be and you will travel there," Turr said deep in Banain's mind.

Banain imagined that he was with Lepe. For a moment, nothing happened. Then everything went black, replaced a few seconds later by a vision of landscape passing by. Banain realised that he was seeing what his friend was seeing.

"Can I talk to him?" Banain asked.

"When your skills have developed, you will be able to talk to some creatures over distance Banain, but only if the receiver has had training. We can see what a creature is seeing by picking up the small transmissions from their mind. It is more difficult to send a message than to receive one."

Banain imagined he was with Krask and immediately the scene changed to a view from high above the ground. The vision was so real that Banain felt his head spinning as he looked down. He could see the figure of Lepe running below towards his home mountain in the distance. It was an incredible experience and he wished that like Krask he could soar in the sky, detached from all the problems below. Seeing Lepe running towards home also made him sad, as he wished he were going there as well.

After a few minutes, the picture dissolved, replaced by his real view of the cave. Given the choice Banain would have preferred to stay flying with Krask.

"Go with Grindor, Banain, and think about what you have learnt. If you wish to train, come back here tomorrow and we will start."

The image of Turr disappeared and Grindor entered the cave. Banain followed him back to the entrance and then to a small building. Inside, Banain found himself in a chamber with a small comfortable nest on one side and a window that looked out towards the north on the other side. A garment lay on the bed, made from a material he had not seen before, although it seemed familiar somehow. It was grey in colour and accompanied by a belt.

"This will be your room, Banain. The robe on the bed is like those made by humans, from plants. It is more practical than what you are wearing. You just pull it over your head, put your arms through the small holes at the top and tie the belt around your waist. Training will begin at first light. Is that clear, Banain?" the large ape said, staring intently at the small child and grinding his teeth, something Banain had noticed the large ape did when he was annoyed.

"I am not sure... Turr said I had time to decide. I miss my friends. I am not sure if this is what I want, Grindor," Banain said, close to tears again.

"Well, you will stay or go. Let me know when you have decided, human." As he spoke the last words, Grindor turned and left the room, leaving Banain on his own, unsure of everything.

"Don't worry about him, he is always grumpy... Mind you he is grumpier with you than with most. Hmm, maybe he doesn't like humans, but I don't know why. Hmm, perhaps it is because he spends so much time in that cave with the jellyfish... Hmm, anyway, you should not worry. It's quite nice here really... Is your name really Banain?"

The voice belonged to the ape sitting in the window ledge. Before Banain could answer, the ape continued. "It's a strange name, Banain. I have a friend called Boredom, but I think that's because he is, well, a bit boring. He talks and talks but what he says is not very interesting most of the time. Many of us apes receive second names after a while from the elders; they decided to call me Jabber for some reason."

As the ape continued to talk, he dropped into the room and inspected all the contents, finally coming to a rest before the robe. "Can I try this on?"

Without waiting for a reply, Jabber leapt into the robe, trying to push his arms through the holes, but he ended up completely tangled in the garment. Banain could not help but laugh at the animated robe without a head leaping around the room.

Finally, Jabber freed himself from the garment and sat looking at Banain.

"You don't say much do you, Banain?" Before Banain could answer, Jabber continued. "Anyway, do you want to see where I live? Come on, it's not far."

With that, he hopped out of the window again and disappeared. Walking over to the window, Banain looked for the ape, but he could only see a sheer drop below and flat walls on either side.

From above a voice said, "Come on, Banain, it's up here."

Looking up, Banain could see Jabber hanging onto a small ledge by his fingers. As he watched, the ape swung his body upwards, landing further up and out of view.

Then Jabber was standing behind him in the doorway. "Of course, you humans can't climb like we can. No problem, you can come this way."

Banain just stood staring at the door. All he wanted was to think about what to do, yet he had this nonstop-talking ape pestering him.

"Hey Banain, that's not fair. I don't talk a lot. You need to learn how to control your mind, Banain; I can hear everything you think. Your friends are fine. They have gone home, and you will see them soon. We have waited for you all our lives, many generations of us. You are very important, Banain, very important, but rude," Jabber said, leaving the room.

Banain moved back over to the window and looked north; he could just about make out the outline of Krask Mountain in the far distance. His young mind was trying to come to terms with what was happening. A big part of him wanted to be back at the nest with Krask and running with Lepe. However, another part, the subconscious part that had kept him alive so far, was telling him that he must stay.

Chapter Thirty-Two

Many miles to the north-west, in the remains of the once great city of Seville, Lord Erador was not happy. He sat, flanked by two of his guards, in a large ornately carved chair in the recently completed great hall of his castle. No other complete buildings existed in the once powerful city. They had been ravaged by the great storms and then nearly washed away completely by the tidal storm surges that came up the Guadalquivir River. Over the last three hundred years or so, his ancestors had built this castle to protect them from both humans and other creatures. Lord Erador had continued to build the fortress and increase the size and power of the army, which he was using to claim more of the country back from the wild.

He was a tall, thin man, dressed in a bright red shirt and trousers with red boots made from brushed and dyed leather. He had a narrow, cruel face, and his hair and beard were dyed bright red. Standing beside him was a massive man wearing plain leather armour. He stood rock still, as did the guards. They all stared down at a visibly shaking scout, who had just returned from an outpost on the eastern border and was reporting on the attack on the camp and the loss of the livestock.

"So if I understand you, Sergeant Fermin, the camp was attacked by thousands of wolves. In addition, this same army of canine devils is attacking and killing my highly trained and armed soldiers. Is that correct?" The question was rhetorical.

Lord Erador knew the man was lying. He knew when all men were lying to him because he could read the minds of other humans. He also had another skill, which he used now.

The sergeant who was standing at attention suddenly fell to his knees, his body not under his control. He then pulled a knife from a scabbard and held it in front of himself, blade pointed towards his own stomach.

"You are lying, Sergeant Fermin; there were not thousands of wolves, just a few who are making fools of my highly trained soldiers. Do you think you can lie to me, Sergeant Fermin? What sort of message would go out to the rest of my subjects if I allowed that? No, that will not do. "

As Erador talked, against his own will, the sergeant drove the knife inwards and then slowly upwards. As Erador finished his sentence, the hapless messenger fell face forward, dead.

"Take his body and display it where all can see, so that none will lie to me again," Erador said coldly to his guards, then he turned to the mountain of a man standing beside him. "Izotz, the sergeant was lying about the number of wolves, but there is something strange going on. However stupid the commander of the camp was, a handful of wolves should not have been able to do so much damage, or act in the seemingly coordinated way they did. In addition, I am worried about these raids. Take a troop and find out what is going on, Commander, and send me back some of the animals that are attacking our troops."

"Yes, my lord," General Izotz said and marched from the room.

Lord Erador walked to a large window looking to the south. When he killed whilst connected to the victim, it was always accompanied by a warm pulse of power beating in his head. Had he not killed the messenger today, he would have sentenced one of the many occupants in his dungeon below the castle. He was finding that he needed more and more kills to provide the feeling of euphoria and power it always gave him, but that was no problem. He had plenty more.

Looking towards the south, he could sense something out there; he was just not sure what. He had been having strange visions and hearing a strange voice in his head for some time. Lord Erador liked to be in control of everything, so with these concerning reports coming in, he needed to find out exactly what was going on.

Chapter Thirty-Three

Bodolf and the three whites had arrived at the new den in the foothills of Krask Mountain, selected by Brek. He could not help but be impressed. There were a selection of two large and six small caves set into the sheer rock face of the mountain. From the back of one of the smaller caves, a tunnel led up all the way to the small valley with the lake. Although a small river ran through it, it was a short cut to the valley and an escape route. After commending Brek on his choice of den, Bodolf updated him and Honi on the events that had transpired, including the situation with Arkta.

"Nardic is not going to be happy with this news, Bodolf. She is due to pup very soon. Did Arkta not send a message for her?" Honi said.

"He did not. I think his experiences with the humans have upset his mind. He is not the same wolf that any of us knew," Bodolf said sadly.

"If Arkta and his pack are out attacking humans, there is going to be trouble. We greys have always avoided the humans and on the whole they've kept clear of us, but now..." Brek said, clearly worried by the news.

"Now, we keep watch and protect our young, Brek. We are not going to war with the humans, although we will protect ourselves from them if we need to. For now, they are well to the east and we saw no sign of them close to these mountains. Have you seen any sign of the eagle I spoke of, Brek, or that goat?"

"No, Bodolf, but we kept clear of the mountain interior as you asked and have only been hunting game close by on the plain. You may not want war with the humans, Bodolf, but I think it will come to you anyway," Brek said and then loped away.

"I will go and talk to Nardic and then go and see the eagle," Bodolf said to Honi.

"Let me talk to Nardic, Bodolf. We have been quite close recently and the news may come better from me." Bodolf agreed and went in search of Krask.

Once each day for the next couple of days, Bodolf followed the trail up from the valley to the ledge below Krask's nest, but the eagle was not there.

After hearing the news about Arkta from Honi, Nardic agreed to stay at the den for the sake of the pups, but was withdrawn and morose. She had not spoken a word to Bodolf.

On the third day, Bodolf was making the journey to Krask's nest again, going over recent events in his mind and trying to work out the best course of action. In reality, he quite enjoyed the solitude of these daily trips and spent much longer than necessary on the ledge looking out towards the frozen ice cap. A big part of him wished he had never gone south.

Arriving at the ledge, he called for the eagle, but again got no response. It was a crystal-clear spring day and the ice cap was a pure white horizon calling to the wolf.

"Hey wolf! What you do here?" Bodolf recognised the voice at once – it was that cheeky sheep.

"What is it to you, sheep? Have you come to beg my mercy?" Bodolf said, peering around, trying to see where the sheep was.

"Pah, Lepe no apologise to stupid wolf. Stupid wolf should apologise to Lepe!"

"Show yourself sheep and you will never call me stupid again!" Bodolf said, his hackles rising.

"Here I am, wolf, come and get me then," Lepe answered, stepping out from a boulder on the other side of the ledge from Bodolf.

The ledge was only just wide enough for Bodolf to turn on, and the gap was too large to jump without a run-up, but Bodolf was just about to try anyway. Then Krask's piercing keen stopped Bodolf and Lepe, and the big eagle landed with a flurry of large wingbeats between them.

"If you two will stop annoying each other, we have much more important matters to discuss," Krask said to the pair, who stared hard at each other across the gap.

"Lepe and I have just returned from taking Banain to the immortals, and I have just scouted the plains to the north of this mountain. The news is not good," the eagle continued.

"What have you seen, eagle?" Bodolf said, turning to get more comfortable on the small ledge, but keeping an eye on the sheep in case he came into range.

"There are many humans. They travel on horses at great speed towards the east. However, they also send smaller groups out to each side, and such a group is coming towards the mountain and your den, Bodolf."

"How many in the group and how long before they get here?" Bodolf demanded, all thoughts of Lepe immediately gone from his mind.

"Not long, Bodolf, but if you attack them they will go back and bring more humans to the mountain. There are six of them."

"And if they see our den they will come anyway! Okay, we need to try to conceal ourselves from them, but if they do find us, they all need to die. None can return to the main group and give our position away," the wolf said, already turning to start down the mountain.

"Agreed Bodolf, good luck," Krask said, launching into the air again.

"Good luck, wolf. Can I help?" Lepe said, regretting some of his earlier comments.

"Just stay out of the way, sheep," Bodolf said as he charged back down the track towards the den.

Arriving at the den, Bodolf immediately called a hunting meeting. As the pack stood in a circle nose-to-nose, Bodolf informed the group of the situation and his plan to deal with it.

"Okay, Honi. You keep the very pregnant and the pups with you in the water cave. Brek, you take the greys to the north and shadow the humans if they come close. I will say with the whites and mixed in the large cave, as we cannot conceal ourselves as well as you greys. We will kill the humans if they come into the camp. Remember, if they discover us and are able to return to the other humans, many more will come very quickly."

Waiting inside the large cave, Bodolf went over the plan in his mind again. With one grey and two whites close to giving birth, he had twelve wolves left to deploy.

"Bodolf, they are very close and heading straight for the camp. I think they have our trail!" Brek said.

Peering out of the cave entrance, Bodolf could just hear the familiar sound of humans riding on horses, and it was getting louder every moment. Then six humans rode into the clearing in front of the cave and halted, looking around. Bodolf froze absolutely still, tensed and ready to spring.

One of the humans climbed down from his animal and walked towards the small cave where the mothers, babies and small pups were hiding. Bodolf had put them in there so that they could escape through the tunnel at the back if need be. He regretted not putting some of the whites with them. The human walked towards the entrance and peered inside. Bodolf could smell fear in the human and realised that he did not want to enter the cave to discover what might be inside. After a cursory inspection of the entrance, the human turned back towards his horse and was just about to leap in the saddle, when a four-week-old mixed pup charged out of the small cave towards the human.

In a second, everything changed for Bodolf. He saw the small pup emerge from the cave, the human riders pointing at it and pulling out their weapons and the man on the ground spinning around and running towards the pup.

"Attack!" Bodolf screamed as he powered out of the cave and headed for the human on the ground. He already knew that he was not going to be in time. The human was swinging his shiny weapon towards the small wolf, who was still charging bravely at the invader.

Then he saw Lepe leap from behind a large rock above the small cave entrance. Landing around five metres behind the cub, he too charged at the startled human. Reaching the cub just before the human's weapon, Lepe batted the small animal to the side with his head. Missing the cub, the weapon found Lepe's left horn and sliced straight through. It then continued to bury itself halfway into his other horn.

The impetus of his charge carried Lepe into the human, and they both collapsed onto the floor. Pulling his weapon free, the human slashed at Lepe again.

Bodolf could not believe the scene unfolding in front of him as he closed the distance. It was the bravest act he had ever witnessed. As the human was about to slash for a second time, Bodolf reached him, his jaws closing around the human's exposed neck, and barrelled him to the floor. The human's weapon, deflected by Bodolf's attack, sliced into Lepe's front right leg, and the young sheep who was just struggling to his feet, collapsed in great pain on the floor.

After finishing off the first human, Bodolf took stock of the situation. Of the four humans torn from their horses by the wolves, only one was still fighting. It looked like two of the greys and one mixed were either dead or wounded.

Most worryingly for Bodolf, the one remaining human had managed to escape and was departing as fast as he could.

"We must catch the last human!" Bodolf shouted and started after the disappearing rider, with six wolves streaming after him. Travelling as fast as he could, Bodolf was not making ground; in fact, the rider was pulling away from the chasing pack.

Then a series of keening screams tore through the air, and the shapes of three large golden eagles flashed over the heads of the wolves towards the fleeing rider. In seconds, the first eagle's talons hit the rider's head, unbalancing him. Before he could recover his balance, the second and third eagles hit, and he fell from his horse to the floor, where he was easy prey for Bodolf's wolves.

Exhausted, Bodolf checked that the youngsters were able to deal with the human and his horse and then looked up at the circling eagles.

"Thank you, Krask," he said grudgingly.

"We did it for all of us, Bodolf. We cannot only look after our own concerns anymore if we wish to survive against the humans." Krask turned to head back towards the den.

At the den, Lepe was trying to get to his feet, but every time he tried, he collapsed to the floor again. Around him, a group of wolves were gathering. They had not witnessed Lepe's rescue of the cub and were about to add sheep to the menu.

Lepe had never felt pain like this before and his right leg would not follow his commands. Looking up, he saw the circle of wolves closing in on him.

"Come on then ugly wolves, Lepe not scared of you!" he shouted, actually feeling very scared. For the first time in his life, he was without options.

He watched as if in slow motion as the first of the wolves jumped in, and he felt powerful jaws close around his neck and start to squeeze.

"Leave the sheep; he is mine!" The wolf that was just about to end Lepe's life let go and backed away, along with the rest of the pack. Bodolf stalked up to Lepe who was struggling to get back to his feet again.

"So sheep, will you call me names now?" Bodolf said as he stood over the wounded Lepe.

"You still stinky wolf. Lepe prefer another not stinky wolf kill him, although you all pretty stinky," Lepe said, realising it was a mistake, but he never could stop using his mouth before his brain.

Bodolf put his head right next to Lepe's and said very quietly, "You are the bravest animal I have ever met. I will be forever in your debt for saving the life of one of our cubs. I offer my friendship if you can stand to be friends with a stinky wolf?"

Lepe looked at the big wolf, not sure if he was serious. Then his world turned black as he passed out from blood loss.

Chapter Thirty-Four

When Grindor arrived at Banain's room at sunrise the next morning, he was surprised to find Banain standing by the window dressed in his grey robes, the belt tied securely around his waist and his long mane of hair tied behind his head. On the table, an empty bowl showed that Banain had eaten his fruit and wild grain. The child seemed to Grindor to have changed overnight. Gone were the tears; those steely blue eyes instead held a look of intelligence.

"You have decided then, human?" Grindor asked.

"Yes, although you know already," Banain replied.

"That is not the case. Jabber told me of his conversation with you. I imagine it was one-sided. It is not our custom to read minds, although we have the ability. He is young and has a lot to learn, but he will regret his mistake. In fact, his punishment is that he will accompany you on your training, child. Now, if you are ready, follow me," Grindor said and leapt out of the window.

Banain ran to the window and looked up to see Grindor perform the same feat as Jabber had the day before. He was not going to be humiliated again, so he jumped through the window, trying for the ledge above him. He did not even get close before his upward momentum stopped, and he started to fall.

Two strong hands reached down and grabbed his flailing arms, pulling him to the safety of the ledge above.

"An impressive attempt, Banain, but let this be your first lesson. Being brave is good, but it can kill you. Always weigh the risks before committing. What is a little humiliation compared to death, eh?" Grindor started down the trail towards the bottom of the mountain.

Banain followed as fast as his short legs would let him and was almost out of breath by the time he reached the bottom.

Grindor was crouched waiting for him. As he approached, the ape shouted, "Jabber! Jabber, where are you? He was supposed to be here! This is not a good start."

The next moment, Jabber ran up, chewing on some berries.

"Sunrise Jabber, sunrise I said. Banain was ready, why not you?"

"Ah well, Grindor, Jabber heard your instructions, but thought you probably got mixed up with breakfast. So Jabber having breakfast first. As you know, you need lots of fo–"

"Shut up, Jabber, I do not have time for one of your speeches," Grindor interrupted, grinding his teeth in anger.

"Now listen Banain, the reason for these exercises is to help you use your powers, without damaging yourself. Krask told me that when you used them on the trip here, it almost killed you. This is because your brain requires a tremendous amount of energy to accomplish what you are asking it to do. Energy comes from glucose supplied by your blood and your brain requires oxygen to process the glucose and other essential chemicals. When these support systems to the brain are not up to the job, there is insufficient oxygen in your blood to feed your brain, so the heart pumps faster, raising the pressure of the blood system. When you had that nosebleed last time Banain, it was because the blood pressure in your head was so high, the vessels in your nose started to burst. My job is to get your body fit, so that your brain can receive the oxygen it needs. The immortals will explain more of this later. Let's start."

Banain was still trying to take in all that Grindor had just said when the ape started running back up the mountain trail again. "Come on Banain, Jabber, to the top of the rock and back three times."

After the exercise, Banain and Jabber sat together exhausted.

"Sorry Banain, I should not have read your mind yesterday. It was very rude." Banain waited for the talkative ape to continue, but Jabber just sat watching him.

"That's okay, Jabber. I was not very nice to you and now you have to do this with me. I can try talking to Grindor if you like," Banain said, noticing that the big ape was approaching.

"No Banain, I will exercise with you," Jabber said as he pushed the last piece of fruit into his mouth and ran off in the opposite direction.

Grindor led Banain back down to the deep cave, and once again, he sat in front of the image of Turr, floating in the water in front of him. To one side of the cave there was a collection of items ranging from small sticks to large rocks, Banain could not remember them being there the day before.

"Okay, Banain, for you to be able to control your gift, you must master the art of relaxing," Turr sang.

"So far you have mastered the basics, but to fully appreciate your gift you need to understand what is happening. Most people's brains can only connect with and control parts of their own bodies. However, some beings possess the ability to connect with external entities. Your gift is very strong, and with training, you will be able to influence much of the environment around you.

"The mechanics of the gift have similar requirements both in and out of your body, however when you control your own body, your commands are carried out by your muscles. When you want to perform a task outside of the body, you need to find a replacement for that muscle, and that is what most species cannot manage. Banain, with your mind, lift the small stick over there and keep it in the air," Turr instructed.

Banain looked at the stick and imagined it hovering above the ground. Instantly, the stick leapt into the air.

"Very good. Now pick up the medium size rock next to it as well."

Banain thought about the rock and imagined that in the air as well. The rock started to rise, but the stick fell to the floor and Banain started to feel dizzy. Then he felt the soft chanting grow and swell in his head. The rock steadied in the air, the stick floating beside it.

"Did you notice that when you tried to lift the second item, it was difficult to control both and the heavier item made you feel tired very quickly? This is because, like using your muscles in the body to carry out activities, you need mental muscle to use your gifts. Moreover, the bigger or the more objects you attempt to control, the more muscle or power you require. Now you have the power of millions of immortals helping you hold these two items in place. Please put them down, Banain."

Banain envisaged the rock and stick floating back to the ground and they followed his wishes.

"Another part of your gift is the ability to communicate in the minds of other creatures. Again, you have a very strong gift that opens up receptors in those exposed to you, allowing them to communicate as well. Communication through mind contact does not require the knowledge of languages, as it works by translating feelings and thoughts into data that both sender and receiver can decipher. You need to learn to control this gift, Banain, as there may be some creatures that you would not wish to endow with the gift of communication.

"Grindor has told you that you need to exercise to build your physical strength, but you also need to build your mental strength, and that is what we will be doing a lot of the time. Do you have any questions?"

"I think I understand, but what of the control of other creatures' minds? I have been able to control insects and smaller animals. What training do I need to master these skills?"

"These are very dangerous skills, Banain, and we do not recommend you use them even though your powers are strong. You have the ability to influence other creatures and in many cases cause them to carry out your wishes, but the immortals consider this an abuse of power. If you control another creature against its will, you are responsible for its destiny. If it dies whilst you are connected, it can be very distressing. If it dies whilst you are in control, it can corrupt your mind very quickly, and you can become addicted to the sensations it causes.

"You must also never use the power to move yourself. Although it is physically possible, it would be very easy to do terrible damage to yourself. For instance, you may imagine yourself in another place, and your body would try to travel there by the quickest route, regardless of what lay between! However, do not worry Banain, you have much time to learn all these things and develop your skills. Let us begin."

Chapter Thirty-Five

Six months later, Arkta was crouched low on a small hillock. He was watching a group of four humans who were lying asleep wrapped in furs by a burnt-out fire. Right next to them was a large structure that rose over ten metres into the sky. He and his pack, drawn by the smell of the humans, had been watching them for several hours. It looked as if they were going to build a new outpost there, as Arkta could see many areas where the ground had been disturbed, leaving scars in the snow where they had been digging.

"Do we attack, Arkta?" Brosk, one of the wolves in his pack, asked.

"Wait Brosk, something is not right here," Arkta snapped back. He was not sure why, but his wolf sense was telling him that there was something wrong. He had sent scouts – there were no other humans close by and these ones did not even have the protection of fire.

"They are defenceless, Arkta! Let us kill them," Brock insisted.

"Okay, attack with caution," Arkta instructed, rising and starting down the hill. Twelve other greys also rose from their places of concealment in a circle around the humans and started towards them.

As they got closer, sensing no danger, they broke into a run, trying to close the gap with the humans as soon as possible.

At ten metres from the humans, Arkta's instincts were screaming at him to stop the attack. He sensed the ground was not as it should be; the snow felt all wrong, as if the earth was hollow.

"Abort the attack! Abort the attack!" he yelled, turning as fast as he could. The other greys either did not hear or ignored his order and kept running towards the four.

Arkta had only just begun to turn away from the four humans when the ground disappeared below him. He felt himself falling. He tried to reach the edge of the large pit which had opened up beneath him, but it was too late.

With a noise of screaming wolves and falling debris, the pack landed on the floor of a circular pit with an island in the middle. On the island, the four humans got up from where they had been faking sleep, walked to the large structure and started unfolding and lowering it across the pit, until it came to rest on the outside, allowing them to leave the centre.

Arkta was not hurt, but several of the greys were dead or dying impaled on stakes set in the ground. Some of the uninjured wolves were leaping at the smooth earth walls, but they were just too high.

"There is no point trying to jump out of here. Pick one point and start digging out," Arkta instructed, indicating a location to start digging. At once, two greys started attacking the wall.

After only a few minutes, the beginning of a small tunnel leading upwards was taking shape. Then a volley of arrows flew from the bows of the humans above and the two digging wolves lay dead on the floor of the pit.

Immediately, a second pair took their place, but within seconds, they too were dead.

"Do not approach the walls," Arkta ordered, looking up at the humans who were waiting with their weapons aimed at the remaining three wounded and five uninjured wolves.

For many hours, the humans did nothing except light a large fire. Then Arkta felt the vibration of the hooves of many horses followed by the clashing, banging and smells of horse warrior humans.

A giant human appeared at the edge of the pit and looked down at Arkta with cold eyes. Arkta immediately sensed the cruelty in this man; he had seen similar cruelty in the eyes of his previous captors. The human made a command, and the archers raised their bows and fired at the trapped wolves.

Arkta leapt at the wall, trying to draw the fire away from them, but one by one, they killed the greys, leaving only Arkta. Moving back to the middle, Arkta looked at the large human and snarled, showing his teeth and a feral stare.

The humans lowered ladders and around ten of them swarmed down, surrounding him. Selecting one, Arkta charged, taking the man by surprise and barrelling him to the floor by the throat. Before he could rise to attack the others, Arkta felt familiar nets restricting his movements, and then the weight of many humans who bore him to the ground and tied him securely.

A few hours later, Izotz stood by the cage transporter looking at the great white wolf within. Arkta stared back at him, showing no fear.

"Take him back to Lord Erador as quickly as you can. If you let him escape, your deaths will not be pleasant," he informed the small troop of soldiers.

The journey to Old Seville took around eight hours. The soldiers did not stop when it got dark. They lit fat burning lamps more to keep away potential attackers than to aid navigation – they could see by the full moon well enough. The track was well worn and rutted, cutting through the snowfields covering the tundra all the way to the outskirts of the once great city. Drawing closer to the centre, Arkta could see and smell many humans and animals. He could also smell death and fear.

A short while later, Arkta was in a small cage, alongside several greys, in the dungeons below the castle.

"Hey Arkta, is that you?" a grey two cages away asked.

"How do you know my name?" Arkta asked, not recognising the smell or appearance of the questioner.

"I do not know you…but I know of you. Your fame has spread to most packs in the tundra and many greys fight against the humans because of you. You have been captured before, Arkta. What will they do with us?"

"They will make us fight, either each other or other animals, or humans they do not care about," Arkta said, not really wanting to remember what was in store for him.

"I will not fight you or another of my kind," the grey said, looking around at the other wolves in the area.

"How long have you been here?" Arkta enquired.

"Only since yesterday, all of us here arrived together. They captured us when we attacked a small group of humans. The ground opened up and swallowed us. They killed many of the group, but for some reason they brought the five of us here."

"You will fight each other and anything else that you get near when they have finished with you. The only food you get is what you kill. They will beat you every day until hate and the need for revenge consume you. You will not recognise friend or foe, only food. Now leave me in peace." Arkta circled the cage several times before lying down to sleep.

The next day the door crashed open and two humans marched in. They approached Arkta's cage and stood a safe distance either side. Then a tall, thin human with a brightly coloured hide approached Arkta, again stopping at a safe distance. The thin man communicated with one of the other humans, but Arkta could not decipher what they were saying. Since his experience with the baby human, his communication skills had improved greatly and he could pick up the meaning of some of their mind talk, but hardly any of them used it, relying mostly on verbal communication.

"So you are the wolf that has been giving us so much trouble."

The voice in Arkta's mind came from the tall, thin man he was sure, before he could think or stop himself he said, "Yes. Release me from this cage and I will tear your chest open and eat your heart."

The thin man's eyes widened and he took a deep breath, clearly shocked that the wolf could talk to him. He looked around the room, talking verbally to the two humans and looking everywhere for a source of the voice in his head. Finally, he looked back at Arkta and stared into the wolf's unblinking eyes.

"So you can talk, wolf. This is a surprise and it explains a lot about what has been happening recently. Can all you wolves talk?" Lord Erador commanded.

Arkta realised he had made a mistake letting this human know that he could communicate, so he did not reply.

"Oh, come now, it is too late; I know you can talk. But it's okay, you do not need to tell me what you know, I am sure I can find out."

Suddenly, Arkta experienced a jolting, lancing pain in his head. It was as if someone was inside it, ripping it apart. He fell to the floor, legs scrabbling, screaming with pain as Erador probed his mind.

After a few moments, the pain stopped. The lord looked at him and smiled. "I could extract everything I want from you, Arkta. I already know much of what you can tell me, but I want you to tell me yourself. I will come to you each day and when you answer me again, the pain will stop and you will have food. Do not be stupid, Arkta. I punish stupidity."

The lord spoke again to the two humans and strode from the dungeon. After he'd left, the guards opened Arkta's cage, pulled him out by his chains, secured him to a wall and beat him until he collapsed.

For the next five days, Arkta suffered more physical punishment from the two guards, and each day Lord Erador visited and extracted more information from the tormented wolf.

On the fifth day the lord visited, Arkta had lost all will to live. When the lord asked him if he was going to talk, Arkta answered, thinking he had nothing more to hide from this human anyway.

"Yes, I can talk, human," he said simply.

"I know that, but it is good that you have decided to stop being stupid," Erador said, and then issued instructions to the humans.

"What do you want from me?" Arkta asked, pushing himself to his feet so that he could look at his antagonist.

"Well, I want you to be my friend, Arkta. There is no need for all this pain and torment. No, I want you to be my loyal companion, to walk beside me, to show all that I am friends with the wolves. Can you do that, Arkta?" As the lord spoke, the humans brought in a large tray of meat and laid it in front of the famished wolf. Arkta could not help himself. He tore into the flesh – it tasted better than anything he had ever eaten before.

"And if I refuse?" Arkta said as he ate.

"I will kill you without a thought, wolf; I can make you eat your own body if I wish. However, let us not think on these negative things… You are not going to refuse me, are you Arkta?"

"No, human. You are now pack leader, although the pack is small."

"You will call me 'my lord', wolf, and the pack is not small. Oh no, not small at all."

Back in the great hall, Lord Erador asked for General Izotz, who he had recalled to the castle. The news he had dragged from Arkta's mind had both excited and frightened him, and he did not like to fear anything. He needed to find and kill this child, which would deal with his fear, but he also wanted to find out more about the immortals and that Bodolf, another wolf with strange powers.

"I have to find that child, Izotz. How long before the main army can march?" the lord asked, pacing impatiently beside his throne.

"My lord, the main army is stretched thin; we have garrisons in the east and west which demand a constant supply of troop replacements. In addition, my lord, you must consider the weather. It is the beginning of winter and we will not be able to fight effectively in the frozen tundra. Also, my lord, with respect, you do not know where the child is. According to the information taken from the wolf, Banain was going to the south to train, but he did not know where. May I suggest my lord, that we find out more information about the child and his location before taking further action?" Izotz was very tired – he'd only returned in the early hours of the morning. Normally he would have noticed the warning signs when dealing with his very unpredictable master. In this instance, he did not know how close he came to death.

"As usual, Izotz, you make sense, but be more careful in future when questioning my decisions," he said finally. He had not divulged any information regarding the immortals to his commander.

"My lord," was all Izotz said. He chided himself for allowing this mistake and re-checked the mental shield that he had built up over the years, which protected him from the lord's casual mind probes. Whilst no match for Erador, the commander had learnt several skills over the years which had helped him to keep his deepest thoughts protected. He was a pragmatist and realised that the lord rewarded loyalty, but was also wary of any being who could challenge him. Izotz knew that the lord's method of dealing with a threat was to remove it.

"Over the winter, you will build an army that by spring can sweep into the plains and then south in search of this child, Banain. I will be accompanying you."

"Yes, my lord," Izotz said and marched from the room.

Chapter Thirty-Six

Banain woke at sunrise and leapt out of his bed. Donning his grey robe and tying the belt quickly around his waist, he stuffed his pillows under the bed covers to make it look like he was still in bed and stood beside the window, waiting. Over the last six months, the effects of training with the immortals had aged him by just over five years. He had to have new robes almost every week to keep up with his growth. He stood almost one and a half metres tall and weighed forty kilos. His young body was well muscled, and his blond hair was cut to shoulder length and kept out of his eyes with a leather headband.

After a few moments, Jabber appeared in the window, and in his customary manner, started shouting insults at the figure in the bed that he thought was Banain. After not receiving a response, the talkative ape leapt into the room, rushed over and pulled the covers off the bed, revealing the pillows underneath. During this time, Banain had climbed onto the window frame.

"Good morning Jabber. What are you doing looking for me there?" Banain said and then threw himself out the window and to the right. In mid-air, he located the rock he had moved to a ledge a few metres below his window the night before and envisioned it just under his feet. The rock flew under him and he used it to spring himself to the ledge above, which until now, only the apes had been able to manage. Grasping the ledge with his fingertips, Banain pulled himself upwards and onto the top of the rock. Then he sprinted down the short trail to his door and burst in to surprise Jabber…and Grindor.

"Very impressive, Banain. However, what if you had miscalculated, eh? What use would all the training have been if you had ended up dead on the floor? Do my teachings mean nothing to you?" Grindor said, his eyes blazing with anger and his teeth grinding together making a grating noise similar to fingernails scraping across a chalkboard.

"They do, Grindor. But you are the one that set this challenge for me, and I knew I was able to do it," Banain said, holding Grindor's gaze.

"Use the door in future, Banain. If you need more challenging exercises, I am sure we can find them for you," Grindor said and left the room.

"Oh well done, Banain, now Grindor will put us through hell!"

"Ha, you don't have to do it, Jabber, but who would you talk to all day without me? Come on, how bad can it be?"

For the next two hours, they both found out. Grindor doubled their routine and added new exercises. During their morning food break, neither of them had the energy to speak, and it took all of Banain's reserves to concentrate on the very complex lessons with Turr.

Halfway through a mind exercise, involving holding five rocks in the air whilst erecting a shield against other stones that were hurtling towards him, Grindor entered the room, interrupting his concentration. During the six months he had been training with the immortals, no one had entered the cavern. As he dropped his guard, several of the flying rocks hit Banain on the body and one on the temple sending bolts of pain shooting behind his eyes.

"Let that be a lesson to you, Banain. Never let your guard down, even if the unexpected happens. In fact, especially when the unexpected happens," Turr sang, with what Banain sensed to be amusement.

"Grindor, we assume there is a problem?" Turr enquired.

"There is no danger, but I need Banain's help with a rather unusual situation. Our sentries have discovered an injured human warrior. If they approach, the human may attack them in defence. But Banain may be able to approach safely," Grindor said.

"Banain, go with Grindor and see what you can do, but be careful, you humans can be very unpredictable!"

Grindor led Banain out of the cave and down the mountain, the way he had arrived a few months ago. He had been some of the way back during his exercises, but not this far. Along the way, Jabber had also joined them, asking question after question.

"Jabber, you need to be quiet, we are nearly there. Banain, the warrior is in that ruin on the right. Be careful!" Grindor said quietly.

Banain walked slowly towards the building, looking for any sign of the warrior. There was an entrance on the right hand side, and he noticed a trail of blood leading into it.

Following the trail, he entered the doorway, stopping to allow his eyes to adjust to the gloom.

Slumped against a far wall, he could just make out the figure of someone, then as quick as a flash, a bow raised and an arrow flew towards Banain. Months of training had honed Banain's reflexes. He imagined a shield around his body and sent a tendril of energy shooting towards and around the bow. The arrow bounced harmlessly off the shield and the bow pulled itself from the warrior's grasp, flying away to the other side of the room.

In desperation, the warrior tried to rise but collapsed onto the floor, unconscious. Banain closed the gap quickly, removed a sword and dagger from the body, and called Grindor in.

"Well done, Banain. I see the immortals are training you well. It would have been a pity if your life was ended by the arrow of a girl!" Grindor said, examining the warrior's body.

"A girl? I did not notice. She is wounded, Grindor. We need to get her back to the mountain," Banain said, worried about the amount of blood flowing from wounds above the warrior girl's right eye and on her left shoulder.

"I am not sure that is wise, Banain. We do not bring humans to the rock."

"Well we cannot leave her here, Grindor; she will die from blood loss. Send your scouts to find some sticks and I will make something to carry her on," Banain said, ripping some of his cloak off to make bandages for her head and shoulder.

Teague opened her eyes and was surprised to find herself in a large, sparsely furnished room. Her head and shoulder were hurting badly, and she realised that although she was under a cover, she was naked and she could not see her clothes. Worse, her weapons were on the far side of the room, next to a young boy who looked to be around ten years old.

"Are you okay?" she heard in her mind. The voice could only have come from the boy who was looking at her – the boy with the amazingly blue eyes.

In fact, on closer inspection, she could see that there was something special about him. He was sitting cross-legged on the floor and had an aura of calm and control about him, which belied his age. She had to use all her warrior training and skills not to let her guard down and to keep looking for opportunities to get her weapons back. The problem was she was naked under the sheets.

She decided to talk before acting to see if she could distract him in some way.

"Who are you?" she said.

"I am Banain. You do not have to mouth speak, I can hear you very well, and you should rest your face so that your wounds can heal. I am sorry. I have had to read your mind a little as you did try to kill me. I checked with the immortals and they said for now it was acceptable. You do not need your weapons, and I am not easily distracted. I wish you no harm."

Teague was dumfounded. This boy had read her mind; he knew everything she was thinking, but she did not know how he was communicating or how to answer him.

"It is simple, just think what you want to say and I will hear it. It is easier, at first, to look at the person or creature you wish to communicate with, but after a while you will learn how to focus what you want to say, and to whomever, in your mind alone."

Teague was getting annoyed; he was reading her every thought. "Stop reading my mind!" she said in her head, looking at Banain.

"There is no need to shout, Teague; if you promise not to get your weapons and hurt anyone here, I will stay out of your mind."

She considered for a moment and decided there was no immediate threat, if this child or the monkeys had wanted to kill her, she would have been dead already.

"Okay I promise Banain, but do you have a female healer? I need to talk to her about my wounds and the best way to treat them. Apart from being a warrior, I am also a healer, and I can help her find the correct ingredients to mend my wounds," Teague said, uncomfortable being naked under the covers with this boy present. In her village, they would never allow such a thing.

Her vision started to mist as she remembered the awful events of a week ago when her village had been attacked. She had been on sentry duty and had called the alarm in plenty of time, but there were just too many of them. She had only just escaped with her life, leaving behind the sounds of the attackers forcing her loved ones, those who were still alive, into trailers. She had looked back to see her burning village lighting the night sky.

"Are you okay, Teague? I am not reading your mind, but I can tell you are upset," Banain said, rising to his feet and walking over to the bed.

"Yes, I am fine. Please call the healer," Teague said, more fiercely than she intended, but she was upset by the memories and uncomfortable with Banain so close to her.

"I am sorry, Teague, there is no healer. In fact, I am the only other human here. I hope I have treated your wounds correctly. I sought guidance from the immortals before proceeding. You have a large cut above your eye which I stitched using the mandibles from large soldier ants. A puncture wound in your shoulder, I think from a spear, I cleaned and dressed with a honey compress. You had some other cuts and grazes over much of the rest of your body, which I cleaned and treated with aloe vera sap. I –"

Before Banain could continue, Teague interrupted. "You undressed me? You cleaned me? You did everything?" She couldn't believe this boy had done all this, and she didn't know how to respond. She looked at her shoulder and could see that Banain had done a good job, but…

"You are shouting again, Teague. Of course I treated you, who else would? I wouldn't let Jabber loose on you, his healing skills are not good, and the main ape healer here was not very keen to treat a human. Anyway, it was interesting for me. Yours is the first female body I have seen. It is quite different to mine. I should check your wounds," Banain said, reaching to pull Teague's covers down.

"No, you will not, Banain," she managed to say without shouting, pulling the covers up to her neck and holding them tight. "It is not right for a male to look upon the body of a female unless they are joined. Don't you know that?"

"I do not understand. I cannot look at your body?" Banain said, standing back from the bed and running one hand through his hair, which he tended to do when perplexed.

"Of course you can't. Didn't your parents or village elders teach you anything?" Teague asked.

"Well Krask, my father, never took off his feathers. I think it would have been impossible for him to, and I don't have a mother or a village, just my friends. You are the first human I have met. I only wear this robe to keep warm and to protect my human skin from injury. It's a shame we humans don't have permanent coats like other creatures. Do you feel more comfortable now?" As he finished the sentence, Banain pulled off his robe.

Teague's hands flew up to cover her eyes. "Put it back on, now!" She was yelling again, which probably meant that she would prefer him to wear his robe, Banain realised. His first encounter with another human was not going well!

Pulling his robe back over his head, Banain walked to the window and said,

"Jabber, it is not that funny; if you are going to spy on people, try to do it properly. You might as well come in. I am not doing very well it seems."

Jabber leapt into the room from his hiding place just outside the window, looking curiously at the girl in the bed.

"Teague, I have my robe back on so you can uncover your eyes. This is my friend Jabber."

Teague put her hands down and looked nervously at the ape sitting in the middle of the room.

"Hello Teague, I am Jabber, although it's not my real name, just one given by the elders. I do not know why they call me Jabber, but the elders give us a name and that is what we have to use. Where did you get your name? It is very strange. Did an elder give you the name? Do you think it was for a reason or just because the–"

"Okay, Jabber, give Teague a chance to reply," Banain said, breaking into the ape's prolific opening speech.

Teague was even more confused. She could hear the voice of Jabber in her head and she could see the ape staring at her. However, she could not bring herself to believe that it was actually the ape talking.

"What trick is this, Banain? Animals do not talk. It is you, isn't it? You are putting this in my head, which is a very cruel trick," Teague said, feeling confused and angry.

Banain did not understand any of this. He thought that his first contact with a human would be great, but this was not great at all!

"All creatures can communicate, Teague; they just have different languages. I have communicated with creatures that use a whole variety of methods. Just because you cannot understand them, does not mean they cannot understand each other. I have the ability to bridge the communication gap between creatures, allowing different species to connect at the level of the mind. I have facilitated this between you and Jabber, and it was Jabber who was speaking to you!

"You need rest if you are to heal properly. We will leave you. Please try and sleep, I am sure everything will become clear after a while." With that, Banain turned and jumped out of the window, followed by Jabber.

Teague tried to sit up, testing her wounds, and found that she could, but with some pain. Swinging her legs over the edge of the bed, she managed to get to her feet and walk over to where her weapons lay. Her bow and quiver with six arrows, her bronze sword and her dagger were all there. She picked up the dagger and moved to the window. Looking out, she could not see where Banain could have gone, but then there was so much about the boy she did not understand. Then she noticed a mirror on the wall; a damaged face stared back at her.

At seventeen years old, she had dark brown almost black hair and almond shaped blue eyes. She had refused many suitors, looking for that special something in a partner. "Who will want me now?" she thought, feeling sorry for herself.

She felt a wave of weakness wash over her and looked down to see that the wound in her shoulder had opened up again. Moving back over to the bed, she lay down and placed her right hand over the wound. Concentrating her mind, she envisaged the wound repairing. In her weakened state, she just managed to stop the flow of blood and repair the recently ruptured blood vessels but could do no more in her weakened state.

Exhausted by the effort, she started to slide into a very deep sleep. Her last thoughts were of Banain's body. Although she had pretended not to look, she had peeked. For a young boy, he was already well muscled, but what caught her attention was the scarring on his chest. The scars were similar to those inflicted on one of the men in her village by a large mountain bear.

Chapter Thirty-Seven

Lepe was getting short of breath; it had been a mistake to come off the rocks and into the snow-filled valley, and the three young, mixed blood wolves were gaining on him with every bound. Cutting hard to the right, he attempted to head back towards the safety of the mountains, but his pursuers anticipated his move and split up, one cutting in front and the other two staying behind, closing the gap every second. Frisk, the lead wolf, evaluated the distance and leapt for the sheep's neck, judging the move perfectly. His jaws clamped tight and the weight of the seven-month-old white and grey mixed wolf forced the sheep to collapse into the snow. This gave the other two the time to catch up and leap on the prone body of Lepe.

"Okay, okay, you win stinky wolves. All get off before I crushed," Lepe said from under the mound of wolf bodies.

"Ha, you are getting slow, Lepe. You should never have gone into the snow, you are no match for us here," Frisk said, gloating.

"Well if Lepe not injured saving smelly wolf pup, you not catch me!" Lepe said, relying on his well-worn excuse. Pushing himself up to his feet, the sheep gave himself a shake to get rid of the snow. In reality, the wound to his leg did slow him down a bit, and he was still having problems balancing properly due to the loss of one of his horns. The other one had survived, but there was a large lump missing where the soldier's sword had nearly cut that one off as well.

"Sorry Lepe, we forget sometimes that you are not as fit as you used to be. I will ask all the new pups to be gentle with you," Frisk said, easily avoiding the anticipated jab from Lepe's remaining horn.

"You cheeky and ungrateful Frisk. I teach you all a lesson."

Before anyone could say another word, a new voice spoke. "Why don't you kill that sheep, what is the matter with you cubs?" The new, deep and harsh voice came from a large white wolf who had stalked up to the group and who was looking menacingly at Lepe. Frisk and the other two wolves turned and moved between Lepe and the newcomer.

"This sheep saved my life, and Bodolf our pack leader has granted him the friendship and protection of the den," Frisk answered, every fibre of his young body alert and sensing danger from this white wolf, but also something else, something familiar.

"Bodolf was always soft. Sheep are prey. Move aside, pup. I have travelled far and I am hungry," the white said, preparing to attack.

"You will have to kill me first," Frisk said, going into full aggressive mode. Although larger than a grey, he was no match for the mature white, but he would protect Lepe with his life.

Sensing what was about to happen, Lepe sprang forward whilst the white was distracted by Frisk, jabbed the white with his one good horn and ran as fast as he could for the sanctity of the rocks, which looked a long way off.

The white wolf barrelled past Frisk in pursuit of Lepe who, already exhausted, was having problems moving through the deep snow. In his element, the white gained with every second. Frisk and the other two mixed were also tired and were having problems keeping up.

Sensing that the white was about to leap, Lepe stopped and turned, pointing his one good horn at his attacker. Not expecting this move, the white stopped, assessing the situation. He then bunched his muscles to jump at the sheep's neck.

The delay had given Frisk time to catch up, and he leapt straight onto the back of the attacker. The white twisted his head and grabbed Frisk by an ear, ripping the youngster from his back. Blood flew in all directions, and the force nearly severed Frisk's ear. Ignoring the pain, the plucky cub began to rise in order to attack the white again. Not giving him the opportunity, the white straddled the smaller, younger wolf and drove his jaws down towards the exposed neck.

"Arkta! What are you doing?" Nardic shouted. She and a group of wolves, including Bodolf and Honi, had just returned from hunting. They had charged unnoticed across from the valley entrance to where the bloody scene was unfolding.

"The wolf you have just mutilated is your son. If you do not back off, I will kill you!" Nardic growled, moving towards Arkta. The white looked up from Frisk, bloodlust still in his eyes.

"And if she doesn't, I will!" Bodolf added, also moving close to the bloodied white.

Arkta, seeing the odds were against him, backed off from the cub and sat down, looking carefully at the group of wolves surrounding him.

"Can you get up, Frisk?" Nardic asked, licking the blood from the youngster's lacerated ear.

"I am okay, it is just a scratch," Frisk replied, although he was in great pain.

"So what are you doing here, Arkta? The last I heard was that you and your pack had been captured," Bodolf said.

"We were. The humans have become very cunning, but I managed to escape. I had nowhere else to go and didn't think my father would refuse me a place to rest," Arkta said, but something in his manner worried Bodolf.

"It is not a good way to ask for sanctuary, attacking my pack and your own son. I am not sure you are welcome. You will stay here and I will organise a pack meeting to decide. Frisk, can you make it back to the den?" Bodolf asked the young, wounded cub.

"Yes, I can make it, Bodolf. Please do not banish my father. He did not know who I was!" Frisk said, confused over the situation but feeling a loyalty to the large, white wolf.

"It has to be discussed by the pack, Frisk. You can be involved if you are well enough," Bodolf said, turning back towards the den. "Lepe, I wouldn't stay here if I were you!" Bodolf added.

"Lepe come with Bodolf, not stay here with nasty white wolf!" the sheep agreed, moving alongside Frisk to accompany him back to the camp.

Sometime later at the den, the wolves were concluding their meeting.

"So we are in favour of letting Arkta stay, but until I have talked to him and I am convinced he has not been affected by the humans, you must all be careful. I will go and tell him," Bodolf summarised to the group of senior wolves and Frisk.

"Bodolf, would you mind if I went instead?" Nardic asked.

"Of course, Nardic, you must be so pleased to have him back again," Bodolf said, sensing doubt in her.

"Well, I would have been happier had he not attacked our son, but I suppose he did not know," Nardic replied, turning to the youngster and licking his ear again. "Frisk, you stay here and rest. I need to speak to Arkta alone."

Some hours later, Nardic and Arkta came back to camp. Bodolf waited a while before approaching Arkta and taking him some distance away from the den.

"So what happened to you, Arkta? I heard much about your raids on the humans, in fact you were becoming quite famous. Then I heard the humans had captured you."

For the next hour, Arkta told Bodolf the whole story of his raid on the humans, the pit and the treatment he received from Lord Erador.

"After a few months he thought he had me under his control, Bodolf, and to be honest, with longer to work on my mind, I think he would have. After I agreed to be his lap dog, he took me everywhere with him, but always close enough to keep control of my mind. Then yesterday he took me hunting for bulls on the plain. He was riding his horse, which stumbled, throwing him to the floor. In the confusion, I ran and managed to escape. I do not know if he was hurt, but I have not felt his presence in my mind since."

"And you say you know nothing of Lord Erador's plans?" Bodolf enquired.

"No. I was not told of such things. I do not think he is a threat, however; he has many problems on the plain. I think he is planning to leave the animals here alone in future, especially now he knows that we can communicate and are organised."

"Perhaps, Arkta, but he sounds like he is very dangerous to me." Banain said still not convinced.

Chapter Thirty-Eight

Teague lay pretending to be asleep, but watched Banain as he rose from his bed on the floor, stretched and donned his robe. Since their first encounter, he had been careful not to go naked in front of her and had erected a screen for her to change and wash behind. However, in the early mornings when he thought she slept, he would be less modest. The changes in him were unbelievable. It was as if he was growing up in front of her eyes. Every time he came back from a training session with the immortals, she could see that his body had aged a bit more and, due to the rigorous training routine provided by Grindor, he was extremely well muscled. She had been at the rock for four months now and was still not sure why she stayed. Although her people were gone and her village was destroyed, she knew of other villages where she would be made welcome. But something about this place and Banain in particular intrigued her.

Teague had been to see the immortals on several occasions, and they had helped her with her healing and her other gifts, but she had not wanted to sacrifice more of her youth for experience. She had, however, been teaching Banain some skills, including everything she knew about soldiering and the human language. He was like a sponge, soaking up knowledge, but he also had a creative flair for finding ways to use it. Mastering her language quickly, he spoke it as if born in her village.

She was looking forward to today and was just contemplating rising from her bed, when Jabber burst in through the window, leapt on her bed, threw the bedding everywhere and then danced around the room, causing mayhem as usual. Realising the ape had left her in her nightclothes again and that Banain was watching with a wry grin on his face, Teague grabbed the bedding and moved behind her screen to get dressed.

"Jabber, I have told you, do not burst in through the window; do not leap on my bed, and do not pull my covers off!" She knew she was wasting her time – when Jabber was excited he could not help himself – and she felt a bit sorry for shouting at him…but only a bit.

"My apologies Teague, but it is so exciting! Today is the final selection day for the ape elite guard!" Jabber said, still leaping around the room.

"Yes, we know, Jabber, you have talked of nothing else for months. I don't know why you are so nervous with all the training you have been doing you will win easily," Banain said, smiling at the ape.

"Yes, but only one will be selected, and I am the youngest ever to be entered!"

"You will be fine, Jabber. Now we have another important thing to attend to, don't we, Banain," Teague said.

"Yes. They should have arrived last night. Let's go!" Banain said, leaping out of the window and up to the ledge above, closely followed by Jabber. He did not need to use his gift to make the leap anymore; he was almost as strong and acrobatic as the apes he trained with daily.

Teague sighed and exited through the door, doing her best to catch up with the pair. Banain led the group up the path to the old campsite where he, Krask and Lepe had stayed those first few nights almost a year ago. Although he had seen Krask on regular occasions, Lepe had not yet made the long journey and he was looking forward to seeing his friend again.

Rounding the last corner, Banain spotted Krask and then Lepe standing next to him. Krask had told Banain of the events that had caused Lepe's injury, but he still was not prepared for seeing his friend this way.

Lepe was also in shock. Where was the small child he had carried most of the way from Krask Mountain? Who was this nearly two-metre tall, muscled man? Of course, he knew it was his friend Banain, but the changes were incredible.

Banain only hesitated for a second before running up to Lepe and throwing his arms around him. "Lepe, my friend, I have missed you so much. Krask told me some of what happened to you, but it has not prepared me. You were so brave!" Banain said, continuing his bear hug.

"You not prepared…Lepe not prepared! Where nice child gone? Who is big stinky human trying to squeeze Lepe life out," the sheep said, managing to free his one good horn and give Banain a solid poke with it.

Banain backed off, looking at the sheep, worried that his friend did not recognise him. "Lepe, it is me. Krask must have told you that I had changed," Banain said, looking at the eagle, who had not had a chance to say a word yet.

"Ha! Banain grow bigger, but still stupid!" Lepe said. He leapt at Banain, licking his face and giving him another, friendlier poke.

"I like your friend, Banain. He knows you very well," Jabber said from behind him.

"Yes, maybe now he is here he can teach you some manners," Teague joined in between gasps; she was still smarting from being left behind, again!

"Lepe, this is Jabber and Teague. It looks like they will be joining you in giving me a hard time!" Banain announced.

The five of them spent half an hour with pleasantries and then the conversation turned to recent events at the mountain and the return of Arkta.

"Does Bodolf trust Arkta, Krask?" Banain asked the eagle.

"I do not think so, although Arkta has not been a problem and has fit in well, Bodolf still seems very wary of him. I think he is the only one who is. I think if Arkta was going to do any harm to the pack, he would have done so by now, but you know Bodolf, once his mind is made up, it is hard to change."

"Yes, I know how relentless Bodolf can be!" Banain said, remembering the events of last year and shuddering inwardly.

"Shouldn't you two be somewhere?" Teague asked, looking at Banain and Jabber.

"Oh yes, the sun is quite high. Come on, Jabber, or we will be late. We will talk more after the challenge!" Banain said, turning to run down the path to the bottom of the mountain.

Chapter Thirty-Nine

Almost every ape not on guard duty gathered on the large open expanse between the Rock of the Immortals and the mainland. Grindor and ten of the elite guard stationed with him stood on the top of what was left of the air traffic control tower. The apes had no visual method of rank recognition, but once accepted as elite, all apes knew who you were.

Grindor stood up. Every ape chattered their teeth and then fell silent. "Today is elite selection day, as happens every spring. The ape selected will join the ruling council and help with the responsibility of guarding the Rock of the Immortals. The ten candidates will have to prove that they are worthy of the honour and responsibility this position would bestow on them.

"You will face the five challenges: speed, wisdom, fear, strength and compassion. This year we have created a new chant. You will listen to the chant, which contains all required to complete the challenges.

"Remember, you must not go further than the limits of the old city. There will be elites posted around the area to make sure you stay within the rules. In this way, we will monitor your actions. You have until sunset to complete the tasks. The elites, with guidance from the immortals, will make the final selection. Are you all clear on the rules?" Grindor said, looking at each ape in turn.

"Yes Grindor," the ten apes chanted in reply.

"This is the Chant. Please listen carefully. It will be intoned only once.

How quick the leg, how strong the arm
To climb, jump, run but do no harm
To take what is sweet, and then retreat

To venture in the moving floor
To man-made rock and back once more
To find a weed, is to succeed

That is all. Good luck and off you go!"

The ten apes ran off in different directions.

"Well Lepe not understand any of that. What stupid chant, not mean anything!"

"It all seems quite clear to me," Krask said.

"And me," Teague agreed.

"Ha, well of course Krask know, he know everything. I not know Teague, but if similar to girl sheep, they know everything as well. What about you Banan, I bet you not know," Lepe said, looking at Banain who was sitting cross-legged on the floor eating some dried fruit he had brought with him.

Giving a bit of fruit to the enquiring sheep, Banain sat for a while longer before speaking. "Well, I think the first section is to do with speed, compassion and probably strength. Jabber needs to find a bee's nest and take some honey without upsetting the bees, or receiving a sting in the process. That will require all those qualities. Then he needs to fashion something that will float from driftwood, paddle out to the man-made island out there, collect some seaweed and bring it back, which will cover fear and wisdom. Apes hate the water, and it will take wisdom to figure out that he should use some type of raft rather than swimming. I think we should go and wait down by the edge of the water, at the nearest point to the island." Banain stood and surveyed the coastline.

"Oh you very smart, Banan. You will be hell to live with if right!" Lepe said, shaking his head.

"Sorry Lepe, but I think he is right, and he is already hell to live with, so no change there," Teague said, laughing as she stood up.

"I will go and observe how he is getting on," Krask said, launching himself into the air in search of Jabber.

Some hours later, Banain and Teague stood next to each other trying to skim stones across the water, but a strong wind had risen in the last hour, creating ever-growing waves.

"Jabber not going to like this," Lepe observed. He stood a little way back from the waves breaking onto the beach.

Then Banain saw a figure of an ape running down the beach towards them.
"Quick, let's move back out of sight. We don't want to put Jabber off or be accused of aiding him," Banain said, moving behind a large lump of broken concrete and out of view of the beach.

The first ape was not Jabber, nor the next two, but none of them entered the water, instead they ran up and down the shore, undecided about what to do.

Then Jabber arrived and surveyed the situation. Looking around the beach, he spotted a medium size branch, ran up to it and, without hesitation, dragged it into the waves. When he could no longer stand, he jumped on the log and paddled toward the island, but his progress was painfully slow. The other apes looked around as well but only one of them found something to help them float and followed Jabber.

"Banain, we have a problem. Look out past Jabber!" Krask shouted.

Running from his hiding spot, Banain shielded his eyes from the glare of the spring sun and saw at least six vessels in the water moving towards the land and passing close to the island Jabber was paddling towards.

"Banain, these sea houses are full of humans, and they have weapons!" Krask warned. The boats, or "sea houses" as Krask described them, were moving very quickly. Banain noticed that they had large wings above them to catch the wind and push them along. Many rows of sticks, dipping in and out of the water in unison, also helped to move the vessels. Banain could also see humans lining the bow of the nearest vessel; they wore armour and waved weapons aggressively in the air.

"Krask, warn Jabber!" Banain shouted, diving into the sea and swimming for the flailing ape. He had spent several hours every day for the last year swimming – it was a great strength builder – so he moved easily through the water and closed the gap quickly. However, by the time he reached Jabber, they were only a few metres from the island. Alerted by Krask, Jabber had stopped, not sure in which direction he should go.

"Swim back to land, Jabber," Banain instructed, swimming past the ape and walking ashore onto the island.

One of the vessels had turned towards the island and would soon be close enough for the warriors to throw their spears. Banain ran to a point on the opposite side of the small concrete outpost closest to the vessel and furthest from Jabber.

As the vessel came within range of him, the warriors hurled their spears. Focusing his mind, Banain concentrated on erecting a small personal shield around himself. The immortals had taught him that he should only use the minimum amount of force necessary to achieve his objectives, saving his energy for as long as possible.

The spears bounced harmlessly away from Banain and lay in a heap on the floor around his feet. Confused, the attackers threw again, with the same result.

Banain then concentrated his mind, willing the spears to join. Instantly, they all leapt from the sand, creating one very large weapon. He then envisaged the super spear hurling towards and striking the bow of the vessel at the waterline, which it did with devastating results. The effect on the ship was instantaneous; the sea poured in through the massive hole made by the spears, flooding the front of the craft, its forward momentum forcing more in every second. Within moments, the vessel was sinking. Those soldiers who could swim were making for the island, whilst others clung to pieces of the wrecked vessel.

Banain dropped the shield. He was feeling slightly drained from using his powers, but all the physical and mental training were paying off.

Turning, he ran back towards Jabber who was halfway to the mainland. He dived in and swam after his friend, and they both arrived at the same time on the shore.

"The other vessels are heading towards the rock, Banain," Krask said, monitoring the situation from above.

"Thank you, Krask, keep watching them," he acknowledged.

Banain knew that when the warriors got ashore, they were going to have a bloody battle on their hands. He estimated that they only had around ten minutes before the first ship landed, which was not enough time to organise a proper defence. Along with Jabber, Lepe and Teague, he started running toward the point where they would reach the shore, but it was going to be close.

Grindor had also realised the seriousness of the situation and had arranged over two hundred apes on the beach facing the oncoming craft. Grindor himself was standing by the water's edge, in communication with the immortals.

As the vessels came within range of the apes, the warriors started throwing their spears. With the immortals' help, Grindor erected a shield around the apes, but with such a large area, it was weak, and every now and then a spear would get through.

"Grindor, you need to get the apes off the beach. What can they do against armed warriors?" Banain messaged as he ran.

"We cannot let the warriors get to the rock or all will be lost, Banain. When they come ashore, we will have our chance. Remember the immortals' teaching Banain, kill only to survive!" Grindor sounded very tired and Banain still had some way to go.

"Kill only to survive. What part of this situation is not survival?" Banain thought to himself as he ran.

As the first vessel landed, around twenty-five warriors leapt from the bow and ran towards the apes on the beach. As the howling mob approached, the apes split into two groups so quickly that the attackers did not know which way to turn. Then, with incredible displays of coordination, agility and strength, the two groups flanked and converged on the milling group of soldiers. Instead of fighting, the apes leapt over and dodged under the warriors, tripping and pushing them to the floor. Then they wrestled the warriors' weapons away, running down to the water's edge and slinging them far out to sea. Some apes were killed and more wounded by the first wave of attackers, but by then they had almost totally disarmed them and they started running back to their vessel.

Banain could see that the strategy was working for now, but there were another four vessels almost on the beach.

Finally reaching the battleground, Jabber and Lepe went to bolster the ranks of the apes and Teague found a spot within arrow range of the nearest ship, and Banain ran to Grindor. Teague badly wanted to kill as many of these raiders as she could, remembering what their kind had done to her village, but she respected the wishes of the immortals and aimed to maim rather than kill, most of the time!

The second vessel reached the beach, and although they had witnessed what had happened to the first group, poor communication and bloodlust blinded them to the situation and they too fell prey to the same defence by the apes. Lepe, in particular, found that he could charge through the attackers' legs, knocking them down like ten pins. Jabber would follow him, pulling weapons from the dazed soldiers' hands. However, it was a costly exercise, resulting in the killing and wounding of many more apes.

"Grindor, pull your troops back as fast as you can and create a gap between them and the soldiers," Banain instructed the quickly tiring ape.

"Okay, Banain, but I hope whatever you are going to do works; we are going to be overwhelmed soon," Grindor replied, sending the instruction to his troops.

As one, the apes disengaged and ran a hundred metres inland, reforming and leaving a large strip of sand between them and the attackers, strewn with the bodies of wounded and dead apes. Many of the raiders who had been disarmed in the first attack, had found new weapons on their vessel and were re-grouping with the rest to charge at the apes again.

All the vessels were now ashore and over one hundred and twenty, mostly armed, troops faced Grindor's remaining one hundred and fifty unarmed apes.

From above the battlefield, Krask looked down at the massed ranks facing each other across the sand, the invaders weapons gleaming in the sun, in stark contrast to the unarmed apes. He loved Banain and knew how special he was, but even with his powers, he could not see how a small child could turn the tide of war against such a large well-armed foe.

Chapter Forty

Bodolf stalked through the short tundra grass, which was just starting to send up new shoots as the freezing winter weather receded and spring claimed the plains again. A little way ahead and upwind, a group of humans was standing with a white wolf. Close enough to pick up the mind conversation he listened, his heart breaking as his son betrayed the pack to the humans.

"You have done well, wolf. Are you sure that the child will be returning to your mountain?" Lord Erador asked again.

"If what I have been told is correct, he should be here within the month, my lord. The eagle and the sheep are where he is training now, and the word around the den is that he will be coming back with them."

"This training fascinates me, wolf. Do you not know anything about it, or these immortals?" The lord continued pacing up and down in front of the wolf as he spoke.

"Only that they have some way of training the power of the mind and slowing down time, whatever that means, my lord."

"Go back to the pack and stay until you know for sure when the child is returning. Make sure you find a plausible excuse to leave, so as not to raise suspicion. As I said, you have done well so far, but remember, if you fail me, I can reach you wherever you are! Now go before they miss you."

Arkta turned and loped away from the lord and his escorts. Bodolf shadowed him back to the camp, heartbroken. He had had his suspicions about Arkta since his return, so when he had seen Arkta slipping out of camp a few hours earlier, he had decided to follow him. He wished that he had brought some of the pack with him, so he could have attacked the human who held so much power over his son.

"Do you believe the wolf, my lord?" Izotz asked, as he trotted alongside his leader back towards Seville.

"Yes, why not? My control over his mind is complete. He believes I can control him from any distance, and it is what he believes that matters. The intelligence he gave us regarding the location of the den will help us take the area swiftly. When we return, you will make the final arrangements for the army to travel as soon as Arkta informs us the child has returned."

Izotz grunted his agreement and dropped back into formation with his soldiers, sending one to scout ahead to search for possible ambush. Although he had been informed that the area was safe, he always double-checked everything; this was why he believed he was so successful. He was not happy about relying on the word of a wolf to move his army, but he knew better than to argue with Lord Erador.

Bodolf returned to his den and laid down, troubled. He was bitterly disappointed with Arkta, but what action should he take?

"Where did you go, Bodolf? I looked all over camp for you. You normally let me know when you hunt and take the youngsters with you." It was Honi.

"I needed some time alone, Honi. Sometimes an old wolf like me needs time to think," he replied, deciding not to worry his mate with these problems.

Honi did not believe him, but knew better than to quiz him further. Whatever the problem was, she knew Bodolf had to deal with it in his own way, and in his own time.

Chapter Forty-One

Banain moved to the centre of the beach and stood in front of the line of apes and facing the invaders, who were about to charge. Concentrating his mind, he put the plan he had just discussed with Grindor into action. As one, all the apes started chattering their teeth and pounding the ground with their hands. It was a fearsome noise, even to Banain!

He shouted to the humans in the language taught to him by Teague, "Begone, or face the wrath of the great sand ape!"

The leader of the raiders yelled at his soldiers, trying to spur them on to attack the apes.

"Begone, or die at the hands of the great ape of the rock!" Banain shouted, whilst in front of him the sand started to move and shift as if alive. Several of the soldiers started to point at the sand as it rippled and moved. It seemed as if a large circle of it was flowing like a river inwards. When it reached the middle, it started flowing upwards, creating feet, legs and arms. The sand flowed faster, gathering momentum, creating a giant sand ape that stood over ten metres high!

The giant ape started mimicking the actions of Grindor's apes. But with every chatter of its sand teeth and bang of its sand hands, jets of sand would fire at the petrified soldiers.

The raider's captain tried one last time to rally his troops, but when the sand ape took its first giant step towards him, he ran along with the rest of them for the boats.

There was mass panic as the troops climbed over each other to escape the approaching sand monster. By the time they were all on board, the ape was at the water's edge, his head swelling larger with his mouth opening. With a mighty roar, wind and sand rushed out of his mouth and pushed the vessels from the beach. Taking the hint, the invaders raised their sails and paddled with all their might away from the sand monster, picking up the stragglers from the wrecked craft on the way.

Banain could hold his concentration no longer. The sand ape collapsed into a large pile on the shoreline, and the apes stopped chanting and thumping the ground. Teague and Lepe ran toward Banain, who was having problems keeping on his feet, but Jabber got there first.

"Banain, are you okay? You don't look okay. You need to sit down. That was amazing! Did you see how they ran from the sand ape? It was brilliant, Banain. I can't believe–"

"Hey Jabber, give Banan a chance recover. He very tired, need sit down," Lepe said, interrupting the ape in full flow.

Whilst the two of them argued over what was best for Banain, Teague placed a hand over his forehead and concentrated her healing skills. To Banain, it felt like a cool river flowing into his mind and putting out the fires that were burning there. Within moments, he was feeling fine. He had never realised before how powerful Teague's skills were, but he was very grateful for them now.

"Jabber, stop arguing with Lepe. Banain is fine but many here are not! Go and get my healing bag, please. Lepe, please stay with Banain whilst I attend to the wounded."

Before any of the three could answer, Teague had run towards the first of the wounded apes.

Many hours later, Banain, Jabber, Lepe, Krask and Grindor sat together at the top of the rock, looking towards the setting sun in the east.

"It was a fine thing you did today, Banain. You defeated an army with only a few casualties. I would never have believed it, had I not been there. The message will go back to would-be raiders that the Rock of the Immortals is protected by a fearsome sand monster," Grindor said.

"Yes, Banain, it was impressive. From above, your position looked hopeless. You were outnumbered and without weapons. It is a battle that should be immortalised by song," Krask said, preening his feathers and feeling proud to have raised such a warrior.

"I hope you not going to make song, eagle. That one you sing: 'above the clouds, above the clouds' enough to make anyone want to bury head in sand. In fact, if you sang that song today, eagle, all soldiers run away without need for sand monkey. And why make sand monkey, Banan? Fearsome sand sheep much more frightening," Lepe said, giving Banain a poke with his good horn.

"Ha ha, you are right, Lepe. A sand sheep would be more frightening, but I thought I would save that for a big battle. You should apologise to Krask, though. His song is beautiful and you know it," Banain said, laughing and tugging hard on Lepe's beard. "It was not just my gifts that won the day. Without Krask's eyes, Grindor's skills and Teague's bow and healing, the battle could have been very different! Where is Teague anyway?" Banain enquired.

"She is still healing the wounded; the girl has not stopped since the battle ended. Many of the injured apes would have died without her help." Grindor replied.

"I will go and find her in a moment, but first we need to discuss our plans. I am worried about what is happening with Bodolf and Arkta and have decided that I will go back to Krask Mountain for a while, but Grindor and I need to meet with the immortals to make sure that they can keep the rock protected in future. Krask, can you fly back and let Bodolf know of the plans, please," Banain said, standing up.

"I will go now. I can get there before dark and will return in the morning," the big eagle said, launching from the rock and soaring off towards his mountain.

Down in the lower caves, Banain found Teague laying her hands on an ape with a spear wound on his arm. She had black circles around her eyes, her shoulders were slumped and she hardly noticed Banain as he entered and laid his hand on her arm.

"How many are at risk or in pain?" Banain asked.

"They are all safe, none suffer," Teague replied, standing back from her work to observe the results.

"Then stop Teague, or it is you who will need healing. They are in safe hands here."

Teague looked at Banain and nodded, then her eyes closed and she started to slump to the floor. Banain caught Teague and scooping her up in his arms, he ran out of the cave and up to their room, laying her on the bed.

"She will be okay, Banain. She is just exhausted. We have been telling her to rest for the last few hours, but she would not," Mendalot the head ape healer said. She had followed Banain up the hill and was wiping Teague's forehead with a cool cloth.

"Thank you, Mendalot," Banain said. He still found it funny how the apes were named, but funnier that they did not seem to realise. When he had told Mendalot that she must have got her name because she was a gifted healer, she had dismissed the idea as silly.

After Mendalot left, Banain lay down in his usual spot under the window and gazed up at the moon. He had problems sleeping at night, although his growing mind needed it.

Spending so much time with the immortals had not only aged his body but also his mind, and a part of him was mourning the loss of his childhood. He sometimes felt that he was a product of the immortals' wishes, rather than a person. He was looking forward to going back to Krask Mountain and spending time with Lepe.

He also had confusing feelings about Teague. Just recently, he had found himself looking at her and feeling strange emotions, which he had found quite distracting. He had not discussed this with the immortals as he felt this would be wrong somehow. It had altered the way he behaved with her; he no longer went naked when she was around, as he felt self-conscious about the natural reactions of his body. With all these thoughts running around his head, Banain finally managed to get to sleep in the early morning hours.

"Wake up Banain, you have to see the immortals and Krask has returned. I have brought you some breakfast and your favourite freshly squeezed juice. What time will we leave for your mountain?" Teague said excitedly. The bags were gone from her eyes and she was almost skipping around the room with excitement.

"Thank you, Teague. You are looking much better," Banain said, stretching and rubbing the sleep from his eyes.

"Hey Banain, are you ready?" Jabber said as he appeared at the window.

"Ready for what, Jabber?" Teague quizzed.

"Exercise, of course, and he shouldn't be eating all that!" Jabber admonished.

"Exercise? Banain is not exercising today, Jabber. He has too much to do! He has to get ready so we can start the journey to Krask Mountain."

"That's no excuse. He should exercise every day. You should understand the importance Teague, if he–"

"Okay, Jabber, we will exercise for an hour! Anything for some peace!" Banain said, starting to get up from his bed. He had slept in his robe from the previous day, so was able to leap to the window and follow Jabber as the ape exited.

"What time are we leaving, Banain?" Teague shouted, running to the window to try to hear a reply. However, they were both long gone.

A little while later, Banain arrived at the top of the rock and found Krask standing quietly waiting for him. Banain knew that something was wrong; the eagle looked even more dour than usual.

"Are you okay, Krask?" he enquired.

"I am fine, but there is bad news from Bodolf." The eagle told Banain of the events with Arkta.

"Bodolf is torn, Banain. Arkta is his son, but he has his responsibility for the pack to consider."

"Yes, I understand. Please wait for me whilst I talk to the immortals regarding what we should do," Banain said, standing. He then left to speak with Turr.

"The plan you suggest is very risky, Banain. You did well yesterday, but this will not be so easy. We suggest you stay longer and finish your training with us. We can offer sanctuary to any of your friends who need it," Turr sang.

"I cannot let Krask Mountain be taken by this Lord Erador, Turr. He has already done so much damage; he needs to be stopped!"

"Again, Banain, we advise that you are not ready for this, you should reconsider your plan. However, if you are set on this course of action, we will do what we can to help. Remember all we have taught, keep your mind and body fit and remember you can find us wherever the water flows."

"Thank you, Turr. I have to do this whatever the cost. Please watch over Teague for me. I do not want her involved."

"She will be safe with us. May the strength and wisdom of the immortals be with you, child," Turr sang with the voice of millions.

"I will never be a child again," Banain said sadly and walked from the chamber twelve days older.

"Are you sure you want me to do this, Banain. Shouldn't I stay with you? Shouldn't someone stay with you?" the eagle enquired, ruffling his feathers with worry as Banain told him his plan.

"Why do we not all travel together, eh? That would make more sense. Then we can discuss the defence of Krask Mountain with Bodolf. You can create some monster to frighten off Lord Erador's army, and it will all be fine."

"Believe me, Krask, I have considered that. But I do not believe it will work. No tricks will deceive Lord Erador. No, it has to be as I have said. My mind is set. Please scout for that information I need as soon as you can, my plan depends on it. Then return to Bodolf and let him know what he must do. I am going to leave without seeing anyone as it will be too difficult to explain, and I do not have the time. Ask Jabber to look after Teague and try to convince Lepe to stay here." It was tearing Banain apart having to leave this way, especially when he knew how excited Teague was about going to Krask Mountain, but he could see no other way.

Leaving the eagle on the top of the mountain, Banain returned to his room. Teague was tending the wounded at the infirmary, so he had some time to gather a travel pack together.

As he was just about to leave, Grindor appeared in the window carrying a small bundle. "Going without saying goodbye, Banain? What is it, exercises too hard for you? It's okay, Turr has told me of your plan, which I think is madness by the way. However, you have been a more than average student, and you should not dress as a novice. Try this instead. I made it one evening when I had nothing better to do."

Banain opened the package handed to him by Grindor; inside was a beautifully crafted robe. It was a very deep blue and adorned with gold designs and emblems. It was the most fantastic robe he had ever seen. Despite what the grumpy ape said, Banain knew that this robe had taken many hours to make.

"Thank you so much. It is the best gift I have ever received. However, I cannot wear it where I am going, and I do not want to have it stolen from me. Will you keep it for me please, Grindor?"

"I will. Banain, please take care of yourself. We cannot afford to lose you," the ape said, and Banain thought he saw a tear forming.

Walking over to Grindor and putting his arms around him, Banain said, "With the skills you have given me, I will be safe. Thank you, friend." Then he left.

Chapter Forty-Two

An hour later, Teague was pacing furiously back and forth in front of Grindor and Krask. Lepe and Jabber were standing someway behind her downcast and shaking their heads.

"What do you mean he has left already? I was supposed to be going with him… We all were. Why has the plan changed?" she said, looking from one to the other.

"Teague, we know no more than what we have told you. After the meeting with the immortals, Banain said he had to go alone and that you should stay here. That is all we know. I am sure he will be fine," Krask said. He was not happy about telling the lie but Banain had told him not to mention the plan to anyone except Grindor and Bodolf.

"No, it will not be fine… There is more to this than you are saying. Is Banain going to do something dangerous?" Teague pressed.

"No, he is just going back to sort everything out at the mountain. Then, when all is ready, you can travel there. You will be fine with us here, Teague. We will look after you. Then, when all is prepared, you can travel there with an escort of apes. Now, we still have the awards to give for the competition yesterday. It is too late today so we will do it first thing in the morning. I will see you then," Grindor said, looking at Jabber and then leaving the group.

"Go and rest, Teague. You must be exhausted after yesterday. I need some real food, so I am going hunting for a while," Krask said, and he too left.

The remaining three stood together in disbelief.

"I don't believe them; they are not telling us everything," Teague said, shaking her head.

"In all the time I have known Grindor, I don't believe he has lied to me. But he is hiding something, I can tell," Jabber added.

"Krask bad liar. Banan does something only stupid humans do. He need help I think," Lepe said, looking from Teague to Jabber for confirmation.

"Okay, so how long does it take to get to the mountain, Lepe?" Teague asked. For the next few hours, the three of them discussed what they should do.

The next morning, the area where everyone had gathered for the start of the selection competition was once more full of apes, and there was a sense of expectancy in the air. Once again, Grindor was flanked by his ten officers, but this time two of them sported dressings from the battle wounds they had received. He held his hand up to quieten the chattering apes, and in the following hush, he addressed the gathering.

"This was to be a day to award the honour of member of the elite guard to one of the ten contestants in the selection competition, and indeed it is still that day. Although we were not able to conclude the event, we were able to select a winner. Not based on the competition, although at the point when the raiders attacked this ape was already winning, but based more on the way he acted during the event.

"It is also a day to honour the many others who fought with valour and distinction. I am proud of you all. The immortals are safe thanks to your efforts. Would the tenth candidate please come to the fore?" Grindor asked, noticing that one of the contenders was missing.

After a few moments, no one had come forward.

"Does anyone know where Jabber is?" Grindor asked, looking around the gathered apes.

"No one has seen him this morning. Normally he comes with Banain and Teague in the morning to visit the wounded, but no one turned up this morning. I assumed he was preparing for this event," Mendalot answered.

"Perhaps they got lost when out herb gathering. I did not see them return, but they did leave very close to the end of my shift," another ape added.

"When was this, Sleeper, and who was with Jabber?" Grindor enquired, starting to get a very bad feeling.

"Jabber was with Teague and the sheep. It was late yesterday afternoon; Jabber told me that they needed to collect lots more medicinal materials. They certainly did have a lot of bags," Sleeper answered, getting the feeling he may be in trouble.

"So you just let them go without telling anyone?" Grindor asked, trying to hold his temper but already grinding his teeth.

"They have gone for herbs many times before, I thought nothing of it. There was no instruction to report them leaving," Sleeper replied, trying to hold the furious stare of

Grindor and sensing that all the other apes were watching him.

"That is a fair comment, Sleeper. I think we can assume they are making for Krask Mountain. Officers, assemble a squadron of troops ready to travel in one hour and then report to me. This gathering is dismissed," Grindor barked, and then sprang from the tower in search of Krask.

Krask was in fact far to the north, deep in conversation with Bodolf.

"I am not happy with this plan, Krask. There is so much that can go wrong!" Bodolf said for the third time.

"I know, Bodolf, but it is too late. Banain is committed, and if we do not do our parts, it will fail," Krask said, not happy with the situation himself.

"Okay, I will call a wolf meeting, but this is such a risk… I hope the boy knows what he is doing."

A short while later, every available wolf in the den gathered in a circle, almost nose to nose, in the traditional way.

"I have great news. After almost a year, the child, Banain, is returning to Krask Mountain. In fact, he started the journey today and should be here in three days. I am sure we want to provide a great welcome home for him," Bodolf announced.

"That is great news. I will start organising an event to welcome him home," Honi said.

"Why is this great news? What has this child ever done for us? We know nothing of him other than he is a small child with good communication skills," Arkta growled.

"He is more than that, Arkta; he has been working with the immortals for the last year and will be able to share their wisdom with us. With their help, we can start to rescue the plains from the humans. I thought that was what you wanted?" Bodolf replied.

"If you believe that a child, or the immortals, can stop Erador and his army, then you are all fools. He bends the wills of thousands of humans and animals to his command. What can anyone without an army do to stop him? I at least managed to slow him down and that is what I will do again. I have wallowed in this place long enough. It is time to start fighting again as I did before," Arkta said, backing off from the circle.

"I will come with you, Arkta, as will many here," Nardic announced and moved to the side of her mate.

"No you will not! You and the others here have become soft; you are of no use to me. I will find wolves who still know how to fight," Arkta said, looking coldly at Nardic. Then he turned and loped from the meeting.

"I am sorry, Nardic, but you must let Arkta go. I think he was trying to protect you in his own way. Now that he has gone, I need to discuss something further with you all," Bodolf said.

For the next hour, the leader discussed Banain's requirements, as relayed by Krask, with his pack.

Chapter Forty-Three

Banain was in trouble! Only a day after leaving the rock, he had run into the slave traders, who were taking slaves and animals to Seville. He was trying to lose them in the foothills of the mountains to the south of Seville. Crouched behind a large boulder, he watched the hunting party detach from the main body of wagons to find him. He had alerted them to his presence by the smoke from his breakfast fire and had been running ever since.

He never heard the three wolves that had circled around behind him and now had him pinned to the ground. He would have been dead if not for the wicked looking muzzles keeping the three sets of teeth from mauling him.

A few moments later, the wolves' owners arrived and clubbed him unconscious.

Waking sometime later with very sore head, Banain found himself chained to the floor of a large caged wagon, which was jolting its way along the track from the coast to Seville. Sitting up, he could see several more wagons, both in front and behind, most filled with men, women, and children; the others held a variety of large game animals, including lions. In his wagon were around thirty people. Alongside the wagons, around fifty heavily armed raiders just like those that had attacked the rock, were riding on plains horses.

Sitting next to Banain was a mountain of a man; the fresh wounds all over his body showed that he had not come without a fight. He was about thirty years old and had jet-black hair tied tightly behind his head. He was wearing a leather apron and had old burn marks up his arms. The man was looking at Banain steadily.

"What village are you from, blond boy?" he grunted, in Teague's language and dialect.

"I am from San Roque, or was until the raiders destroyed it and all my friends and family. I have been on the run from the raiders since then, but as you see, I did not make it. And you?" Banain enquired.

"I was captured by these whoresons when they decided to visit my village, and our wise chief decided not to pay the tax they levy on us every time they pass from the coast. That resulted in the raiders burning the village to the ground and the slaughter of the old and young. Those left from our village are in this wagon," he said, his brave face nearly slipping, but only for a second.

"Do you know where they are taking us and for what?" Banain asked.

"We are to be guests of the mighty Lord Erador." The man almost spat the name. "We will be slave labour if lucky, but more likely will be used in the arena to keep the crowds amused. I would not get your hopes up for any type of future, Blondie. These slavers collect most of their human cargo from across the sea in old Africa, but they like to gather some local merchandise on their trip from the coast to Seville, which is our final destination."

"My name is Darcy, and you?" Banain asked.

"I am Wayland; I am a blacksmith…or was."

Over the next three days, Banain talked with Wayland, learning that he had been a mercenary soldier fighting with a lord from far to the west before coming to his village. He had apparently risen to second in command of the army, but he did not like the lord's ruthless methods. Banain made up a story for himself, based on the life of Teague in her village.

The wagons stopped at sunset and set off again at dawn. Every morning and evening, they were supplied with water and food, which surprised Banain. Wayland said that it was because the slavers wanted the best price for them.

On the morning of the fourth day, the wagons drew into the outskirts of Seville, finally stopping at the command of Lord Erador's soldiers.

The soldiers spent some time going up and down the wagons, and then they gave the slavers instructions. They moved on again until they reached a wider area, where the wagons pulled to the side of the track.

After a while, Banain could hear what sounded like a rhythmic pounding getting closer. Soon, he could see the front of a large column of soldiers on horses riding two abreast coming down the track towards them. Riding a little way in front were scouts, then a pair of banner men carrying bright red banners with a gold design depicting the letters LE. Behind the banner men came around two hundred mounted troops. In front of the mounted soldiers rode a thin man dressed in bright red leather armour and a mountain of a man in black-bronze armour decorated with silver trim. Loping along beside the horse carrying the man in red was a large white wolf that Banain immediately recognised as Arkta. As the leader drew level with Banain's carriage, the tall, thin man raked the wagons with his eyes and stopped abruptly when he met the eyes of Banain.

Banain had never felt such a strong and malevolent mind probe in all his life. It took all his skill and training to keep in place the blocks guarding the parts of his mind he did not want the lord to see. He thought that the lord was going to stop and come back to him, but after what seemed to be an age, the cruel gaze moved on and the troops continued to stream past.

After the mounted soldiers came hundreds of foot soldiers, all marching in rhythm to massive drums, which were carried on the backs of large bulls spaced every twenty metres or so. It took quite a while for the soldiers and drums to pass and even longer for the train of wagons carrying food, weapons, tents and all the other requirements of a marching army.

Finally the last wagon lumbered by and the slavers started forward again towards the centre of Seville.

"That man in red was Lord Erador. He seemed to be very interested in you, Darcy!" Wayland said, looking at Banain questioningly.

"Yes, I don't know why," Banain replied.

At that moment, a group of soldiers ran back from the marching army and stopped the wagons again. After talking to the lead slaver, they came towards Banain's wagon and ordered the slavers to open it and unchain him.

Pushing him out and to the floor, the four soldiers surrounded him and marched him in the direction of Lord Erador's castle.

"The lord seems to have taken a shine to you. Not many get an invite to his castle," one of the soldiers said.

"Yes, you are to be his honoured guest," another added, laughing.

"Although once in the lord's castle, not many come out!" the first one said, laughing.

"At least he will have a while to contemplate whilst he waits in 'luxury' for the lord to return from his child hunt. Why he has to take an army to find a child is beyond me," the third soldier added, and the three of them laughed as they marched along.

"You want to be very careful what you say. You know the lord has his spies everywhere. You could end up as guests of the lord yourselves. Now shut up. Let's do this and try to catch up with the column again."

"Yes Sergeant," the men mumbled.

"Hey Sarge, why do we have to go back? This place is hardly defended; wouldn't it be better if we stayed here?"

"It is Sergeant to you soldier, and as soldiers we follow orders. I follow the lieutenant's and you follow mine. Now keep your trap shut and do as you're told!"

"You recognised that blond human in the slave wagon didn't you, wolf?" Lord Erador quizzed Arkta as they travelled. He had already read the wolf's mind before he responded and was pleased to have such a strong hold over this animal. He had proved to be very useful so far.

"He reminded me of the child, my lord, but it could not be. Banain can only be five years old at most and this was a young man," Arkta replied.

Lord Erador had also felt something strange about this blond youth. His interest had engaged the moment the wolf had locked onto him. He had probed him deeply, and although he had found nothing out of the ordinary, he had experienced a feeling that he had only sensed in one other human, General Izotz.

He had long held the vague suspicion that the general was holding back on him, but he could never prove anything. Now he was more suspicious, which was why he had ordered the soldiers to take the blond youth back to his dungeons for interrogation on his return.

"General, you would not hold information back from me, would you?" he queried Izotz who was riding next to him.

"What do you mean, my lord?" Izotz answered, staring straight ahead.

"Well, I sometimes get the sense that you hold back from telling me everything, is that correct?" the lord pressed.

"My lord, I am sorry but I do not know what you mean," Izotz answered, working hard to conceal his thoughts from the probes.

Luckily, at that moment, Arkta broke into the mental interrogation. "I will go ahead and scout Krask Mountain, my lord. Bodolf will have hunting parties out until dusk, so I suggest that is when you attack. You need to secure the dens outside the mountain first and then send troops inside to the valley. Once you are inside, you will have full control of the mountain. I don't know why you need so many troops, my lord. There are only twenty or so wolves to take care of."

"It is not your place to question my reasons, wolf, but it amuses me to tell you. Taking Krask Mountain and finding Banain is just the start of this campaign. I intend to carry on all the way to the coast and find the mysterious home of the immortals. Now go and do your job."

Chapter Forty-Four

After throwing Banain in a cell, the guards left. He sat down, concentrating his mind on locating Krask. So far, his plan had gone well, but he had not counted on Arkta being there. He was also not with the main group of slaves as he had intended, but he was sure he could still improvise from here.

"Krask, where are you?" he sent.

"I am high above the castle, Banain."

"Good, are you sure you do not mind me melding with you?"

"As we discussed, it is fine. Let us do this so that we can get back to the mountain. I am worried what will happen to my home, Banain!"

Banain used the techniques he had practised with the immortals, and after a few moments, he was looking down on the city of Seville from Krask's lofty viewpoint.

"The main human holding pens are there, Banain, and the animals are all kept over there," Krask said, whilst looking at the locations on the ground underneath him.

"I calculate that there are about one hundred soldiers left in the city, just enough to keep order. At this time most are active, but at night many will be asleep in the guardhouse, which is there." Krask continued slowly circling above the city.

"Thanks, Krask. Can you go back to Bodolf and let him know the plan is proceeding well and that he should carry on with his part. I will contact when all is ready here," Banain said, withdrawing from the eagle's mind, his visual images changing from Krask's world of freedom, back to the small, dirty cell.

Lying down on the filthy floor as comfortably as he could with the restriction of the chains, Banain forced himself to sleep and conserve energy for the task ahead.

Bodolf's scouts had already reported the approaching army, and Bodolf himself was halfway between them and the den. Hidden downwind of a small gulley, he knew his prey would have to travel this way to reach their target.

After a couple of hours, Arkta loped into view. Being careful to make no noise and keeping downwind, Bodolf followed the traitorous white to the outskirts of the camp.

After several minutes of watching, Arkta turned and loped back in the direction he had come.

When he was sure he had gone, Bodolf ran into the camp to set the final plans in place.

Chapter Forty-Five

"If we hurry, just make valley before dusk," Lepe said as he continued at a steady pace towards Krask Mountain. They were just going through the last narrow pass before entering the plains. Having participated in many of Banain's exercise regimes, Teague was having no problem keeping up the pace with Jabber and Lepe. Because of the number of raiders about, they had moved cautiously during the days and used no fires at night. They were just a couple of hours away from the mountain and were keen to finish this journey and quiz Banain as to why he had left without a word.

"You will love mountain, fresh grass, cool water, fruit…better than stinky rock!" Lepe said, sensing home was close and picking up the pace.

"I will love anywhere we can lie down and rest! It's a long time since I have travelled such a distance in such a short time," Teague replied.

"I have to admit, my hands and feet have never been sorer," Jabber added.

As they finally entered the plain, they saw an advance scouting party of fifty mounted soldiers sent to secure the southern approaches to Krask Mountain. The party was quite a distance away, but they were charging at full gallop towards them.

"Run for rocks!" Lepe shouted, heading towards the nearest outcrop. Although far away, the mounted soldiers were closing the gap alarmingly quickly. Lepe, being the fastest, pulled ahead of the other two. His vision allowed him to see both in front and behind, and he could see that Jabber was moving very fast, but Teague was not going to make it.

"Come on, Teague, they are close behind! Run faster!" Lepe encouraged, but it was the worst thing he could have done. As he watched, Teague turned her head to see how close her pursuers were and tripped over a boulder.

Jabber also looked back. He turned immediately, running back towards her. Before he could get to her, the leading rider threw a spear. It drove into her body, pinning her to the ground.

Jabber leapt at the rider, knocking him from his horse. The pair of them landed in a heap on the floor.

By this time, the rest of the soldiers were milling around, and Lepe could no longer see what was happening. He wanted to turn and go back, but knew he could not help. With tears misting his vision and an ache in his heart, he ran on into the rocky outcrop where the heavily armoured horsemen had no way of following.

An hour later, he reached Krask Mountain and climbed up the secret trail, only accessible to mountain sheep and cats. When he went through the small entrance near the top of the southern mountain, he could not believe the sight that greeted him.

Chapter Forty-Six

Banain woke clear-headed and feeling refreshed. He made contact with Krask again to make sure that all was going to plan, then stood up and looked at his leg and arm shackles. They were a simple threaded lock type so it was an easy job for him to unwind the locking pins and let them fall to the ground.

Walking to the door, he looked through the barred peephole and saw two guards sitting across the hall. Much to their amazement, the large bunch of keys lying on the table between them lifted in front of their eyes, flew towards the door and through the opening. Both guards rushed to the door and looked in, but they could not see the keys.

Then the lock clicked and the door swung slowly inwards. They could now see Banain shackled to the wall on the far side and the keys on the floor near his feet. Moving forward with their weapons in front of them, they approached Banain. He looked at them and smiled.

"You like chaining people up, but have you tried it yourselves?" As Banain spoke, further manacles on either side of him flew out and clamped onto the arms and legs of the soldiers.

At the same time, his own dropped away and he stepped forward, picking up the dropped weapons and placing them against the back wall, out of reach of the manacled guards.

"If you shout or say a word I will have to kill you, is that clear?" he said to them. They both nodded.

"Give me the answers to the next questions and your lives may be spared," Banain said.

When he had finished questioning the guards, he unchained each in turn, made them remove their uniforms, and then re-chained them.

After leaving the cell, Banain walked down the long corridor, stopping at each cell to open it and free its occupants. Some were too sick, injured or mentally damaged to move, so he found a person with some healing skills to set up a temporary infirmary before moving on.

Of the sixty-three people in the main cells, forty-two were fit to help with his plan. Banain quickly told them what they must do. On his way to the cells, Banain had memorised the route and the number and location of the guards in the main castle. From the information provided by Krask and the guards he had questioned, he knew where the main guardroom and the slave pens were located – all the information was imprinted on his mind like a map.

The two men he had instructed to go back to his cell stood outside the inner guardhouse, dressed in the guards' uniforms. Standing on either side of a slumped Banain, one rapped the correct code on the door. The small inspection hatch opened, but the view from within was limited, allowing the viewer the sight of the slumped Banain and half of each guard only.

"What the hell are you two idiots doing with that prisoner? You know Lord Erador has a special interest in him. And why are you standing so close to the door?" the sergeant of the guards said, trying to get a better view.

"We think he is dead, Sergeant, so we thought we'd better bring him to you. Thought you might want to see him?" the fake guard said.

"You have to be the most stupid pair I have ever come across. If that boy is dead we are all in trouble, and you don't want trouble with Lord Erador. Stand back from the door!"

The peephole slammed shut and the main bars holding the massive door closed released from within. As the door swung open, the sergeant came face to face with the smiling figure of Banain standing alone, his hands held in front of him as if in an attitude of prayer.

Before the sergeant or any of the other ten soldiers in the guardhouse could move from their beds or gambling tables, Banain spread his arms wide. Every weapon in the room leapt into the air and flew into the tunnel behind him, clattering to the floor. At the same time, the far guard door swung closed and locked, effectively stopping the guards from escaping to raise the alarm. From the cells either side of the tunnel, the prisoners streamed out and ran into the guardroom, overpowering the guards. Then, stripping them of their uniforms, the prisoners pushed the guards none-too-gently into the cells. Ten more of the prisoners donned the guards' uniforms and the group, led by Banain, moved up into the main castle.

Over the next two hours, using the same methods, Banain's growing army took over the whole castle. Of the one hundred and thirty people in the castle, twenty-three more were soldiers (of which eight immediately said they wanted to join with Banain), sixty-three were slaves and forty-four were very young girls, found in a large hall in the lord's private quarters. Banain knew it was a risk to trust the soldiers, but he had to take the risk. He had sensed genuine feelings from them and he needed all the armed help he could get.

Banain's biggest problem was trying to convince so many badly treated people not to kill their former captors outright. He had to put the soldiers in the dungeons and post his own guards to protect them, such was the anger. Knowing he was short of time, Banain appointed a prisoner called Garfled who was an ex-soldier sergeant to be in charge of the castle until he returned, with the orders to let none but him back in. He had been immediately impressed with the man – he was quick-witted and had a strangely calming effect on those around him, a natural leader.

Taking thirty uniformed men, Banain left the castle and moved towards the building housing the bulk of the human slaves.

Manacled again, with soldiers either side and equipped with the correct passwords, the group raised no suspicion from the sentries posted along the route.

On reaching the gates to the slave holding pens, the gate guard challenged them. "What the hell are you doing here with that prisoner? Does it take so many of you to guard one man?" the guard sneered.

"This prisoner has been interrogated. He has divulged that one of the wagons that arrived today contains weapons that the occupants intend to use against us. He is going to identify the wagon," the lead ex-prisoner guard said.

"Pah, what rubbish. We search each wagon when it comes in here. We would have found the weapons if they had been there," the guard answered, although he didn't sound entirely convinced.

"Well, if you do not want to cooperate, we will have to inform Lord Erador that it was your fault that the weapons were not found, if in fact this information is true," Banain's guard continued.

"Very well, come in and look, but you are wasting your time and more importantly mine," the guard grunted, opening the gates to let the group in.

"You had better bring any troops you have here with us just in case. Now prisoner, show us where this stash of weapons is supposed to be, or things will not go well for you," Banain's guard said, standing aside so that Banain could walk between the rows of carriages.

As planned, Banain's men allowed the twelve genuine guards to walk in front of them, just behind Banain. He did not want them examining the false guards too closely, in case they realised they did not recognise any of them. One of the reasons Banain had planned this event at this time, was that the failing light helped reduce the risk of that happening, especially there in the darkened interior of the slave building.

Reaching the trailer he had arrived in, Banain met and locked eyes with Wayland through the bars.

"Hello blacksmith," he said, smiling. "How would you like to get out of that cage?"

As he spoke, he threw his arms upwards, his shackles flying into the air, and set up a personal barrier around himself. From behind, his fake guards attacked, clubbing down the real guards before they had time to react. Banain had cautioned against killing unless there was no choice. The guards on the floor would live to tell the tale, but would have massive headaches.

Banain soon got his men opening the carriages and freeing the occupants, again sorting out who was fit and willing to fight and who needed caring for.

Banain himself opened the wagon he had travelled in and grabbed the meaty arm of Wayland as he jumped down to the floor.

"You are full of surprises, Darcy!" the big man said, looking at Banain with a quizzical expression.

"That is true, although the name I gave you was not. Had you known the truth and Lord Erador had searched your mind, he would have known too. I hope you understand."

"I understand nothing youngster. How have you been able to do all this?"

"How is a long story, Wayland. I will tell you when time permits. My purpose is to take over the city of Seville and raise an army to attack Lord Erador's, before it can do any more damage."

"And when do you intend to do this?" the giant of a man asked, looking in disbelief at this boy who was standing confidently before him.

"We need to capture the city tonight and leave with an army by midday tomorrow, so if you have finished questioning me, we have much to do. I take it you will accept the position as acting general? I know where there is a suit of armour just your size!"

Chapter Forty-Seven

"Bodolf...Bodolf, where you?" Lepe sent as strongly as he could. He was still in shock after the event with Jabber and Teague. Looking down over the valley, he could still not believe what he was seeing. It was full of animals of every type, but what was amazing was that the animals that would normally be hunting and killing each other were standing side by side! Wolves next to bulls, big cats next to sheep... Sheep! There were at least one hundred of his kin in the valley.

"Lepe, is that you? How come you are here?" Bodolf replied. He sounded very tired.

"It long story, Bodolf, but have bad news. Teague and Jabber captured by many raiders. Lepe no help them, Bodolf, think they both be dead!" Lepe sent, his world falling apart again as the words triggered memories of the event. He had let his friends down.

"Did you see them die, Lepe?" Bodolf asked.

"No see die but wounded with spear. I should have stayed, helped."

"Listen, Lepe, it sounds like you had no choice; as soon as this battle is over we will go and look for them, okay?"

"What battle, Bodolf, and what all these animals doing in valley?"

"Sorry Lepe, I don't have time to explain everything now, but I am glad you are back. At any time, we are expecting to be attacked by a large army, and I need you to take charge of the sheep," Bodolf said. Then he explained what he wanted Lepe and his four-legged troops to do.

As the sun started to set, Bodolf had positioned all his resources as discussed with Krask. Then he waited.

"Is everything ready, General?" Lord Erador demanded. He was not sure about Izotz and wanted to get this over with so he could interrogate him properly. For now, he needed him to run this campaign.

"Yes lord, the troops are in place awaiting your order," General Izotz answered, calmly as always, which infuriated Lord Erador more.

"Then attack, General, attack, or it will be dark and we will not be able to fight at all. I hope this plan works for your sake."

"With respect, my lord, the plan is based on the word of the wolf. If his information is correct, then it will succeed," the general replied, looking calmly at the lord.

"If not it will be your fault, you are the general. Now get on with it," Lord Erador screamed.

General Izotz signalled to a messenger, who raised a horn to his lips and blew the signal for the attack to commence. Then he spurred his horse on and headed towards the front of his troop of fifty mounted men. With Arkta leading the way, the troops galloped towards the wolf den.

A short way from the target, the general signalled his force to split, so that the attack would come from both sides.

The other one hundred and fifty cavalry, accompanied to the rear by Lord Erador, charged towards the entrance to the interior of the mountain, with the five hundred foot soldiers following at a quick march. The plan was to take the dens and the interior before the enemy knew what was happening, and then use the mountain as a base for further expansion into the south and east. When Lord Erador had interrogated Arkta and had learnt of the mountain and its interior valley, he had realised he had made a mistake not securing it beforehand. A mistake he would soon rectify.

As Izotz's group converged on the wolf dens, they found nothing. The soldiers with the nets jumped from their horses and spread the nets across all the entrances to the caves except one. Izotz and Arkta led a group into that cave, which had the tunnel through to the interior of the mountain, but found it to be like the rest of the den…empty! The small tunnel inside had been filled with earth and rocks, making an impenetrable barrier. There were no signs that wolves had even been there recently.

"What sort of betrayal is this, wolf?" Izotz said, turning to the wolf, his sword drawn.

"I was here not a few hours ago and it was a thriving den! I do not understand," Arkta replied, backing away from the furious human. All his instincts told him that Izotz was going to attack him.

"You are in league with these wolves, and you have led us into a trap. I knew you were not to be trusted. Because of your actions, Lord Erador will turn on me. Well, you will not be around to see that." As he spoke, the general swung his sword at the crouching wolf, but with lightning speed, Arkta leapt at the general, nearly knocking him to the floor, and ran out of the cave, past a group of startled soldiers and into the foothills of the mountain.

Izotz recovered his balance and charged outside, but the wolf was gone. Looking down, he saw a trail of blood leading into the mountain.

"You there, take five men and track, catch and bring the wolf to me. Do not kill him! The rest of you, form up behind me. I think Lord Erador is going to need us!"

The main body of mounted soldiers had just reached the bottom of the long trail up to the entrance, changing formation to two abreast, the widest they could manage in the narrowing canyon. They charged up the hill, hoof beats reverberating off the narrowing walls.

As the lead soldiers came around the final corner at the top of the trail, they could not believe their eyes. Where the trail widened into the valley, over a hundred plains bulls stood shoulder to shoulder. From the soldiers' point of view, it looked like a wall of horns on black heads with wicked, staring eyes. As one, the bulls charged towards the mounted soldiers.

Lepe and the other sheep were hiding in the rocks on either side of the canyon. He was at the top of the trail and could see the bulls starting their charge. There were also about thirty cougars waiting, tails lashing from side to side. As the bulls closed the distance on the lead riders, they panicked, turning their mounts and trying to force their way back through their own troops. With nowhere to go, the whole charge came to a disorganised halt, with soldiers milling around, not able to find a way forwards or backwards.

At that moment, Lepe shouted to attack, breaking cover and charging towards the soldiers closest to him. The cougars also broke cover, leaping straight at the riders, raking at them with their claws and pulling them to the ground.

Lepe headed towards the top of the trail where the bulls had stopped the charge. With most of the still mounted riders trying to urge their mounts down towards the bottom of the trail, the horses without riders were milling around towards the top, as far away from the carnage of battle as possible

"Horses of plains, you want live, throw human, follow me!" Lepe shouted as he charged through the legs and hooves, risking his own life several times. Bodolf had told him that because of his exposure to Banain, he would be able to speak to any animal, so he hoped that it was working.

A large black warhorse, standing nearest to the bulls and looking for a direction to run, pawed the ground, threatening to charge at Lepe.

"Look, stupid horse, you want die, okay, but Lepe show you a way to live."

"How can you speak? What is this trick?" the horse replied in Lepe's mind.

"No time explains now, but you follow me and live free…otherwise die here."

Lepe looked once more at the very nervous black horse, and then ran towards and through a gap between the bulls. The horse stood for a while longer, looking down the track at the mayhem, then he made his decision.

He neighed the horse equivalent of "follow me" as he turned and galloped towards the gap between the bulls. Hearing his call, the other horses in range also followed, each sending the message further down the trail. Those who still had riders bucked and kicked so savagely and unexpectedly, that they dismounted their riders before they realised what was happening. The cougars targeted those who managed to stay mounted, making short work of pulling them from their horses.

The surviving soldiers on the floor bunched together in a defensive formation and backed down the mountain. The cougars and sheep continuously harried them and forced the dwindling group to retreat further down the trail.

Lepe waited inside the bull barrier to see if any plains horses appeared. After a few moments, the black charged through and stopped, eyes staring wildly at the collection of deadly foes within the valley.

"Not worry horse, no harm you, animals here truce. Follow Lepe," the sheep said and ran towards an area close to the edge of the lake, away from most of the other animals.

The black horse did not need much encouragement. He galloped after Lepe followed by a stream of horses, as they too entered the valley.

"Bring the horses over here, Lepe, and line them up quickly!" Grindor said, emerging from the trees by the side of the lake.

"Hello Grindor, nice see you too! Lepe need go back. You line up horse, good luck!" Lepe turned to gallop back to the pass and collect any strays.

"Where is that idiot Jabber? I want a word with him, you and Teague when this is over. The actions of you three nearly caused this plan to fail completely."

"Lepe not have time explain now, we talk after," Lepe said as he ran out of range of the ape, his heart sinking as the excitement of battle faded, replaced by grief and guilt over the loss of his friends.

At the bottom of the pass, the main body of foot soldiers had met up with the retreating ex-mounted soldiers. Some of the foot soldiers were laughing openly at the sight of their dismounted comrades, harried by what looked like sheep and a few large cats.

"Okay, the next soldier to laugh will be sent into battle on his own. Now line up in battle formation. You newly promoted foot soldiers, form up at the back and let the real men do the fighting," the foot soldiers' captain shouted.

"Captain, get up that hill and kill those animals. I will deal with those cowards who turned and ran myself, after you have done the job they were supposed to do," Lord Erador instructed.

"Yes lord… attack!" he screamed at his troops, and charged towards the retreating sheep and cougars.

At a point just before the trail narrowed, the sheep and cougars turned to face the enemy again. From behind them, a stream of wolves poured out of the trail and moved to either side. Within a few moments, over two hundred wolves, headed by the massive shape of Bodolf, faced the charging soldiers. With their staring eyes reflecting the last of the fading sun, their mouths open and teeth bared, they must have looked like the army from hell to the advancing soldiers.

Just when Lord Erador's army thought things could not get worse, the eagles attacked. Numbering over two hundred, they dived at the exposed heads of the charging soldiers, causing panic amongst the troops. None of the soldiers' training had equipped them to deal with this, and the charge faltered, then stopped completely.

With piercing howls, the wolves launched themselves down the valley at the disorganised soldiers, who were trying to defend against attacks from the eagles. For the next few moments, a deadly battle ensued, with many casualties on both sides. But the ferocity of the attack by the animals had sapped the morale of the soldiers, resulting in more and more of them running from the battle.

At that moment, General Izotz turned up with his mounted troops. The general instantly weighed up the situation. "Sound the retreat, before we lose the whole army!" he instructed.

The captain, glad not to be responsible for ordering the retreat, called his men and organised a tactical withdrawal. The soldiers still faced the wolves, but now they worked together. Those troops thinking of running realised that the safest place to be was with the group, so order returned to the ranks.

As soon as the troops started retreating, Bodolf stopped the attack and reformed his wolves at the entrance to the pass, which was alien to his hunting instincts. Normally when prey runs, a wolf attacks, but Banain's instructions had been clear and reluctantly Bodolf pulled his wolves away.

He had, in fact, disobeyed Banain's instructions by attacking at all, but he did not think the humans would have stopped without the extra threat from the wolves. Taking a quick count of the bodies he could see in the gloom, he calculated that he had lost over twenty wolves in the battle. When the enemy had retreated, he would check for wounded.

"Come to me, horse, and I will remove your human trappings," Grindor said to the large, black horse.

The horse stood looking at this very strange creature, almost like a small hairy human, and considered whether to run again.

"Where would you run, horse? Let me help you. You will feel so much better without all that heavy stuff on you, and with that thing out of your mouth." Grindor continued talking calmly and slowly walked up to the side of the big horse. "How do you take these things off?" Grindor tugged at bits of leather and buckles.

"Well not like that! You have to undo the strap under the flap where the humans sit," the horse said, turning his head to grasp the flap of the saddle with his teeth and lifting it to expose the buckle.

"Ah I see," Grindor said, pulling hard at the end of the exposed strap, which just tightened the strap more.

"No, no, you need to pull a little upwards and then let go," the horse said, regretting letting this creature near him.

"Okay, I think I have the hang of it. Are you others watching?" Grindor said, as the buckle released and the strap fell away. From behind Grindor, another fifty apes appeared from the trees.

"Okay, how do I take your head gear off, like this?" Grindor said, climbing onto the horse's neck and trying to pull the bridle off over the top of his head.

Unnerved by the appearance of the other apes and the actions of Grindor, the black shook his head, throwing Grindor to the floor. He shook his whole body, throwing the saddle on top of the ape.

"Hey, horse, I am trying to do you a favour here!" Grindor complained, pushing off the heavy saddle and looking up at the skittish black horse.

"How do we know that? You could just be preparing to eat us. This is just so strange. I was a cavalry horse, looked after by my human owner, now what am I?" the black horse said, but he had started to calm down again.

"You are a free horse! You may be a cavalry horse again if you wish, or you may run with your friends on the plain. Alternatively, you may do both! There is a new world coming, all will be explained, but for now would you rather keep this thing on your head or get rid of it?" Grindor said, trying to soften his normal gruff approach.

"There is a buckle on the side of here," the horse said, lowering his head to Grindor, who swiftly undid it, letting the bridle fall to the floor.

"Okay, now we just have to do the others!" Grindor said, moving towards the next horse. His troop spread out and picked animals to help.

"Why have you ordered the retreat, General? Send those men back to fight. These are a few animals against well trained, heavily armed men!" Lord Erador screamed at General Izotz. They were standing in front of the re-formed army, which had mainly suffered the loss of its cavalry horses. Now only the fifty horses from Izotz's party remained, and around twenty of the group which had charged through the pass.

"My lord, had I not stopped the action when I did, you would have lost your army. As it is, we have lost many mounts, but retained a considerable force of soldiers. There was no way to finish the planned attack before nightfall. The enemy are far more organised then we were led to believe and seem to be able to work together. With respect, we need to re-think our strategy."

"This is your fault, General. You are useless! I will lead the army from now on, and I will find out what is going on in that mind of yours. I know you have been holding back, General, and I will enjoy extracting every secret and plot you have, after I have defeated these few animals. Guards, take this traitor away." Without pausing, Lord Erador turned to the waiting ranks of soldiers and shouted, "Who is the senior officer here?"

At first, no one responded, and then a grizzled captain reluctantly stepped forward. "I am the next in command, my lord," the man said.

"Then I order you to attack these animals and win this battle for me. Is that going to be a problem?"

"That depends, my lord. If we attack in the dark, without knowing the lay of the land and the number or type of force facing us, then it will be. There could be thousands of wolves, who have excellent night vision. I suggest, with respect, my lord, that we make camp, reorganise our forces, scout the area and attack tomorrow in the light...my lord!" the captain said. Having weighed things up, the captain had realised that death was a certainty if they attacked, whilst there was a small chance that the lord would heed his advice.

As usual, Lord Erador had not waited for the man's response, instead reading the soldier's mind and the minds of several other soldiers around him. He realised that he would have to wait another day for his victory.

"Okay Captain, make camp and brief me in the morning with your plan. What is your name?"

"I am Hunner, my lord."

"Well, Hunner, do well tomorrow and you will be my new general. Fail me and...well, I think you know the answer to that, Hunner!"

As Lord Erador strode away, Hunner breathed a huge sigh of relief, and then went about the job of setting up a camp in the dark.

Chapter Forty-Eight

"You are crazy, Banain; we can't do this in the time you are proposing!" Wayland said, flexing his muscles in Izotz's spare set of armour.

"I told you the armour would fit, Wayland, and we have to do this. At this moment, Lord Erador's men are regrouping and will attack Krask Mountain again tomorrow. So far, Bodolf and the other animals have managed to hold off the attack, but they can only last so long without reinforcements. So, now you look like a general, it is time to act like one," Banain said, pacing up and down and playing his plan through his mind again, searching for flaws.

"How do you know what is happening at Krask Mountain? And how can the animals fight together without killing each other? I still do not understand!" Wayland said, rubbing his chin, again wondering what it was about this childlike man that was making him follow his strange methods.

"There is a lot to take in, and as I said before, very little time. You just have to trust me, Wayland," Banain said, his steely blue eyes meeting those of the dubious warrior.

"You have my trust, Banain," Wayland said, reaching for Izotz's spare short sword and helmet.

Situated a little way from the castle and the slave pens, the barracks currently housed around two hundred troops, the bulk of the force being away on the Krask Mountain campaign. Banain and his growing army had already captured fifty-three guards, so that left around one hundred and fifty in the guardhouse.

"I think we should barricade the doors and burn the devils as they sleep!" Wayland said, as he strode through the halls with Banain.

"If we do that we are no better than them, Wayland. No, we must try my plan first. If it doesn't work, then we will have to be more aggressive," Banain said. The immortals had said he should only kill as a last resort, but the instructions were becoming increasingly hard to follow.

"If it doesn't work, I don't think there will be many of us left to be aggressive, lad! But we will give it a try," Wayland said, as they reached the doors to the large inner yard. Outside, a group of uniformed soldiers, comprised of fifty ex-prisoners and some of the converted guards, waited. They looked the part, but most, except for the ex-guards, had had little training. They would be of little use if this did not go well. Behind the group of men was a large, covered carriage, pulled by two horses.

Striding to the front of the group, Wayland issued a command and they marched out of the castle towards the barracks. Leading his soldiers, Wayland pulled his helmet visor part way down and prayed.

"You there, open the gate and then rouse the guard. I want them all out here. I am going to select further troops to assist Lord Erador. Tell them to bring their weapons and place them in the middle of the drill square here. They will then be able to select new, improved weapons for the campaign from the wagon," Wayland shouted at the gate guard.

"Yes, General, at once," the flustered guard said, opening the gate and running towards the barracks. Wayland moved the wagon into the middle of the square and positioned his soldiers in a line behind it.

For a while, nothing happened, then the barracks door opened and a fully armoured captain stepped out. "General, with respect Sir, I am not sure I recognise your voice, or some of your soldiers, and I have been here a long time. Would you mind removing your helmet please, just so I can verify you are who you say?" the captain said.

As he spoke, more fully armoured soldiers exited the barracks and lined up behind him. Wayland knew the plan had failed. As soon as he lifted his helmet, the deception would be exposed and they would be fifty mostly inexperienced men facing one hundred and fifty fully trained soldiers!

"Charge them boys!" Wayland shouted as he pulled up the visor and ran towards the captain, sword in hand. He hoped to kill the troops and block the doors before more entered the fight.

On seeing the stream of fully armed soldiers pouring out of the barracks, many of Wayland's untrained troops just dropped their swords and raised their arms in defeat. Most of the ex-guards, realising that Wayland was beaten, switched sides and started attacking the slaves, leaving only six seasoned ex-slaves running with Wayland towards the captain and his growing number of soldiers. Reaching the heavily defended man, Wayland used his bulk to charge the man to the floor, then slashed across his exposed neck. Without pause, he moved to the next man, dispatching him in a short time as well.

"Form a defensive circle!" Wayland shouted and manoeuvred himself so that he was fighting back to back with his six companions. More and more guards poured out of the barracks and piled into the melee of soldiers trying to defeat Wayland's small group.

One by one, the sheer force of numbers overcame the small group, until bloodied and exhausted, Wayland stood alone.

A large soldier raised his sword and was about to hack down at Wayland, when his sword leapt out of his hand and stabbed him! It then flew through the air, slashing and stabbing at the ten closest soldiers to Wayland, and continued into the hands of Banain.

Realising that his plan was going horribly wrong, Banain had come out from his hiding place in the wagon. He stood on the top, searching for some way to scare the soldiers away from Wayland, but events had happened so quickly that his mind had taken over, and before he knew it, he had killed the soldiers attacking Wayland. Although shocked by what he had just done, he was becoming more and more enraged by what the soldiers were doing to his men. Those next to Wayland, still stunned by what had happened, stopped attacking for the moment, but those who had pledged allegiance to him and then reverted, were still slaughtering the escaped slaves.

As the soldiers next to Wayland started to raise their weapons again, cold fury took over Banain's mind.

Leaping from the carriage, Banain ran with incredible speed towards the soldiers attacking the remaining liberated slaves. With a bloodthirsty scream, he leapt onto the back of the closest soldier, his sword swinging below him, grabbing another sword from the man as he stabbed downwards with the first. Using the soldiers' backs and heads as springboards, Banain leapt through the group, leaving a trail of collapsing, dying soldiers behind him. For Banain it was like fighting in slow motion, every jump, thrust and sweep of the swords carefully performed. To anyone watching, it was a blur of deathly acrobatics.

Before the last soldier had dropped to the floor, Banain was halfway to the larger group who were starting to attack Wayland again. Given a few seconds respite, Wayland had managed to dispatch a few more soldiers, but he was exhausted and could hardly swing his sword.

Banain reached the outside of the pack and sprang over the heads of the soldiers towards Wayland. A trail of soldiers dropped to the floor as he dealt death from above on his way. Landing with more agility than a mountain cat, Banain became a blur of steel lightning as he cut through swathes of men like human straw. He was so fast and agile that not a single enemy sword came close to touching him.

Wayland watched the spectacle in amazed shock. As Banain had leapt in, he could hardly recognise the features of the boy. The normally smiling face was contorted with rage, and the eyes! Banain's normally blue eyes were inky black, showing Wayland a frightening glimpse of the darkness within. Wayland would never forget that face.

Already the boy had killed many men and showed no sign of slowing down.

The soldiers were trying to find some way of escaping this death-dealing devil, and most had thrown their weapons down.

"Banain…Banain stop, they are done!" Wayland shouted, running up behind the boy and grasping his shoulder. In an instant, Banain spun and brought one of his swords down towards his friend. Using every ounce of his remaining strength and experience, Wayland managed to block the blow, but he knew he only had seconds to live.

"Banain, please stop. It is me, Wayland!" he shouted in Banain's face.

For a moment, he thought Banain had not heard, but then he saw a change in the lad's face. His eyes slowly turned back to a deep blue again, deeper, Wayland thought, than they had been before.

"Wayland, what have I done?" Banain said, looking at the carnage around him, and then he collapsed to the floor, unconscious.

Chapter Forty-Nine

Hunner took a last walk around the temporary camp perimeter. The soldiers had constructed a makeshift wall, and he had posted guards every ten metres. With three large fires burning in the middle of the camp and the remaining wagon and cavalry horses picketed, fed and watered, he hoped that the lord would be happy with his work.

"Come in Hunner," Lord Erador shouted from inside his grand tent. Entering, he found the lord sitting in a chair naked to the waist; two scantily-clad female slaves from his personal harem were gently rubbing scented oils into his shoulders and chest.

"Ah the rigours of war, Hunner. Is everything prepared for the night? What are your plans for the morning?" Erador said, motioning for Hunner to sit opposite him.

"Um, I have prepared camp as best I can, my lord, and I intend to send a scouting party out at first light to assess the situation," Hunner said, his concentration interrupted by the presence of the slave girls.

"Assess the situation!" Lord Erador shouted, jumping to his feet, pushing the girls away and striding over to glower down at Hunner. "We are an army, they are a bunch of animals; what is there to assess, Hunner? They were lucky that it was getting dark or they would all be dead. At first light, you will take the soldiers, march them up that hill and kill or capture every animal in the valley. Is that clear?" Lord Erador screamed the last three words only centimetres from Hunner's face.

"Ye...yes, my lord, if that is your wish, of course, but I have been speaking with the cavalry soldiers and they say that the animals were organised and were acting together," Hunner said, knowing he was risking his life questioning the lord.

"I know what they think, I know what you think and I know the animals are communicating and acting together. I am not stupid, Hunner. However, what chance do they stand against well-armed troops who are ready for them? We know what to expect and we will not be surprised and run away, will we, Hunner... Now, go and prepare for an assault first thing in the morning and bring me your plan within the hour."

"Yes, my lord," Hunner said, rising from his chair, grateful to be able to leave this man's presence for a while. Then he stopped, listening intently.

"That is all, Hunner. Go!" Lord Erador said, becoming impatient. Then he too thought he could hear something strange. Like a growing rumbling noise.

"What the hell is that, Hunner?" but the acting general had already sprinted out of the tent and was calling the general alarm.

Chapter Fifty

Bodolf's excellent night vision was almost useless in the dust and debris thrown up by the charging bulls in front of him. For the hundredth time, he ran his plan through his head and just hoped it would work. Since Krask had returned with the news that Banain was unconscious after a battle, it had been up to Bodolf to decide what to do next. Banain had said they would have to modify the last part of the plan to take into account how the attack on Krask Mountain went and if he could bring reinforcements from Seville in time to help.

Not having any further instructions, Bodolf had decided to make a bold move and take advantage of the animals superior night vision. He had not wanted to face the alerted soldiers in the light of the next day. Therefore, there he was, only metres from the soldiers' camp, following the charging bulls with two hundred of his kin.

Behind Bodolf and his pack, Grindor was equally uncomfortable, hanging on for dear life to the mane of the galloping black horse grandly named "Emblazoned Star of the Lord's army" which Grindor had shortened to Star.

"For God's sake, Grindor, stop pulling on my mane! Even with all the tack on, it was more comfortable to ride with a human," Star complained for the tenth time.

Grindor and around thirty other apes were riding the horses who had volunteered to help with Bodolf's plan.

In front, the lead bulls had reached the point picked out by Bodolf as the weakest in the human camp's perimeter. Approaching the small earth wall constructed with sharpened stakes, the bulls just lowered their massive heads and shovelled their way through like crazed bulldozers.

Once inside, they split into two groups and charged through the lines of tents and weapons stands, keeping clear of the three large fires and the picketed horses.

Since Hunner had sounded the alarm, only a few men had managed to emerge from their tents and the sights that greeted them were enough to put terror in the hearts of the strongest of them.

Behind the bulls came wave after wave of snarling, biting, killing wolves. Those men not killed or maimed in their tents, faced the fury of Bodolf's temporarily enlarged pack, and not many were to survive the encounter.

Grindor and the rest of the horse-mounted apes made straight for the picketed horses, who were trying to run from the mayhem going on around them.

"Try and calm the horses so we can get them untied," Grindor instructed, leaping from the back of Star and running to the nearest horse to untie it.

All the horses were there, except for those belonging to Lord Erador and his elite guard. As soon as Lord Erador had realised what was happening, he had summoned his guard and horses. "Bring the prisoner and get me out of here!" he commanded. By the time he had donned his clothes; his horse was standing outside accompanied by his elite guard of twelve men, some only wearing nightclothes.

Leaping into the saddle, he took one last look at the slaughter of his men and headed out of the camp through the escape route planned by his guard. Lord Erador always ensured he had an escape route, and he thanked his own thoroughness on this occasion.

"Get me back to my castle," he instructed his senior guard.

"It will not be possible at night, my lord. I have identified a safe location where we can wait for this to die down, then we can leave at first light."

Erador was going to argue with the guard, but then he decided that the man was probably right and just grunted his agreement.

On hearing the general alarm, the guards posted beside the mobile cage housing General Izotz ran to help with the fight against the animals. The general leapt to his feet and tried to force the cage door, but even with his great strength, he could not move it. The sounds of the stampeding bulls grew louder until he saw a wall of them smashing their way towards him, destroying everything in their path. Even facing his own death, his warrior instincts were impressed with the job these animals were doing. He realised that this was a well-executed plan and he respected the mind of whoever was behind it.

The first of the bulls hit the cage with a glancing blow that nearly pushed it over. Before it had time to recover, more bodies barrelled past, and the wagon holding the cage crashed onto its side, throwing the general against the bars, which bent under the pressure. The bulls streamed around either side of the solidly built wagon, saving the general's life for the moment.

Seeing a chance of escape, Izotz grasped two of the loosened bars of the cage and, using his considerable strength, managed to bend them far enough for him to squeeze through. Hearing the baying and growling wolves getting closer every minute, he knew he only had seconds to find a way of escaping. The only option he could come up with was almost suicidal, but he was out of ideas and time. Running towards the nearest bull, he leapt for the animal, grabbing onto the hair on the back of its neck and holding on with all his might.

Chapter Fifty-One

Banain woke once again with a thumping ache above his eyes; he squinted against the early morning sun streaming through the window. He was lying in a large bed and looking around, he noted the fine furniture and pictures on the walls depicting stern looking men in uniform looking down at the world with disdain, all dressed in elaborate armour. By far the biggest picture was of Lord Erador himself, dressed in bright red armour with matching hair and beard. Banain sensed the man's malice even from the picture. Tearing his eyes from those of the lords, he tried to remember what had happened and where he was. The last thing he could recall was Wayland engulfed in a sea of Lord Erador's guards, then he…he had killed them all!

The full memory of every sweep and cut came back to him, replaying in his mind. The noise of men screaming as his twin blades of death carved through them, the metallic taste of their blood as it splattered his lips, the looks of fear on their faces as he stole their lives. He felt revolted by his own actions, but worse, he recognised that a part of him had enjoyed the power over the mortality of others.

Getting up and moving to a bowl of fresh water by a large mirror, Banain splashed his face and looked at his reflection. Looking back were the dark blue, troubled eyes of a five-year-old boy, trapped in the harsh realities of a grown up world.

"Banain, are you awake?" It was Krask.

"Yes, Krask, I am. Where are you?" Banain answered, trying to gather his wits.

"I am outside on your balcony."

Striding over and opening the double doors, Banain walked out onto a grand balcony that overlooked the old town of Seville. He realised that he must be in Lord Erador's quarters. The man had certainly looked after himself.

"Are you okay, Banain? We have all been so worried about you. After the battle last night..." Banain knew from the tone of the eagle's voice that he was worried.

"Do you know what I did, Krask?" Banain said, walking over to the ornate railing and looking down over the grounds of the castle. He recognised the barracks. It looked like someone had removed all traces of the carnage he wrought. It would not be so easy to remove the memories.

"The human Wayland told me of the battle, and of how you saved his life and those of many others. Yet I sense you are not happy, Banain."

"I used my powers to slaughter, Krask. I ignored all the teachings of the immortals, lost control and killed without thinking. Until last night, I had not purposefully killed anyone, now I am a mass murderer!" Banain said, his vision blurring as tears of remorse streamed from his eyes.

"From what Wayland told me, you had no choice, Banain. He and what was left of your group were about to be slaughtered; your actions saved them. You were not fighting unarmed humans or animals Banain, you were fighting soldiers trained to kill. The immortals taught that you should only kill to survive, which was what you did," the eagle said, hopping along the rail to be closer to the clearly suffering young man.

It was hard to believe that this was the baby he had cared for just over a year ago. His life and the lives of all around had changed once they had encountered Banain.

At that moment, there was a loud rap at the door. Moving back inside, he opened the door to Wayland, who swept into the room accompanied by a host of slaves from Erador's harem.

"Good morning, my lord. These ladies are your slaves, as are all the inhabitants of Seville. They are here to wash and dress you, as befits a lord. I have had them working since the early hours to make some clothes befitting your status," Wayland said, striding further into the room. The girls followed, each with eyes downcast and carrying a piece of ornate clothing.

Banain could sense the fear in the girls and a wary respect from Wayland.

He watched the girls file in and then kneel on the floor in front of him. "Please get up. You don't have to kneel in front of me, and you are not my slaves," Banain said, moving to the nearest and pulling her gently to her feet.

One by one they rose, looking even more frightened.

"Do not be frightened. No one is going to harm you here, you are free!" he said, smiling, trying to put them at ease.

"Free, my lord, free to do what? The only life we know is here. I came here when I was six years old. The story is the same for most of us," one of the girls said, not daring to look at her new lord. She had heard of his terrible anger and ability to kill hundreds of armed men single-handedly, and so she did not want to anger him.

"Free to make your own decisions, but now is not the time to explain."

"But do you not need bathing and dressing, my lord? What shall we do?" the girl asked, looking at Banain. The young man could not understand why these girls would want to help him with his bath.

"The lord has told you he will explain and explain he will in good time. Go back to your quarters and wait until you hear further from me," Wayland said, ushering the girls out of the room.

"Yes, my Lord Wayland. Will you require another bath?" the girl enquired, smiling at Wayland as she left.

"Ah, uh, no thank you, Jasmine. I am fine for the moment. Please tell the guard that we are not to be disturbed." Wayland closed the door and ignored a searching look from Banain.

"If you two have finished with the important matter of who bathes whom, can we discuss some more serious matters please?" Krask said from outside, flapping his wings in impatient irritation.

"Yes, of course, Krask. I am sorry. It seems that much has gone on during my sleep," Banain said, walking out onto the balcony followed by Wayland.

"Listen, Banain, there is much news from Krask Mountain and not all of it good," Krask said, and for the next hour he explained the details of the battle, ending with the bloodthirsty slaughter in the humans' camp.

"It seems that I have not started very well as a leader. First I kill all these men, and then the army I inspired kills hundreds more!" Banain said, his head bowing in shame.

"What is the matter with you, boy? The men you killed would have butchered all of us, and what could Bodolf have done? Given daylight and organisation, those men could have wiped out all the animals in Krask Mountain. Bodolf made a decision, a hard, wartime decision, and most of your friends live because of it," Wayland said, walking over to put his hand on Banain's shoulder.

"What do you mean most of my friends? Who has died?" Banain said, realising that both Krask and Wayland were holding something back from him.

"Teague and Jabber were captured, we believe by Lord Erador's scouts, just before the battle for Krask Mountain. Lepe managed to get away; he could not be sure if they were killed or not, as he was being pursued," Krask said.

Banain felt a stab of loss, almost like a physical pain deep in his chest. The thought of Jabber and Teague not being around was something he could not accept. They were important parts of his short but accelerated life.

"How could they be captured? I left them at the rock. They were safe," Banain said to Krask, his fragile world crumbling around him.

"They must have tried to follow you, Banain. Nobody knew they were gone until too late. Grindor set straight off after them, but they covered their tracks well. Bodolf has sent packs out all over the plain looking for them. I am sure he will find them," Krask said, but Banain sensed the doubt in the eagle's mind.

"Banain, I am sorry to trouble you with all this going on, but unless we establish rule here, Seville could slide into anarchy. We have established temporary marshal law, but people want to know what is going on and what is going to happen to them," Wayland said, his hand still gripping Banain's shoulder.

"I don't know what to do. It all seemed so clear before, but everything has changed!" Banain said, pulling Wayland's hand from his shoulder and leaping onto the balcony rail. To Wayland's astonishment, Banain then leapt from the rail to the corner of the building and climbed down the ten metres to the floor in a matter of seconds. Leaping over the large courtyard gate, Banain disappeared from sight. Wayland turned and started for the door.

"Leave him, Wayland. He needs time to deal with this. He has been through so much in his short life, more than any man, never mind child, should have to deal with," Krask said, his words stopping Wayland in the doorway.

"What is he, Krask? I have never seen such actions before, yet he seems so…so vulnerable," the big man said, looking in the direction Banain had gone.

"He has a rare gift, but he needs our help and support if it is not to become a curse," the big eagle said gravely.

Chapter Fifty-Two

Izotz woke later the next day lying under the overhang of a riverbank, the ground churned up all around him. Sitting up, waves of pain from his left shoulder and arm assailed him. He looked down to see that his whole arm was at a strange angle and that he had a large gash. He remembered the wild ride on the back of the charging bull and the moment when he finally lost his grip on the animal and flew over the beast's head, ripping his arm on a sharp horn as he passed, landing heavily. He guessed that he must have knocked himself out when he landed; a large bump on his head confirmed his suspicions.

Remembering his field training, Izotz brought his knees to his chest, managing to get a grip with his hands on both legs just below the kneecaps with his thumbs pointing upwards. Grimacing against the pain, he slowly leant back, stretching his arms out until with a pop, his shoulder went back into place.

"Very impressive, human," the voice was in his head but the wolf that spoke the words was standing over the ex-general. Arkta was in a bad state. He had a cut down the side of his face where Izotz had caught him with his sword in the cave and various other wounds from his fights with the soldiers sent to kill him.

"So you are still alive, wolf, but only just it seems. You are ready to exact your revenge on me, I take it. What happened to the soldiers I sent after you?" Izotz said, stalling and searching around for any type of weapon he could use against the wolf.

"Oh they nearly had me, but I managed to lose them eventually. The two that are left are wandering around somewhere. Yes, I would like to take revenge for what you did to me and my greys, human, but at the moment I need information more than I need to kill you," Arkta said, settling to his haunches and licking one of his many wounds.

"I am surprised you need information from me, wolf. You and your brethren seem to be communicating very well, judging by the way you were organised last night. I have never seen animals working together before. They wiped out a whole army of fighting men. Okay, it was at night and we were unprepared, but it was an amazing feat for a bunch of animals," Izotz said, realising that if the wolf wanted to kill him, there was very little he could do about it.

"I know nothing of this human. All I told you last night was true. When I checked on the den it looked just as it should have. Bodolf must have been on to me from the start. What I do not understand is where the animals have gone and what they are doing. I have not found a single fresh wolf scent this morning, but it is clear that many hundreds of bulls have passed this way recently."

Izotz considered the situation and realised that the wolf was telling the truth. Deciding he had nothing to lose, he told Arkta of the events of last night finishing with his wild ride on the back of bull.

"And what of Lord Erador, human, was he killed?" Arkta asked.

"I don't know, wolf, but I would be surprised if he were not. Your kin were finishing off everyone the bulls left behind from what I could see," Izotz replied, rubbing his shoulder, which was stiffening after its rough treatment.

"Well it looks as if we are outsiders then, human. Any wolves here will know of my betrayal and you will be known to all humans, who will probably kill you on sight," Arkta said, looking at Izotz and considering whether he should kill him or if he could be of some use. Arkta knew he could communicate with animals thank to his exposure to Banain but he also knew how deadly and efficient the humans were at making war. It was not their strength or speed that he admired, it was their ability to make weapons and their intelligence. Perhaps he should not kill this human, but it was a great risk.

"If I were you, wolf, I would be wondering if I could use this human in some way, but would also be worried about trusting him. Well if it's any help, I have no interest in harming you, quite the opposite in fact. With your skills of animal communication, and mine of humans, maybe we could raise an army of our own. However, it would have to be far from here," Izotz said, looking steadily at the wolf.

"I don't trust you, but these are strange times and what you say is true. For now we need to find somewhere to rest up and let our wounds heal, and then we can see about raising an army."

Chapter Fifty-Three

Banain ran through the streets of Old Seville as fast as he could. It felt good to let his body expel pent up frustrations. His mind was a different matter altogether though. The teachings of the immortals had not prepared him for the anguish of taking lives and losing friends, and he wished he could keep on running, leaving everything behind him. In front, the remains of a large bridge loomed, his forward progress halted by a river almost a mile wide, swollen by melting water from the ice pack.

Standing at the very edge, Banain closed his eyes and let his body relax. Then he walked into the fast moving stream. As he went deeper, the current around him stopped and the water moved away from either side of him, forming a vertical wall of water. One moment the water was brown, full of debris and rushing towards the sea, the next it was quiet and crystal-clear.

Slowly the form of Turr materialised in the wall. "You are troubled, Banain. You have found putting our teachings into practice difficult. This was only to be expected and you have learnt a harsh lesson," the familiar voice of Turr sang in Banain's head.

"I have killed hundreds of men, caused the death of many animals and my friends, it is more than harsh!" Banain said, his anger spilling over.

"Banain, you will not always be able to control situations, and you will not always be able to solve problems without loss of life. It is in the nature of animals and men to kill each other and this will not change. Every day our predators kill thousands of us. We realise this is the way of things, just as you must, this was your first real test and the experience will help you to control you anger better in future."

"But what is my point?" Banain said.

"You are here to stop the world from self-destructing again. You are here to establish an environment wherein people and animals can co-exist, with respect for each other. Lord Erador is just one of many who would enslave all creatures and use them for his own purpose, creating the same environment that destroyed this world before."

"The world!" Banain said, interrupting Turr. "This is just a tiny part of it, how am I to change the world?"

"Believe us, you can, Banain, but let's concentrate on what we must do. Although many of us have travelled here to communicate with you, we can still only manage to do so for a relatively short time."

For the next few hours, Turr and Banain spoke, then Banain turned and walked out of the river. The wall of water containing the image of Turr collapsed and melded back into the river once more.

"So what do you want me to do?" Wayland said, wondering if the lad had completely lost his mind. The boy had walked back into the castle a short while ago and had been talking to Krask, who had flown off, and then to him, explaining his plans.

"I want you to help form a governing council made up of all beings capable of coherent communication. I want to meet with their representatives so that I can explain the new laws to them. Krask has already gone to the mountain to tell Bodolf. And I want you to select officers for the freedom army," Banain said calmly, realising that Wayland was having immense problems taking this in. He needed the large man's support and cooperation to make the immortals' plan work.

"Okay, Banain, can you explain the bit about the animals having a choice. You are saying that if I want a cavalry, I have to ask the horses, and if I want to eat meat, I have to kill it myself?"

"Yes, Wayland. Please sit down and let me try to explain better," Banain said, moving to a large table and sitting down next to his perplexed general.

"All animals capable of communicating will be offered the freedom to choose between living a wild or protected existence. Most of the land in the country will be set aside for those animals wanting to live their natural existences. Some will be set aside for growing crops. There will be no enslavement of animals for produce, such as milk or eggs, but some animals may choose to live under the protection of humans, or perhaps other species. They would need to contribute something. For example, cows will have the choice to go back to the wild or stay and provide milk. Horses will be able to choose between living a wild existence and serving in the cavalry, or both."

"How could they do both?" Wayland said, not really grasping these principles. These ideas were just so strange.

He had never considered animals as anything other than food or tools, now he was trying to deal with the concept that he had to afford them the same type of rights he would give to another human.

"Before humans knew that animals could communicate and think, we forced our decisions on them. In the future, if you need a horse to ride you will ask one. In return for letting you ride, the horse receives your protection and care. The horse may decide that it wants to be with you full or just part time, living free for part of its life," Banain continued.

"But what of the food, Banain? How are we going to feed the people without breeding the animals and killing them to eat?" Wayland said.

"There are no easy solutions, Wayland. We must find a way to share this world with the animals without abusing them. Many animals hunt other animals for food, but we are the only species that enslaves them. That is what must change," Banain said, running his hands through his hair, realising that even to him this was a strange concept to grasp.

"I will do my best, Banain, but it will be no easy task to change the ways so many people live! What of the castle and Lord Erador's slaves?"

"All slaves are to be freed and given the opportunity of employment in the castle. I intend to convert this into a place of learning and a communication portal for the immortals. This will involve creating an underwater tunnel from the river to underneath the castle, so we need to find someone with building skills."

For the next few hours, Banain and Wayland talked, but Wayland could see that the boy's mind was on other matters.

"I am sure Bodolf will find your friends," he said, interrupting the flow of conversation, knowing from the boy's expression that he had guessed the problem correctly.

"I have to go, Wayland. Can you manage here without me?"

Before Wayland had a chance to answer the question, a guard entered the room. "My lords, I am sorry to interrupt, but there is a soldier outside who says he has a message from Lord Erador. He is unarmed. What do you wish done with him?"

"Take him to the dungeons and chain him, we can talk to him at our leisure," Wayland said, dismissing the guard.

"One minute please guard," Banain said.

"Wayland, he may have information about my friends. I must talk to him now." Banain stood and turned towards the door.

"Okay, bring him in, but make sure he is unarmed," Wayland said, drawing his sword and standing between Banain and the door.

A man wearing the uniform of Erador's army was marched in between six guards. He looked very frightened and Banain could sense no malice in the man. "What message do you bring from Lord Erador?" he asked, looking at the man with his penetrating stare.

"Please, my lord, I am just the messenger. I have been told to tell you this on pain of death, or worse," the man said, torn between his fear of Erador and this strange man with the piercing blue eyes.

"Spit it out man… What is your message?" Wayland said, moving towards the man.

"The Lord Erador says that he has your friend and unless you follow his instruction, she will die."

Chapter Fifty-Four

"Are you mad? You cannot go alone!" Bodolf said to Banain, echoing the concerns of everyone gathered outside the dens at Krask Mountain.

Banain had already had this argument with Wayland when he had informed him that he was going to go alone to see Lord Erador, as instructed. In the end, he had agreed to an escort as far as Krask Mountain. Now he had to go on alone, otherwise he believed the lord would carry out his threat and kill Teague.

According to the messenger, Jabber was not with Teague when the scouts re-joined with Lord Erador the night of the Krask Mountain battle.

"If I take anyone with me, Teague will be killed. I cannot risk that. Please do not worry. I am capable of taking care of myself, as you know! Where is Blazon?" Banain said. He had talked to the horses at the Seville stables, and a young stallion had agreed to take him as far as Krask Mountain; now he hoped Blazon would take him the rest of the way.

"The horses have been talking and Star, who is the most senior, has decided to carry you. He is a fine animal. I will find him and get the messenger," Grindor said. He was feeling sad that the big horse was going; he had formed quite an attachment to him.

A short while later, the messenger arrived with his heavily armoured warhorse, both dwarfed by Star who walked alongside them. The mighty animal was impressive to Banain; he stood almost eighteen hands high and weighed over eight hundred kilograms.

"I am Star, formerly of Lord Erador's cavalry. I thank you for setting me and my kin free, Banain. I pledge my service to you for life and share the breath of friendship with you." Star trotted up and lowered his nose to within centimetres of Banain's, and then he exhaled in the traditional horse greeting.

"I thank you Star and accept your pledge. I would be honoured to ride with you," Banain said, breathing in the air of the big horse and returning his own. "You understand that this is a dangerous quest and that I cannot guarantee your safety," Banain said, looking for any doubt in the horse. He found none.

"My kind welcome danger; it is where we differ from our wild cousins. We charge in, whilst they charge away," Star said, a deep sense of pride evident in his words.

"Do you require a saddle and bridle to ride me, Banain?" he asked.

"No, thank you. I think I will be fine." With that, Banain leapt nimbly onto Star's back.

"I think you will!" Star said, amazed. He could hardly feel the well-positioned and balanced rider. "If Grindor is to ride me again, perhaps you could give him lessons, Banain." Star gave the equivalent of a horse chuckle.

"I heard that, horse," Grindor said, his sadness turning to indignation.

"I am only joking, Grindor. You rode well...for an ape!" Star replied as he disappeared from view, following the messenger.

After around two hours of riding, the light was beginning to fade. As the messenger kept up a steady pace, Banain had tried to quiz him about what Lord Erador wanted, but it was clear that the soldier did not know much. All he did know was that Teague was unharmed. That would have to be good enough for the moment.

"I smell horses nearby. I know most of them from my stables and there are several either side of us. Do you wish me to run?" The message from Star broke into Banain's mind and he could feel the big horse's muscles bunching.

"I would not if you wish the girl Teague to live. In fact, why don't you let Banain walk!" The cold voice of Lord Erador cut into both Banain's and Star's minds.

Still in connection with Star, Banain felt the sickening jolt of power as Erador entered the great horse's mind, causing him to buck and kick violently. Banain flew through the air, landing nimbly on his feet. His concern rose – he heard Star nickering in despair as Lord Erador applied more and more pressure to his overloaded brain.

"I will not tolerate mutiny. Every single human and animal who has supported this boy will feel my power, and you, my ex-cavalry horse, will be the first to satisfy my need for revenge." The big horse was rolling on the ground, his eyes filled with the pain.

Banain entered the tormented horse's mind and pushed back against the will of Lord Erador. He could see the malevolent tendrils of force tearing into Star's brain. Focusing, he cut across the main channel of Lord Erador's power, pushing it backwards whilst sending his own healing tendrils in.

Freed of the pain, Star leapt back to his feet and ran towards Banain.

"Go back to Krask Mountain, Star. I will be okay, but I cannot protect you for long. Go, it is an order!" Banain managed to message to the large horse.

Star hesitated for just a moment, then thundered away.

"Very impressive for a four-year-old, Banain. Shall we stop fencing, or would you like me to kill your little friend?" Lord Erador snarled in Banain's mind, clearly angered by missing his revenge on the horse.

Hoping that Star was far enough away, Banain withdrew his block, only to be instantly assaulted by a powerful mind probe.

"Ah, now I understand, Banain. You really still have a lot to learn, don't you? Now I know everything you do and more. Did you realise that the immortals locked information within you that you cannot access? They did not have to age you Banain, that was a lie. They just did it so that you would be a better tool for them to use. So that you could change the world the way they want it. Well that is not going to happen! You, my young man, are going to help me live forever!" Lord Erador boomed. Then the young man felt a vicious burning pain and saw a flash of light as he lost consciousness.

Sometime later, Banain opened his eyes. The face of Teague slowly swam into view; she looked drawn and pale, her normally lively eyes dull and tear-filled.

"Teague, are you okay? The last thing I remember was Lord Erador in my mind and pain," Banain said, struggling to sit up.

They were in a small cave, sitting on the opposite side to Lord Erador.

Erador smiled. "How touching! The girl is fine, Banain; she will remain that way as long as you follow my instructions to the letter. I know you have gifts, but believe me, you would not be able to save her if I decided otherwise. In fact, Banain, if anything happens to me, she will die. You see, I have rather rewired her brain stem. It is quite clever really. Instead of making independent decisions about her heartbeat, respiration, actually all of her auto functions, she depends on me being close to live. I haven't tested the range yet, but I suppose now is as good a time as any." Erador stood and walked out of the cave.

It was only then that Banain noticed a length of chain tethering Teague to a large rock. After a moment, Teague started to shudder and have difficulty with her breathing.

"You had better not let her get too far from me, Banain," Erador shouted back into the cave.

"Teague, get as close as you can to Lord Erador. I will carry the rock," Banain said, jumping up, hefting the large rock from the ground and following Teague. Outside, Lord Erador was standing by his horse. Behind him were the fifty troops that had captured Teague and Jabber.

"Are you okay?" Banain whispered to Teague. She was breathing better but he was worried.

"I am okay, Banain. I thought I would never see you again!"

"Do not worry; it will be okay," Banain said, trying to reassure her, to give her the spirit to keep fighting.

"You will have no energy for whispering soon, Banain! Do not fall behind or you know what will happen to your young friend," Lord Erador said, climbing onto his horse and smiling down at the pair. Kicking his spurs, he galloped to the front of the group and signalled them to move on at a fast walk. Banain and Teague ran after them, finding that they had to keep amongst the horses for Teague not to feel the effects of being too far from Lord Erador.

For hour after hour, Banain kept up the gruelling pace, his whole body wracked with pain from carrying the heavy rock. He had tried carrying it in all different ways, but after a short while, the pain became almost intolerable, and he had to adjust his grip again.

Then he tripped and fell to the floor, the rock rolling off in front of him. Struggling to his feet, he bent down to pick it up again and felt a soothing sensation on his back that travelled through his whole body.

Realising he was close to exhaustion, Teague used her healing skills to rejuvenate him and now she helped raise the rock. Carrying it between them, they hurried after Lord Erador, as Teague began to lose her breath again.

At dusk, the group stopped and made camp. They did not bother tying Banain and Teague up, leaving them to collapse close to the tent erected for Lord Erador.

For the next three days, they followed the same routine; both Teague and Banain were kept on the verge of exhaustion. It had become clear to Banain that Lord Erador was not trying to kill them, as on several occasions he had called for a stop on some pretence or other when they were too exhausted to continue.

After making camp on the third night, he approached them. "Tomorrow we will be at the rock, where I will meet with your immortal friends. I know, from what I have read in your mind, that they will not hurt me. I will let you and the girl go when they have given me the gift of immortality," he said, smiling down at Banain.

"There is no such thing as immortality, and you will not be able to enter the rock to speak with the immortals," Banain said, meeting Erador's cruel gaze with his own.

"Your mind tells me differently, Banain. I told you that the immortals hid things from you, but you could not hide them from me. They will let me in, and they will grant what I wish in exchange for saving you," Lord Erador said, smiling confidently at Banain.

The next day they completed the last part of the journey to the rock. On arrival at the outskirts of the old town, there were no guards, and the group moved cautiously forward until they reached the closed entrance to the tunnel. Again, there were no guards.

"Tell your master to let me in, or I will hurt the girl. Perhaps they need a demonstration?" Lord Erador said, but as he finished the sentence, the entrance to the tunnel appeared in the solid rock face.

"Captain, post men at this entrance and at intervals all the way down the tunnel. Only I will enter the final chamber with these two," the lord said, striding ahead. Teague and Banain ran to keep up with him.

In the final chamber, Turr was floating gracefully in its raised water chamber.

"So Lord Erador, you have travelled a long way to meet us. What may we do for you?" Turr sang in the lord's head.

"You know what I want; I have been through the boy's mind and know what he does not. I have to say you would make a worthy ally. I like to work with people who are ruthless and will do anything to reach their goals," Erador said, walking closer to and smiling at the image of Turr.

"Ah well, all may not be as it seems, Lord Erador. Banain is averse to killing, so he came up with a plan to bring you here, where this could all be sorted out without further loss of life," Turr continued.

"Rubbish. I am in full command of all of the information in Banain's head. I know of your deceptions, and I can kill the girl at any time. I think you do need a demonstration," Lord Erador said, severing his life support with Teague.

Teague simply stood in place, unaffected.

Lord Erador could not believe what was happening, staring open-mouthed first at the girl and then at Banain, who was also standing calmly watching him.

"That won't work, my lord," Banain said, his dark blue eyes boring into the lord's. "In fact, it hasn't been working for several days. I dismantled your control over Teague the moment I came into contact with you. You have no control over anyone here."

"We will see. I should have dealt with you earlier, child!" the lord snarled at Banain, focusing his power and sending a ferocious killing blast at him.

Banain just stood smiling at the lord. Erador tried again, but with no effect on the boy.

"As I said, you can't harm us here. Over the last few days, I have learnt much about you. Every time you thought you were probing my mind, you were just feeding me more information. I only allowed you to see information that I wanted you to see, including false information about the abilities and plans of the immortals. I knew you would not be able to resist the chance to become immortal," Banain said.

"Guards…guards to me," Lord Erador shouted.

"They can't hear you, my lord, as you are in a different shift of time to them, but we do need to remove them from our tunnels. Banain, can you manage that without killing them?" Turr sang.

Banain concentrated his mind. From all around the image of Turr, water surged out of the pool and upwards until half of the cavern was full to the ceiling. Then it split into two halves, each going around one side of the cavern, avoiding the group standing in the middle, and converging at the exit. Then the water barrelled down the narrow tunnel. The force of the water was so powerful that it washed the guards posted every few metres from their feet and out of the tunnel. Before they had time to recover, a hundred ape guards appeared from the rocks, some grabbing discarded weapons, others disarming those soldiers who had managed to hold onto them.

Inside, Lord Erador pulled out his own sword and lunged at the unarmed Banain, who in a blur moved away from the sweeping sword, grabbed the lord's arm and forced him to drop the weapon.

"Your days of control are over, my lord. But you wanted immortality and that wish is about to be granted. Let's leave Lord Erador with Turr," Banain said to Teague, taking her hand. They walked together out of the chamber.

Chapter Fifty-Five

"So you could have stopped Lord Erador at any time. We went through hell and he could have killed us – why didn't you tell me what was going on?" Teague said angrily. They were sitting near the top of the rock with Krask, who had been shadowing them the whole journey.

"Yes, I could have, but not without risking further loss of life. I do not believe that I could have subdued Lord Erador and found a way to disarm his soldiers without killing them. If I had told you what I was planning, I would not have been able to stop him from finding the information in your mind," Banain said, wondering again if he had made the right decision. She was right, he had put her life at risk.

"Sometimes Banain, you have to act like a man. You think you can use your magic skills to make everybody happy, but the world is not like that. You should have trusted me and not put me at risk. You are a baby in a man's body, Banain, and one day your actions will cause the deaths of many," Teague said, regretting her words the moment they came out of her mouth.

Banain almost crumpled before her. "That has already happened," Banain said quietly, rising and walking away from the pair.

He had hoped Teague of all people would understand what he was trying to do, but her words had cut into his delicate world like a honed knife. As he walked, he realised that he was on his own. That apart from the immortals and maybe Grindor, no one else could really understand his mission. He could not afford to let any others get close to him if he was going to achieve his goal; he had already caused the deaths of many around him. He realised then that he would have a very lonely existence.

Teague watched Banain go, tears of sadness welling in her eyes. "What did he mean, Krask? What has happened?"

For the next hour, Krask told Teague about the events since she had last seen Banain. As he recounted the massacre in Old Seville, Teague wept openly, knowing how terribly it would have affected Banain.

"What can I do, Krask? How can I apologise after what I said to him?"

"I am not sure any of us can do anything for the moment, Teague. You were correct when you said he is a child trapped in a man's body. The gifts of the immortals are both a blessing and a curse. Banain must find his own way to manhood, and we must support him the best we can. We are living in strange times. Now that humans and animals can communicate, a new rulebook is required. It would seem that the immortals are the authors of this book and that Banain has the immense responsibility of putting their plans into action, although I do not believe he fully understands this yet," Krask said, trying to alleviate the girl's suffering.

The next morning, Banain arrived at the entrance to the immortals' cave with Grindor, who had returned during the night with the rest of the ape soldiers. Dressed in the blue robe Grindor have given him and with his blond hair neatly tied back, Banain looked taller and more regal than anyone waiting by the entrance had ever seen before, including Teague. She had tried to find him during the night to apologise, but he had been with Grindor and would not see her. She tried to catch his eye, but he did not look her way.

Walking to the entrance, Banain turned to face the large group that included Lord Erador's personal guard and cavalry soldiers, all tied to each other and guarded by ape sentries.

"Today sees the end of Lord Erador's reign of terror. He was a powerful man who used his powers to subdue those around him and to enslave both humans and animals. The immortals teach that greed feeds on the greedy and once in its embrace, escape is almost impossible. Lord Erador wanted to be able to rule everything and live forever, that was his greed," Banain said.

He turned and walked into the entrance, re-emerging a short while later with a naked baby in his arms. "This is Erador. He has been granted part of his wish. The immortals have the ability to regenerate themselves and retain their collective memories. They have regenerated Erador, but have retained his memories so that he comes back without the all-consuming greed that made him abuse his powers the first time around. He has many unique skills, and with the immortals' training and guidance, he will be able to contribute to the new world, rather than trying to destroy it."

Banain passed the child to Grindor and walked towards Lord Erador's soldiers. "You have all served under Lord Erador, and I know that not all of you were happy to do so. I will grant all of you amnesty and the choice to either join the freedom army or leave. If you wish to stay, when you are untied, line up on my right, otherwise leave."

As the men were untied, every one of them moved to Banain's right and formed up. Then one man, who Banain recognised as the messenger, stepped forward. "Lord Banain. I speak for the whole troop when I say we pledge our allegiance to you," he said.

"Good. Grindor, can you take these men and find them accommodation until I leave for Old Seville. I need to talk to the immortals." Banain turned to walk back towards the cave.

"Can I talk with you, please?" Teague said, running up to Banain.

"I think you made yourself very clear last night. Perhaps you should wait until I have grown up before speaking with me," Banain said, not looking at Teague and entering the tunnel. It was not what he had wanted to say to her, but he was still angry, and he never knew what to say when in her company. It is safer this way, he told himself.

As he entered the main cavern, Turr emerged from the central pool. Banain sat in the chair which materialised from the floor.

"The girl does not understand your situation, Banain. You need your friends. You will find that being a leader is a lonely path, and you need those you can trust around you," Turr sang.

"I do not understand my situation, Turr. I need some time to come to terms with things, and I cannot think clearly with Teague around," Banain replied sadly.

"Ah, this is something that we cannot teach you Banain, but remember, Teague is very gifted herself and will need your support. Now listen, although you have done better than any of us could have wished for, there are other humans and animals far more powerful than Erador in the world, who are even now fighting each other and moving the world once again towards self-annihilation.

"You need to consolidate your rule in these lands, Banain, and then continue to spread our teachings. Although this sounds like an impossible task, it must happen whilst the new world is emerging. If left too long, a repetition of past events is inevitable. Go back to Seville, introduce and implement the new ways of living and build a communication portal, Banain. Then we will talk about the next steps."

"You make it sound easy, Turr. Trying to get my friends to understand the new way is proving difficult, how I will convince anyone else is beyond me," Banain said, completely overawed by the thought of the challenge he faced.

"You will find a way, Banain; it is your destiny," Turr replied, echoing the beliefs of the billions of immortals.

A few days later, Krask circled above a group of mounted and foot soldiers, who were just leaving the Rock of the Immortals. Leading the soldiers were Banain and Teague –

Banain mounted on Star and Teague on an almost pure white horse.

Krask reflected on the events of the last few days, still amazed at what Banain had achieved. Every horse could choose to live in freedom. Many, like Star and others from the Seville garrison, had decided to stay in the service of humans, but some had decided to leave.

There was a very interesting selection process where the horses chose who they wanted as partners. Those soldiers who had not been kind to their horses previously, tended to find themselves without a mount. Banain had suggested that those horses who wanted to stay in service should accompany them back to Seville, and that those horses who wanted their freedom should travel with the group as far as the great plains, where they were less at risk from mountain predators.

There had been intense arguments, particularly from the soldiers shunned by their previous mounts, but Banain had explained that if they could prove themselves to new horse partners in the future, then they might become mounted soldiers again. Otherwise, they would remain on foot.

A white horse called Daze had gone to Teague as soon as the selection process had started. Within moments, they had shared life air and bonded, and like Banain, she rode without a saddle or bridle. It was sad that she and Banain had not mended the fences broken between them recently, but time was a great healer.

For now, he knew that this amazing child, who his beloved Krys had sacrificed herself to save, needed his love and guidance. As he flew on, Krask started to sing to himself.

*"In red tinged night and golden dawn
Our love, our life, our spirit born*

Above the clouds, above the clouds."

Printed in Poland
by Amazon Fulfillment
Poland Sp. z o.o., Wrocław